SOUL FORGED

BOOK 1 OF THE GIFTING

This is a work of fiction. The characters, incidents, and dialogues in this book are of the author's imagination and are not to be construed as real. Any resemblance to actual events or persons, living or dead, is completely coincidental.

Published by Sevannah Storm.

First Edition 2021

Copyright © 2021 - 2090 Sevannah Storm All rights reserved.

Cover Art by Sevannah Storm

This eBook is licensed for your personal enjoyment only. This eBook may not be re-sold or given away to other people. If you would like to share this book with another person, please purchase an additional copy for each recipient. If you're reading this book and did not purchase it, or it was not purchased for your enjoyment only, then please return to Smashw ords.com or your favorite retailer and purchase your own copy. Thank you for respecting the hard work of this author.

https://sevannahstorm.com

Version_2

Also by Sevannah Storm

The Blood of Legends Series

The Huntress

The Healer

The Gifting Series

Soul Forged

Fate Forged

Sun Forged

War Forged

Star Forged

Shadow Forged

Earth Forged

Lust Forged

Standalones

Xiaxan Fox

Ire of Silver

The Shikari

Sol Survivor

SEVANNAH STORM

Plump Playwright Series

Plump Jane

Seducing Amelia

Loving FinleyKeeping Tessa

Kissing Navy

COMING SOON

Inkoded

Fire Forged

The Crucible of the Eternal

ACKNOWLEDGMENTS

*To my husband, Francois, who encouraged
me to follow my dreams.*

Contents

Welcome to Yithia   IX

1. Chapter One   1

2. Chapter Two   10

3. Chapter Three   17

4. Chapter Four   28

5. Chapter Five   37

6. Chapter Six   47

7. Chapter Seven   64

8. Chapter Eight   72

9. Chapter Nine   87

10. Chapter Ten   105

11. Chapter Eleven   116

12. Chapter Twelve   128

13. Chapter Thirteen   149

14. Chapter Fourteen   171

15. Chapter Fifteen   182

16. Chapter Sixteen   192

17. Chapter Seventeen   202

18. Chapter Eighteen   212

19. Chapter Nineteen   225

20. Chapter Twenty   233

21. Chapter Twenty-One   241

22. Chapter Twenty-Two   248

23. Chapter Twenty-Three   264

24. Chapter Twenty-Four   273

25. Chapter Twenty-Five   283

26. Chapter Twenty-Six   290

Glossary   300

About the Author   307

FATE FORGED   309

SUN FORGED   310

WAR FORGED   312

STAR FORGED   314

SHADOW FORGED   316

EARTH FORGED   318

LUST FORGED   320

WELCOME TO YITHIA

Beyond the ocean seldom seen
beneath the wavy green,
beholden to the mystic sheen,
they crowned the newborn queen.
In the blackest desert sand
as suns of three blared heat,
the Scorpious rose to command
Mascroba's sacred seat.

Welcome to Yithia.

by James Matthew Byers

Chapter One

THE SECURITY SERGEANT'S GAZE blazed a path across Ori's cheeks. He had to see the emotions roiling within her.

She struggled to hide them from him, fighting to remain still and smooth her features. It was hard. Her uncles had insisted she learned impassivity. With how terror paralyzed her, this wasn't possible. Pinching her lips stemmed the need to babble, to demand answers. She wished she could command the news to be good.

Uncontrollable tremors twitched her muscles. The effort to remain seated, to not pace, to strangle the nervous energy drove her insane. The bombardment on her senses was barely containable.

A port guard had brought her straight to this sergeant's office. He grimaced as he met her gaze. His features folded into an expression she recognized—distaste. Either her presence in his office bothered him, or he had news he didn't wish to impart. Judging by the way he pursed his lips, she leaned toward the latter.

"What seems to be the problem, miss?" His calm voice fueled her agitation, ramping the tension building in her chest.

His hesitation had to mean he had received word. No news, or not knowing, would have been a different conversation, one peppered with questions and assurances. Despite the fear gripping her heart, she grappled for control over the despair settling in her soul. Leveling her gaze with his, she steeled her determination. Fine, she could play it his way.

"My uncles haven't collected me. I haven't heard from them either, and this comm silence is scaring me." She jumped to her feet to pace, giving in to the anxiety enveloping her. If her agitation offended him, he didn't say. "Please check the news feeds. Something might have happened to them."

The sergeant sighed at his data tablet, taking time to search it.

She huffed at the pretense. He must think her too young to understand what he was doing. In her sixteen years, she had experienced more loss than many did in their entire lives, helping her to see through his ruse.

Uncle Diso had made certain she could read people well.

"You already know." Her voice spiked, revealing her inner turmoil.

His shoulders slumped, confirming her suspicions. "Yes." Exhaustion slithered through his voice, deepening it. "You might want to sit down, Ms. McKenzie."

"Just tell me." Her knees weakened at the despair in his eyes, and she collapsed into the chair.

"Pirates destroyed a cargo vessel on a return voyage from Mars's military base."

She sat in stunned silence, in disbelief, when he had, at last, voiced her fears. Something large clogged her throat, and she tried several times to swallow past it. Her garbled breaths didn't fill her burning lungs. In the end, she gave up, on the verge of hyperventilating. Her vision blurred around the edges, while ice flooded her face. Grabbing her stomach, attempting to stop the churning nausea, she shook her head. No. It couldn't be true.

"There were survivors?" She squeezed the words past her tight throat, despite the truth weighing on her, telling her not to hope. A tear slipped free to drip onto her jumpsuit, dissolving into the fabric with mesmerizing determination.

"No survivors. The news came from the base. They're salvaging the area. They had taken delivery from this specific vessel. According to the comms, it was a three-manned cargo drifter."

"It could be any three men, not necessarily my uncles." She grasped at straws. If there was any chance the report was wrong, she would cling to it. She fixed her unblinking gaze on his face, desperate for an ounce of hope.

"The transponder beacon belongs to their vessel, the *Ossicles*."

All energy drained from her, her life force choosing to follow her beloved uncles. She stifled a sob as best she could. The sound came out garbled yet recognizable. Clamping her lips shut, she shuddered under the effort to rein in her grief. He granted her a few minutes before coming around his desk to cup his hand over hers. The gesture seemed unnatural and awkward, his skin burning hers.

"I'm sorry for your loss." Compassion drenched his tone, hardening his voice as though he understood her pain. "What will you do now?"

She didn't know what to say.

Her uncles would expect her to grieve, but only when it was safe to do so.

At present, strangers surrounded her with no safe port to call her own. She needed a place where she could sacrifice herself to the burn behind her eyes and nostrils. Peace, absolute silence, time, and God willing, a sense of security before she would let the grief claim her. Sucking in a ragged breath, she squared her shoulders, straightened her spine, and wiped her escaping tears.

"Did your uncles leave you any tokens?" His kind voice irritated rather than soothed her.

She dipped her gaze to hide her rising anger, coating her pain in a thin layer of heated emotion. His gentleness rattled her when she battled to keep herself together. She ran her thumb along the edge of her jaw, needing the tactile sensation to ground her. "Yes, enough to start a new life. I did well in the exams. Finding work shouldn't be hard."

The sergeant typed something into his Optical Data Implant, or O.D.I., embedded in his left wrist, and rose. "Come with me. Universal Parts is always looking to hire." He strolled through his office door, glancing once to ensure she didn't fall behind.

Her leaden feet dragged. She struggled to generate the energy to take each step, her limbs limp, her knees threatening to buckle. Studying the sergeant's back, she furrowed her brow. She trusted him without hesitation when a uniform could be misleading. His kindness was a rare trait in the far reaches of space. But despite this, he probably wanted to pass the problem of a sobbing girl on to a prospective employee, washing his hands of her.

Uncle Diso said it was easy to falsify kindness. Everyone had ulterior motives. Yet here she was, trusting a stranger, even if he was the port-sergeant. He led her along the causeway, past garish food stalls reeking of reheated protein bars. Outside the staid, dark gray facade of a recruitment office, he paused. As the door slid open, he held it for her in out-of-place gallantry.

He ignored the receptionist and entered the office unannounced. "Darrian."

A chubby man glanced at the sergeant as he rushed forward to shake her hand. "Oriana McKenzie?"

She accepted his hand without thought and scrutinized his stature, his too-tight suit, and his forced cheerfulness. Uncle Diso had taught her to analyze the details in a person's character.

"I was about to comm you, but here you are."

"You were?" she whispered in a surprised tone, but kept her face indifferent, hoping to hide her grief.

The sergeant's stiff posture hinted at a relationship that wasn't amicable between the men. "Ms. McKenzie, this is Mr. Darrian—he is the recruitment officer for Universal Parts."

Mr. Darrian claimed to want to recruit her. Like a job mattered, like her life mattered. Her uncles were gone. Gone, like her parents, and she was once again alone. She couldn't shake the idea they had prepared her for this. Since her parents' death when she was six, they had become her guardians. Together, as a family, they had traveled the known galaxy, each uncle a tutor.

Uncle Bos had taught her how to fix anything since spare parts were scarce in outer space. Uncle Gayn had shared his knowledge, teaching her how to read and write, integrity, respect for life, alien cultures, and how to map the stars. Uncle Diso had embodied honor and Hatimaye, an ancient fighting style.

All three had loved her, without a doubt. They had raised her to value love, laughter, and friendship. She couldn't have asked for better fathers.

"We have a position available on Earth. You can start as soon as you like." Darrian's voice droned, slurred, but she caught the tail end of his words and assumed the rest.

"It can't be this simple?" Her tone implied indifference, but at last, she had command of her vocals again. It was best this way, cold...numb, to not feel, or at least, to give the appearance she had no feelings. She ignored the violence of the emotions trapped like panicked bats in her chest.

"Yes, I've seen your results. I've verified your background, and..."

The sergeant shook his head.

When Mr. Darrian stared in puzzlement, tilting his head like a confused piggish dog-cyb, the sergeant typed into his O.D.I. Her anger burst into flame, rising to squeeze her throat. A burning in her chest expanded to fill every inch of her until her hairline tingled. The sergeant must think of her as a child, or worse, an imbecile.

"What the sergeant is trying to tell you, sir, is that my uncles died today. Yes, Bos McKenzie trained me. Yes, I need this job. Yes, I'll take it." She held out a trembling hand.

Tears stained her face, but she met his gaze without flinching. Let him say a single word, and she would show him everything Uncle Diso had taught her. A night spent in a port cell would be a safe place to mourn.

The man accepted her offered hand, conveying his sympathy.

She hated his touch, hated the sergeant's as well. Not the skin on skin, but what their touch implied—sympathy, pity. She gritted her teeth. No one pitied a McKenzie.

"U.P. will receive the notification. The shuttle departs at 0600 tomorrow morning. We'll reserve passage for you." Mr. Darrian patted her hand.

She tugged her hand free before giving them a polite nod. "Thank you."

Leaving the office, she waited for the door to shut behind her. Once it did, she collapsed against the wall. Her gasps interspersed with dry sobs, yet the tears didn't flow.

Time slowed while she fought for strength, for sanity. She wanted to wail at the universe, at the injustice of it all, at the pain lancing through her, snatching her breath, holding her captive. She wanted to wail her sense of loss, to fight the growing void in her chest. Instead, she dove right in, seeking its darkness, its unemotional appeal, needing it to enshroud her in impassivity. As the shroud grew like an unquenchable inkblot, she died inside, numbing the pain that would await her when she resurfaced.

The dimmed lights and the shuttered stalls cast menacing shadows. The sounds of the bartender locking up were faint behind her while she debated what to do next. Not that she had many choices. Keeping to the lit areas, she could amble from food stall to food stall. A few remained open to serve the evening crews. Or she could head to the docking bay and wait outside the shuttle.

At the thought of food, her stomach growled. A sharp pang twisted her gut at her neglect. The nausea demanded she feed it something other than her own stomach lining and alcohol. She chose not to think about her last meal: what it had been, when it had been, and where it had been. That memory was best left alone. She feared it would trigger the pain, remove the cap on the firm grasp she had on her emotions.

One bowl of synthetic noodles later, she took an elevator pod to the docking levels. She activated her magnetic boots according to safety protocol, not wanting to draw attention if she disobeyed. The shuttle had docked, but the exterior door wasn't open, and the ramp not yet lowered. With nothing else to do, she ran an assessing gaze over the dilapidated transport junket and grimaced. The mismatched panels weren't official replacement parts for this Scorpio class vessel. An exterior vent was an issue.

The grooves marking the metal indicated the number of times the panel had needed repairing. The internal ejection of the panel concerned her. Only a serious malfunction in the engine's cooling system could blasted the panel off. Sub-standard repair bots had caused the external damage. Each scar from the many re-attachments indicated a marked lack of respect. Hence the bots.

Uncaring mechanics tended to have a short shelf life in the outer reaches. The added panels had removed sections of the vessel's name. These non-standard replacement parts were in grays, rusts, and greens. Bold colors against the ship's original white frame.

Other passengers arrived within an hour of the ramp's retraction. Shuffling toward it, she assumed her place in the crowd preparing to board. First come, first choice of the operational ketsi seats. She didn't need a seat to adjust to her backside or height when a quiet corner would do. Away from a visiting grandmother with tales of her grandchildren. Away from someone with wandering hands. Away from a nosey neighbor or a traveling salesman.

As soon as the ramp lowered, she rushed in to find an isolated seat. She scanned her O.D.I. over the protective belt to claim it. Once it unlocked, it registered and informed the trip advisor she had boarded. She grunted at his official title. After strapping herself in, she leaned her head on the headrest. Exhaustion slammed into her, draining her, and numbing her mind and heart.

As soon as they retracted the ramp, the exterior door locked, and the vessel's engines powered up, she slumped. Portraying a strong persona wasn't necessary under the dimmed lights. With a smothered sob, she swiped the paypad, purchasing a cryopen. A sharp pinch in the neck, the cold burn of a sedative, and the sweet silence of darkness consumed her.

 Chapter Two

Planet Etteria

The Royal Court at Issneen

12252 years

WARMTH SWELLED ENYL'S CHEST, but he tamped it down, stiffening his shoulders. He ignored the court's high ceilings of white Fuyra stone, the indigo and gold tapestries, indicative of his lineage.

"This year's Gifting did not have a single pairing. None of the presented females were able to summon the Ethera," King Xeus of Etteria announced. Glancing around the court, he met the blue gazes of his council members and ambassadors.

What mattered was his father's words, and the crisis they were in. The Gifting was a ceremony held every year for unclaimed females, sixteen years of age and older. They paraded before seeking males in the hopes of finding their life force. It had failed again, with yet another year lost.

The heavy burden of their failure and its effect on their future weighted his father's shoulders. "It is time we search beyond our borders. We have no other recourse left to us."

At his announcement, dissent rippled through the crowded court. Enyl hid his deep sigh, wishing the weight of his people's future rested on his shoulders, more so today than ever before. Each lineage had representatives in attendance. The rainbow colors of their cloaks were vivid against the white and blue of Etteria's court. A few males he respected, others he found taxing, but all were honorable as expected of Etterians.

"Taint our bloodline with inferior species?" The angry comment came from Ambassador Brenin.

Enyl was not surprised. He had not experienced intense emotions since he was a *damu*, but if he could, he would hate this male. Brenin's sole purpose was to object to every decision the king made. Enyl would admit though, Brenin did make his father consider his decisions with more care. Alongside him stood his niece. Enyl suppressed a scowl, making a mental note to steer clear of her today. Not that she was not beautiful or precious as an Etterian female. She hoped for more between them. He was not so inclined.

"We are at sixteen males to every female, Brenin. Three years ago, it was nine males, and twelve years prior, it was four males to one female." Anger and frustration tainted his father's voice. Enyl understood his father's struggle. Without Dar Eths, the Etterian nation would fade into obscurity. "Our numbers are declining. We need to diversify. A single male lost is unacceptable. I am informing you out of courtesy. Etteria has released the DNA to all known worlds in the form of a blood test." He drew in a slow, deep breath. "The void is growing within us all. We need to find our mates and birth daughters before we sacrifice ourselves in meaningless death."

Father swept his gaze across the court, portraying a firm and unrepentant stance. From the side of the dais, Enyl searched for discontent. Brenin's pursed lips meant Father had won this round. Remaining calm, Enyl maintained his stoicism since it was an expected Etterian trait. 'To feel was to fail' was the Etterian mantra they lived by. Father strode off the dais to where Enyl waited.

"I see you do not agree, Enyl." Anger seeped into his voice, his implication clear.

"I may not have voiced this earlier, Father, but I trust your decision, believe and pray it will work. I am a male eager for a pairing and intrigued with any compatible species we will find. Would they have biological or physical similarities?"

"I am as concerned. We have our best minds devising tests to ensure compatibility. We are not certain a compatible species will spark the Ethera in our people."

In the final stages of training as *damu*, all Etterians' ice-blue eyes darkened to indigo when the last volatile emotion drained from them. Paired with a non-Etterian Dar Eth meant her eyes would not pale as his would when the Ethera struck. To prove a successful pairing would rely on his own eye color conversion. He sucked in a sharp breath, hope claiming control of his emotions before he tamped it down.

"I wish for you to have the relationship I had with your mother, Enyl. Our females have evolved to pursue many *damu* and with countless males. Your mother's value improved greatly by her birthing you."

Father ran a hand over his face, revealing his inner turmoil. His father had spent days and nights making this decision, dragging Enyl into it. Yet, that single gesture mimicked the restlessness churning inside him. The void might be expanding deep within them both, threatening to consume their souls. And once it conquered, they could no longer feel nor care. Pursuing kills was the only way to feel again. The sweet rush was why the older males died on the battlefield.

Darkness engulfed his chest. He examined his father's face—so like his own. Yes, shadows had formed under his father's eyes, but there was a hint of sorrow. Alodon's balls, no, it was too soon for the void to take him.

"Numerous males sought her, and she left to pursue this, believing she did so for Etteria. This cost you the influence of a female in your formative years. It is unfair to ask our females to judge their value by their fertility. They deserve to find lasting contentment." Father sighed. "I believe we have yet to feel the full impact of the decisions we made centuries ago."

"A bold move," a female said, squeezing Enyl's shoulder.

Father spun at the intrusion, but his stern expression softened.

"Mother." Enyl grinned, covering her hand with his. "It is wonderful to see you. How fares Odoal and Morial?"

"He is why I am in Issneen. His training begins with yet another son leaving my arms. I mourn while my daughter enjoys the Crustiiu pools." She flashed a smile, placing her other hand on Father's shoulder in greeting.

The warmth between them was a familiar one. Her serene presence and bold beauty remained even at her advanced age. Had she called forth the Ethera in his father, she would have made a memorable queen.

"It is good to see you, Arazyl. Are your *damu* well?" A full smile split Father's cheeks before fading into the usual indifference.

"Yes, my sons are as well as can be with such a fine king as their liege. Today, I placed Odoal into your care."

Father accepted the compliment with a nod. "If he is anything like Droal, he will be an honorable male. You are not disappointed with my decision?"

Enyl folded his arms across his chest, observing their interaction. The attraction was still there, along with respect and compassion. Father valued Mother's opinion like she reigned alongside him. Her response would be an honest one. She had never allowed anyone's rank to sway her opinions.

"No. Etteria needs females. I sacrificed much for our world, my king, but I wish for a different life for my sons and any more females I might birth. Maker willing."

"Maker willing," Enyl said. Once a female birthed a daughter, she would remain with that male in the hopes of birthing another daughter. In the eyes of Etteria, Droal and her were paired without the Ethera or life force bond occurring. "I insist you and Droal join us for dinner."

"It would be our pleasure." She gave both their shoulders a squeeze and sauntered off. The silver and green of her ceremonial robe glimmered under the court's lighting. Her ebony braid was a stark contrast to the silver fabric.

Father's joy faded. Something cold slithered into Enyl's stomach, though what it was, he could not say. Perhaps he should have held off on leaving Etteria, just for a day or two. His travel attire revealed his intentions. It was similar to their standard military uniform but denser for further protection. He had pinned his indigo cloak with gold thread to his shoulders. The colors indicated his house and rank.

"You leave for Calustrum?"

"After dinner." Enyl arched a brow. "Unless you have need of me?" He had spent the last week performing royal duties, the weight of it draining his soul. He needed something, some way to ease the tension burning between his shoulders.

Father shook his head. "I will send for you should anything arise."

"I will head for the Galactic Council first and manage the search for a compatible species from Calustrum."

"I assumed as much." Father pursed his lips. "You do not seem yourself."

Enyl sucked in a sharp breath. He had not hidden his struggle well. Alodon's balls. "I have felt...restless of late, Father."

At his confession, his father stilled. "Then go with my blessing, my son." He flashed a grin but the humor did not reach his eyes. "You've grown into the perfect Etterian warrior. Tall, well-trained, battle-honed, and your thick braid states your honor. You have surpassed all my expectations and will make a great king."

Enyl frowned at the finality in his father's words like this was goodbye. He forced a chuckle, hoping to remind him they were alive and well. "Perhaps, one day soon, you can travel to Calustrum and challenge Remi?"

"It is a day I look forward to." Father offered a pained smile before striding away. "See you at dinner."

Despite his father's stilted response and rough movements, there was nothing Enyl could do about it. He was eager to walk away from the sadness and concern he read in everyone's eyes. Eyes that were still the indigo of unmated males and females. Within a few years, those expressions would diminish. Without mates, Etterians would cease to feel, cease to respond with civility, no matter the situation.

The darkness in his chest leaped with greedy delight. His own void had become more imminent in the last few days. But it should not be consuming him for a male of his age. Alodon's hell, he hoped to find a species soon and a pairing for his father. Before it was too late for them all.

Chapter Three

Planet Earth
Universal Parts, Maintenance Division
Year of 2252, March
Six years later.

IN THE SHADOWED JUNCTION to the engine rooms, Ori stared at the man, steeling her features. The yellowed lighting did nothing to enhance his attractiveness. She suspected she looked as jaundiced. Regardless, she knew better than to show an expression of any sort; he took it as encouragement.

Simon Ballard had harassed her since she had started at U.P. She had managed to ignore his jibes, his advances, him. The mourning numbness encasing her heart had thawed, and she was, at last, acknowledging his existence. When he had touched her backside, she'd thrust him against the wall. With a firm grip around his esophagus, she dug her fingernails into his skin with enough force to form bleeding half-crescent wounds. The temptation to rip it out had been overwhelming.

Thank goodness, she had the forethought to report his unwanted advances. Since management had done nothing, she assumed they hadn't read them. Or they had read them but planned to do nothing. U.P. had forsaken her, and judging the situation, she would need to defend herself. All the horrid interactions with Ballard had led to this unavoidable confrontation.

"This is your final warning, Ballard. Stay. Away. From. Me."

His partners in crime sniggered, flushing Ballard's face a ruddy color. The pink wasn't pleasant combined with his pale-blond hair. He had charmed her female colleagues who swooned at his feet. Ori wasn't one of them and had no intention of ever filling that role.

She disrespected him at every opportunity and could read him like a vacuum-kills label. Simple and predictable. Embarrassed, he did what she expected him to do—he rushed at her. She lunged to shorten the distance, gripped his shoulder with both hands, and kneed him in the groin. This required minimum effort on her part.

He doubled over in agony, giving her the opportunity to bring her fist down on the back of his neck. If she utilized too much force, it might do irreparable damage. After he collapsed to the floor, she crouched next to his groaning form. His vermillion uniform pulled tight over a well-defined body that roused no appreciation within her. She knew him, his type, and what he looked like on the outside mattered not. At his extended groaning, no sympathy rose, and she conveyed none when she arched an eyebrow. He had called her a cold-hearted bitch, and for him, she was. Her indifference, any number of dismissals hadn't stopped him from bothering her.

"Next time, I will break something." She kept her voice soft and lethal. With as much confidence as she could muster, she rose to her feet and sauntered off, appearing as impassive as before.

The second she sauntered through the thick fire-retardant door and out of their line of vision, she plastered herself to the rough, concrete wall of the passage to eavesdrop. Instinct screamed this wasn't over, that she had worsened the situation. She clenched her teeth. There was no other way to handle this. U.P. ignored her complaints, and despite the number of times she had put Ballard in his place, he rebounded with more determination.

"I hate her," he muttered.

She huffed. *Well, the feeling is mutual, idiot.*

"I don't know why you bother with the frigid bitch, Simon," one of the twins said.

There was something unstable about the twins. Nothing based in fact, more what she had heard on the buzz. They were snakes in the grass and untrustworthy.

"I say we get rid of her and earn money on the side," the other twin said in a tone she would recognize anywhere.

He delighted in the harming of others less fortunate than him. She had no qualms drawing blood, which was why he hadn't bothered with her. They ruled by fear yet were fearful of her. She smothered a snort. Deep down they were sad, lonely cowards.

"What do you have in mind, Alex?" Ballard sighed as he picked himself off the floor, grunting in the process.

"I have this connection who's looking to trade old parts for new ones. How about we let her take the knock?"

Her brow arched, and she fought a smirk. Oh, so that was how they wished to play this.

"That would mean she'd leave. How do I sleep with her then?"

"Huh? Did you not hear her?" Anger infused Alex's voice.

"Alex is right, Simon. She's never going to do you," slimy, untrustworthy Max said.

She held her breath. *Listen to them, Ballard. For once, they know best.*

"So what? We make a few tokens and frame her until she's arrested? Is that the plan?"

Silence descended, and for a second, she thought they had left. But there had been no footsteps, disappearing or otherwise. Her heartbeat pounded in her ears, affecting her ability to listen, enhancing silence until it beat at her eardrums. Taking in a deep yet soundless breath, she waited for Ballard's decision.

"You're right. Let's get her," he said.

She pushed away from the door, making a beeline for her engine room. After she latched the metal door behind her, she ran her thumb along the underside of her jaw. If she had some confidence in U.P., she might've left Ballard to cast aspersions on her character. Having documented everything upon arrival, she would continue to do so. Her line of fire would be transparency. She couldn't bring the twins' plan to the U.P. supervisors without evidence since it was hearsay.

But she couldn't stand by and let them do this to her. Her work was of a high enough standard to be of a value to U.P. With exhaustion thrumming through to her toes, she started her routine with one thought forming: her time at U.P. was ending.

SOUL FORGED

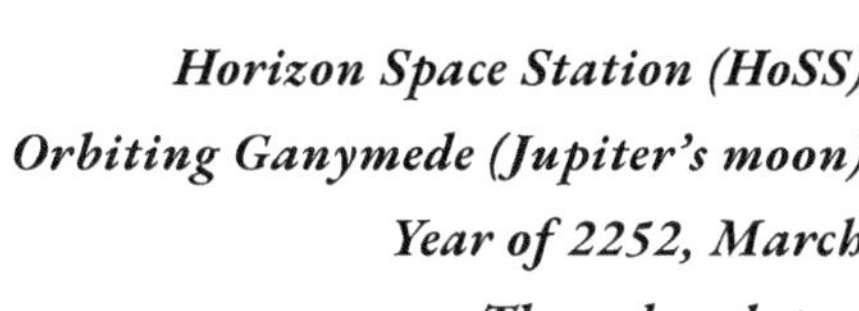

ORIANA'S LIFE HAD COME full circle. Except, it wasn't the luxury of the Lunar Base she'd docked at. No, this station was the worst, by reputation alone.

She stomped down the grooved metal ramp of the ancient transport junket and faced the death trap. Scanning the mottled panels and missing bolts on the exterior surface of the spacecraft, she grimaced. Nothing looked like it had been factory-fitted. The Grecian-class spacecraft's smooth lines carried the scars of inept mechanics, lack of tokens, and desperation. She smiled, grateful to be standing on the ramp. Surviving the journey was a miracle.

Facing the docking bays, she hefted her tattered bag onto her shoulder and sighed. Maintaining an unapproachable facade on the journey included ignoring her disembarking fellow travelers as they slipped past her. She hadn't looked for friendship or other primal connections a few crude passengers had suggested. No one wished her well, or Godspeed, and there was no one to share in her fears, sadness, or

21

loneliness. Had HoSS been a pleasure station, a luau welcoming party would have greeted her.

She straightened her shoulders and squelched her uneasiness. Where the work was, there she had to travel. Horizon Space Station was not a choice destination—a port on the edge of nowhere, last point of known civilization for anyone.

The structure orbiting the moon, Ganymede, wasn't a pretty one. Its initial purpose was a data-retrieval station. Fitted with extensive solar-power adaptors and backup fusion power cores, the station had been the jewel of the outer reaches. Yet its blatant neglect was evident, despite it still being in orbit. It housed an integrated community of various species and most of them suspicious or confirmed illegals. They lived within a patchwork of components, which the station's gravity generators managed to hold together. It would be her task to ensure that miracle continued to happen.

She focused on the plaza situated at the amalgamation of all docking-bay causeways. The elongated spidery pathways reached toward the docked ships. Located in the spider's abdomen were the product stalls.

Jumping off the ramp onto the magnetized causeway, she activated her boots to keep her attached to the floating floor. She thumped toward the bustling crowds, tightening her grip on her bag as she swept an assessing gaze over the area. This was the shit side of the galaxy where shitty people gathered to do shitty things to each other. Anyone like that crossing her path would receive the brunt of her intolerance. Not after having spent the journey in a ketsi seat that had long lost its ability to adjust to her shape. Her diplomatic skills were understandably absent.

She reviewed her concise mental checklist: Get to HoSS. Secure permanent accommodation. Arrive at HoSS Maintenance by tomorrow 0600.

One out of three wasn't bad, well, so far anyway. She stifled a smirk since it didn't pay to show emotion. People tended to approach her if she appeared welcoming. Damn, she hated that, hated making small talk. She knew the gist of it, and no matter which planet or circumstances she found herself in, the same scenario repeated itself.

No, she didn't come here often. No, she didn't have family. Yes, she had work. No, she had no other interests. No, she didn't want to suck him off. No, she wasn't frigid, and yes, she was a bitch. For once, she would like to find a man, strong and handsome, with self-respect and, above all, honor. He must be able to protect her when she couldn't protect herself. It wasn't unrealistic criteria, but dammit, such a man was rare indeed.

Merging with the crowds, she dodged a variety of recognizable species, mechanical pets out for a walk, and other hybrid humans. She ignored the colorful, unhygienic stalls selling a variety of goods, some edible, some lethal. A miasma of smells from the replicated foods and unwashed bodies assaulted her nose. A few odors promised nourishment for various species. Some of it made her stomach recoil. Diverse unknown languages teased her ears, but she had only activated Galactic on her O.D.I.

She hustled past a saloon entrance on her way to the housing unit office. Alcohol, sweat, smoke, and despair bullied her nose and another aroma she hadn't expected caressed across her senses. She reversed a few steps, ignoring the outraged cries from her fellow causeway users forced to weave around her.

Disbelief warred with the ever-present craving as she peered into the haze, past the clichéd holographic saloon doors and the antique gold lettering Bodacious. She pushed through the doors, letting her nose lead her.

The best seat in the bar was at the end of the counter, farthest from the entrance, and with the widest view. Sliding onto it, she waited for the alien bartender, an Algri, to notice her.

The alien was a mottled turquoise green. The shade indicated his extensive age, which was more than a human's maximum lifespan. Of course, they were all tentacles, making bartending easy for them. So many limbs, so many drinks, and those suckers ensured nothing spilt. They were an unemotional species. Uncle Gayn had been clear on this. It wasn't that they had control over their emotions. There was no emotion—an abyss—like a multi-tool had emotional range.

"I smell coffee. Would that be the good kind?" She arched a hopeful brow when he settled one of his six eyes on her.

"Arabica or Robusta—choose."

Those words sent tingles through her chest, more than any sexy man could've roused. "Arabica."

As soon as the metal mug appeared before her, she grinned like a fool. Cupping the mug, a delicious warmth saturated her fingers as she pulled it toward her nose to inhale. The liquid was black, strong, and perfect. She moaned, knowing her addiction was an unhealthy one since she would choose coffee over food any day. With reverence, she brought it to her lips, intent on savoring every drop.

A nudge to her side spilled half of it on her jumpsuit. In utter disbelief, she gaped at the growing dark stain scalding her through the thin white fabric. It looked like mechanical oil. As soon as the horror dissipated, she spun to glare at two grappling males. One was a human man, the other...a Yithian male. The human was insane. If the Yithian bit him—she shuddered—it would be a horrible way to die.

She scanned the inciting crowd for the security guy who had guarded the door. Not seeing him, she slapped the counter, leveling her gaze on the bartender to demand another mug, free of charge. He kept two eyes on the scrabbling pair, two eyes on the customers at the bar, and two searched for someone, perhaps the security guy. The Algri bartender might have to let the fight play out. She huffed, not wanting to intervene, but a cornered Yithian would use his teeth. Cytotoxins would melt the human from the inside out.

"May I?" She gestured to the fighting pair, needing the Algri's permission before she damaged his fine establishment.

His tentacles stopped cleaning the glass as two of his eyes rolled, focusing on her. His six eyes blinked in its version of a nod. She launched herself off the stool, tackling the brawling pair to the dirty artificial flooring.

As intended, she took the males by surprise. Jumping up, she kicked her left heel with precision into the jaw of the human man, knocking him out. The Yithian hadn't hesitated, rising to face her. She dropped to her haunches to dodge his swinging arm. Her jumpsuit pulled tight over her knees and thighs as she threw a forward punch to his groin. Her knuckles hit something fleshy and hard, bringing a twinge of pain to her hand. He crumpled, grabbing at his crotch with a sharp hiss. She jumped up and heeled him between the eyes.

Not winded from the exertion, she hadn't worked up a sweat. While massaging her bruised knuckles, she scanned the unconscious Yithian. She hadn't seen one in real life. He was shark-like, with gray slimy skin and a neck so wide it met his upper arms, like an equilateral triangle. They were humanoid and had a groin to target. Their eyes were wide apart, similar to Earth's great white sharks but inky black. They didn't have a blind spot like a hammerhead shark, despite the buzz to the contrary. Her studies had indicated their weaknesses were their eyes, throat, groin, and knees.

She squinted, trying to recall all the cultural facts she had learned. The cacophonous roar of the saloon returned at once. Snapping out of her deep thoughts, she almost twitched at being the center of attention.

"Here." The Algri placed a fresh cup of Arabica on the counter's surface.

She resumed her seat to savor it while sweeping the room to ensure no one else dared spill it. Both seats to either side of her remained unoccupied. She shrugged, content with that.

When station security removed the limp bodies, she snuck nervous glances at them. Since the officers didn't acknowledge her, she relaxed. Twice now she had jeopardized her freedom and almost earned a night spent in a cell. Missing her 0600 appointment tomorrow morning was unacceptable.

"You need work?"

She jerked, then shook her head at the Algri. "I have work."

"You work evening?" The alien leveled his six eyes on her.

She frowned as she calculated the possibilities. The extra tokens would come in handy. Moreover, all she would have to do is stand around and threaten patrons. This was workable for her.

"For tokens?" She gasped as all six eyes blinked at her. That would be a yes. "What else?"

"One Arabica per shift." Damn, with coffee included. Her mind lingered on the many coffees that awaited her. She must've taken too long to respond, for the Algri spoke again, his voice a monotone, "and a housing unit."

"Deal."

Four eyes stayed on her and two focused on the door. "You start now."

She shrugged, having been sitting and sleeping for three days. Some time standing was what she needed.

"More breasts," the Algri said when she climbed off the stool.

"What?" Maybe she had misheard him in the din of the bar.

"Show breasts, make tokens for bar. Shirt fine, no suit."

Typical. Sighing, she unzipped her jumpsuit, slid out her arms, and draped over her backside. The fabric absorbed liquids, so her white vest remained free of coffee, lubricant, or mechanical stains. This was a plus in her profession, although, she hadn't tested it with blood.

She arched a brow. "Better?"

The Algri assessed her with his six-eyed steady gaze. It didn't make her skin crawl because it was with greed he studied her state of dress. "Will get you uniform."

She scowled. "No skirts." Staring him down, she waited.

His tentacles rippled before he blinked his eyes. "Fine, you stand by door."

She assumed a firm stance at the door. A tall, scarred man appeared beside her. He was the absent security she had seen before. Stunned to see her there, he glared but didn't introduce himself or speak to her. His gaze bored into her, and she stiffened her shoulders against it. Whatever his issue with her, it didn't matter. She was there to stay.

Chapter Four

WITHIN THE FIRST HOUR, she had settled two "arguments." Her knuckles bled on her bruised right hand, but under the circumstances, it was minor. She detained a thief awaiting station security pickup. Holding his arm in a hammerlock, she pressed his face to a wall. If he moved in any way, he would dislocate his own shoulder. Of course, her partner was absent. Again. She scowled, his blatant disregard for his security position angered her.

"You're new," a human man said.

She admired his station-security uniform and the blaster holstered to his thigh. He was tall for a human, broad-shouldered, and the largest muscles in his thighs were well-defined. His uniform—dark gray trousers with a silver, protective armor plate—did his bare pecs and deltoids justice, as well. His face wasn't bad either. An attractive man on Horizon was rare.

"How much is the Algri paying you?"

"He pays me in coffee." Her grin was unrepentant. Despite her determination to remain aloof, the amount of attitude she had endured this evening had called forth her humor. She could lose her patience or gain a sense of humor. The latter seemed less effort.

The man chuckled, shaking his head. "Welcome to HoSS. Here, pass him over to my partner."

Tugging on the thief's twisted arm, she handed him over to the quiet officer standing to the side

"Come by the station sometime. I would love to hear why a beautiful woman like you is in this shit hole."

"You charmer." Smiling, she waved his invite aside. "I've had four marriage proposals this evening. You're offering me a chat when I could be wearing fake diamonds on these well-manicured fingers." She waved her grease-stained hands in front of her face.

His smile dimpled his cheek. "Aw shucks, my missus won't like it if I bring home a new wife."

She laughed, delighted at his teasing response. He wasn't wearing a ring or sporting a matrimonial tattoo which meant he wasn't serious about having a wife. He focused his brown eyes on the thief, the retinae spinning, indicative of bio-optics, or bionic implants. It was the standard practice for security staff to invest in upgrades, the law of escalation, and so forth. In this case, the bio-optics implant strengthened the connection between the O.D.I. and the sec-crime databases. He had the low down on anyone he focused his gaze on.

"In that case, I'll make sure to come see you boys. Always pays to be friendly with men with nice big guns...and blasters." She winked at him.

He smiled as he escorted his new prisoner out of Bodacious. By her shift end, there were no more "arguments." It might've been due to the dwindling clientele than any skill on her part though. Her hand throbbed more than she had expected it to. The bruises and swelling suggested she might need to pay for a medic.

"Good." The Algri glided to her and gestured with four of his twelve tentacles for her to follow him.

She darted over to the lockers to collect her bag, throwing it over a shoulder with her good hand. He traveled fast on those limbs of his, but she managed to catch up. She was curious as he led her along a narrow passage a short distance from the bar. The flickering artificial lights, dirty, white-paneled walls, and filthy grated flooring gave off a sinister vibe.

They breached another door and entered a causeway holding housing units in line with what she had expected a space station to have. After another five minutes, he stopped outside an air-seal door. 28508c in disease-riddled letters embossed the metal.

"Name?"

"Ori," she said, preferring he use her shortened name.

"Boblisknesooput." A garbled sound came from the Algri.

She blinked but didn't ask him to repeat it. Instead, she tried to pronounce his name. Doing so showed respect, even if or when she didn't succeed. "Bob…?"

"Bob good." Six eyes blinked in sequence as he handed her a key card and scurried off.

She stared at the dirty card and shuddered; the urge to sterilize it made her skin crawl. After swiping the key over the console, she peeked into her new home and released a deep sigh.

It was a standard metal cube, five by five by three meters. The side wall was back-lit with the usual soul-sucking UV lights. Creeping inside, careful not to touch anything, she located the bed and called it out of its hidden compartment. She sniffed the mattress, gagging at the odor. The rehydrator and replicator received the same treatment.

Slipping out of the quarters, she shut the door and authorized a sterilization spray. She winced at the cost, but she had foreseen the expense. Projecting a patience she didn't possess, she waited for a green light to flicker before entering the room again.

The subtle sting of antiseptic and bleach greeted her. Better.

Dumping her bag, she left at once, heading for medical. As she strode along the causeways following the emergency signs, she examined her hand. A punch or a deflection maneuver might have caused a sprain. And despite the short spikes of agony when she flexed it, she expected a break to be worse.

Through a sterilization spray, she entered the bright white lights of medical, wincing at the white bulkheads, ceiling, and flooring. Exhaustion summoned a smirk at the thought of asking them to treat her for blindness, as well. Bypassing a male bleeding in a white chair, she ambled to the reception counter and leaned her uninjured hand on its immaculate surface.

"I don't know if you've noticed, but that man is staining your floor." She flicked a thumb at the blood pooling beneath the poor man.

"Shit." The woman, also in white overalls, rushed past her, tugging a device out of her pocket. She scanned him while holding her white-gloved hand to his wound. Her sigh of relief a few minutes later let Ori know he would make it.

"Hello, may I assist you?"

With her focus elsewhere, Ori hadn't seen the male nurse arrive. She sliced a glance behind him at the door marked 'Staff Only' then shrugged.

His sterility mask smothered his masculine voice and hid most of his physical features. If he appeared beside her on the causeways, she wouldn't be able to recognize him. He wore a sort of cap, plastic transparent goggles, the sterility mask, and his white overalls. Well, it was better to be cautious than dead, with the sterilization spray was 99.9% effective against most known germs. Some alien species had blood that was poisonous to humans.

"I suspect I've sprained my wrist." She raised it to show him.

He gestured to a stall. She climbed onto the bed and left the chair for him. He sprayed red foam over her hand, rubbing it in before wiping it off. The throbbing and burning had intensified, and now pulsed to her heartbeat.

"Why is it red?" She indicated the foam canister. "Is it to cover up the blood?"

The medic nodded. He must have heard this question a million times and thought it was easier to agree with her. Sterility had been a subject Uncle Gayn had covered.

"Liar." She paired her soft accusation with a cheeky grin. "Not all aliens have red blood, so if that was the case, you would need a canister for each species on Horizon."

His brown eyebrows arched above his goggles.

"Is the color dependent on the level of contamination?" She wiggled her uninjured hand. "My hands tend to go places no anatomical part should ever go."

The medic chuckled. "We only use yellow and red. Those living in a sterilization unit would use the green."

She offered a smile in thanks as he scanned her hand. The device made her fingers tingle. After a while, he wrapped it with a neo-band with precise yet fast wrist flicks.

She admired his skill. "How bad is it?"

"You should be fine within a day or two. A sprain no longer takes weeks to heal, especially with this new technology. Would you like an anesthetic?"

She shook her head; she didn't need the extra cost. As it was, seeing a medic would be expensive.

"May I ask how you received this injury? Did you fall? Angry boyfriend?"

Anger burned along her veins while she stared at him, not knowing how to respond to his prying. With no partner backing her up, injuries were bound to happen. It made her blood boil, that the other security guard had stood by and let her get hurt. She had glared at him when she returned to her position. His response was an arched eyebrow in a condescending way.

The medic cleared his throat. "My name is Liam. If you ever need any assistance, comm me." The buzz up her arm confirmed her O.D.I. received his details.

"I work at Bodacious, hence the injury, Liam, but thank you for the offer."

"I've been on this station a long time, miss. I've learned not to judge." He cleaned up his mess before giving her space to hop off the bed. "You need to limit your movement for at least twelve hours. Please see the desk for payment."

"Thank you again." As she left, the burn of his gaze on her back added to the premonition she would visit him often.

Within minutes of returning to her unit, she had her bag unpacked. Delighted the previous occupant had left a ration of water, she scrambled to peel off her jumpsuit. She soaped and rinsed before crawling onto her sterilized bed. Her hand didn't ache, which raised the suspicion Liam had administered an aesthetic anyway. The water-resistant neo-band was still dry to the touch.

Spreading out on her back, she stared at the ceiling where the back-lit wall cast lifeless shadows. Her arrival at Horizon Space Station had gone better than she had expected. She had two jobs and a place she could live in. It wasn't home. No place could ever be home again; home had been with her three uncles. She had been alone for so long. After flipping onto her side, she double-checked the alarm on her O.D.I. before sleep claimed her.

ORIANA WAS AWAKE SECONDS before her alarm vibrated her arm. Groaning as she sat up, the aches and pains from the previous day roared their displeasure. Dodging most of the attacks didn't mean the impact of her blows didn't have their own cost. This went without saying when her "arguments" were with cybernetic-enhanced individuals. It had been a while since she had to fight; the unused muscles protested her abuse.

She rubbed her face. Another few hours of sleep wouldn't go amiss. Thank goodness, the artificial lights of the station mimicked Earth days. She didn't think her body could handle the extended days if the station followed Ganymede's rotations. Her twelve-hour shifts were a killer, but she understood the shift length. Someone had to be in the engine rooms to minimize sabotage. Her shift at Bodacious would be six hours long, leaving her five hours to sleep. It was tight, but she could do it for the extra tokens.

Besides, she hadn't found a purpose yet. She lived one day at a time knowing this wasn't what her uncles would've wanted for her. With no other goals, she had fallen onto the idea of purchasing her own craft. A fast one and small enough for a single person to manage. She could be a runner, a courier. If stranded, she could repair most faults and defend herself if she encountered pirates, scoundrels, or lousy clients who could be all or none of those things.

She smirked, unraveled her hair to brush it, braided it, and coiled it into a tight bun on top of her head. It was a hazard if left loose. But she couldn't afford to pay for a cut, nor did she have the tools to do so herself without hacking at it with a laser pen. She sighed; her hair was a separate issue. Neither of her uncles had liked her cutting it, so she kept it long in remembrance of them. One day soon, after she had grieved, she might be able to let go, but that day had yet to dawn.

She slipped on her boring and serviceable white bra. The wide strip of fabric tried to contain her breasts. They were larger than she would've liked, but she wasn't top-heavy. Regardless, they tended to attract unwanted attention from her male colleagues. The year was

2252, and yet men still thought there was a correlation between loose morals and the size of a woman's breasts. On the outskirts of the galaxy, where most of the pioneers were men, she could understand how their thinking was antiquated.

She pulled on her comfortable, blue boy shorts. Over this, she yanked on her cleanest, nondescript, forest green jumpsuit. Completing her designer ensemble, she added her black work boots before zipping up her suit. She slipped her clean key into one of the many pockets of her cargo jumpsuit. The continued use of key cards showed how old the station was. At U.P., she had scanned the pad with her O.D.I. to access her room.

On the way out the door, she grabbed one of the protein bars she had tossed onto the rehydrator's inactivated surface. It wasn't a proper meal, but it was chocolate-flavored and would silence the hunger pains. Now to face the reason why she had come to HoSS in the first place.

Chapter Five

Horizon maintenance was easy to locate. Maintenance offices were always in the bowels of any building or station. For obvious reasons, they needed to be near the engines, generators, and filtration systems. Oriana strolled into the dull green office, ten minutes earlier than her appointment. She liked to be early. It implied she was responsible, competent, and trustworthy. Uncle Gayn had said to be late was disrespectful.

She introduced herself to the Maloidian behind the counter. The alien was pretty with her pale-yellow skin and solid black eyes. Her coloring was startling against her pallor. Variegated gray traditional markings flowed over her forehead and merged into her tentacles. These swayed in a casual way. Their emotions didn't affect the undulation. It was disconcerting when a Maloidian became angry. Dark yellow splotches formed all over their skin. But their tentacles swayed like seaweed on an ocean floor unaffected by the storm above the surface.

The Maloidian stared at her in a curious manner like she recognized Oriana from somewhere. She returned the stare with an impassive face, not bothering to raise a brow in query.

"Mr. Morgan will see you now, Ms. McKenzie." The rise and fall of the Maloidian's voice was startling at first, yet it had a melodic cadence.

"Thank you," Ori whispered, striding into the office filled with a rich soil smell. Pausing for a deep breath, she searched the room for the source. Plants—some of them bearing fruit and others flowers—covered the back bulkhead.

"Mr. Morgan." She offered her hand.

The elderly gentleman frowned as he accepted it. He shook it once and dropped it with his lip curling into a sneer. She fought the urge to study her palm, expecting to find dirt or dried blood on it.

"I didn't expect you to be this attractive, Ms. McKenzie." His abrupt statement surprised her, though she didn't reveal it.

"Since I'm entombed in an engine room, does it matter?" She offered a smile to soften her words.

"I suppose not." He touched his data tab on the desk before him. "You come highly recommended. Universal Parts was sad to see you go."

"They said that?" She barked in disbelief, her voice sounding harsher than she had intended.

"Want to tell me what has you so tense?"

At his calm question, she frowned, debating whether to tell him. In the end, if she didn't and he found out later, he would think her dishonest.

"They accused me of sabotaging their onsite generators. Said my workmanship was of a poor quality. Said I used secondhand parts in order to sell the new ones on the black market." She huffed. "I logged many comms stating the parts as sub-par. I indicated my concerns and included visual evidence with serial numbers. I can't believe they would now endorse me. Do you know they escorted me off the site? Like a criminal."

She took in a deep breath—she was revealing too much. The injustice of it and the treatment she had received spiked her anger which she thought she had dealt with. Ballard had gotten away with this. Transparency had been well and good, yet no fingers had pointed at the culprits. In the end, she looked guilty, covering her supposed sabotage with falsified documentation.

"It states here the sabotage continued after you resigned." Mr. Morgan tapped and flicked at his tablet. She scowled but didn't speak. "They attempted to contact you to apologize and reinstate you."

"I was on my way to Horizon on a death-is-nigh transporter." Her caustic comment brought a twist to his lips.

"Regardless, the position is still available to you." He stilled and waited for her response.

"You don't want me to work for you?" She kept her tone unwavering as she met his gaze.

He had the decency to blush. "I can't spare men to guard you. This is Horizon."

"I'm aware of where we are, Mr. Morgan." She rose, placed her palms on his desk and leaned forward to drive home her next words. "I'm staying. I have accommodation and another position for my evening shift, which you need to be made aware of. If you believe I can't protect myself, visit the Bodacious and judge for yourself."

Now to nail home her point. "I'm prepared to work. I'm a dedicated, conscientious employee, but if you prefer not to hire me, I'll still not return to U.P." She met his gaze for a full minute before he lowered it to his data tab.

"All right, Ms. McKenzie. We'll start on-trial with a security cyborg trailing your movements—station policy, I'm afraid."

She grimaced. A sec-cyb. "For how long?"

"A month. All employees behave in the first few weeks."

What choice did she have? "Very well." She returned to her seat, hiding the relief softening her spine.

A sec-cyb on her ass meant an artificial intelligence would be documenting her every move, would remain within her unit, and would be present at Bodacious. Since it was station policy, Bob shouldn't have a problem with it.

"Your shift is 0700 to 1900. Your shift partner is Joseph Johansson." His lips twisted in displeasure, his dislike of Johansson obvious. "U.P. sent your severance pay." He tossed a chip the size of a thumbnail onto the desk. "It's as close to an apology as you'll get."

She picked it up and frowned. Her first response was to throw it into the disposal receptacle, but a craft would cost a shit ton of tokens. She couldn't afford to be self-righteous; she needed every token she could earn. Sighing, she slid it into a pocket.

"You're assigned to E9. Handover occurs at shift start and end," Mr. Morgan said. "Johansson will complete a full report on your performance, as well."

"You won't regret this, Mr. Morgan. Please call me Oriana or Ori." She stood to leave, glancing at her O.D.I.'s time.

"My name is Andrew."

She forced a reserved smile and left. That had been nerve-racking, and the aftermath had her heartbeat skipping.

Stopping outside the office door, she yanked out the chip. When she pressed her thumb to the back, it read her biometrics before it pulsed a green number. She blinked at the amount. Shit. They must be stricken with guilt. In case they changed their minds and revoked it, she ran the chip over her O.D.I. to transfer the tokens into her account.

"You're hired?" The Maloidian female's excitement was palpable, her smile wide and welcoming. She arched a non-existent brow at Andrew who hovered in the doorway of his office. "Wonderful. Andrew had these ordered for you." She dumped two sets of dark gray maintenance jumpsuits into Oriana's surprised hands. "It's a female's one-size-fits-all." She glanced at Ori's wide hips and thick thighs, and smiled. "Hope it fits."

She had muscled thighs, and Ori wanted to tell her so but knew the Maloidian meant no insult.

"I'm Ssash, by the way."

"Ori." She smiled.

"I saw what you did yesterday." She bounced on her feet, her skin brighter in her excitement with her tentacles trailing every jostle and swing she made.

"What did I do?" Ori tried not to wince. Many things had happened yesterday—she had been busy since she had arrived at Horizon.

"With the Yithian, you know. I would've been so scared. All those teeth." Ssash's smile widened, her excitement making her tremble. Yet her tentacles remained serene. Ori tried not to stare at them with morbid fascination. "Out of nowhere, you floored him. Mikey, my boyfriend, couldn't stop talking about it. We stayed the whole night to watch you."

"It seems I needn't have worried, Ori." Andrew shook his head. "Ssash hasn't been able to shut up about it."

"Epic. We're going back this evening. Bodacious has never been so much fun." She skipped away, not hearing Ori's huff.

"I'm entertainment now," she whispered as she fought the urge to bury her face in her new jumpsuits.

"It's only for a while until they grow bored."

She shrugged at Andrew's comment, sighed, and crushed her jumpsuits against her chest. "Thanks again for the opportunity, Andrew."

He waved, disappearing into his office. She glanced at her O.D.I. again and rushed to her unit, needing to change if she was going to make it in time for handover.

ORI PACED OUTSIDE E9's air-seal door waiting for Johansson. If Andrew didn't like him, she expected not to like him either, but she shouldn't judge. Her uncles had been clear on that. Who knew what circumstances had occurred to make a person the way they were.

At six-feet-four, the sec-cyb loomed, his red eyes glowing. His synthetic skin sagged which placed him as a late 21st century model.

Self-maintenance had become a standard feature in sec-cybs created post 2100. Its manufacturer had suffered a devastating data sabotage and hadn't recovered their market share. Sec-cybs were a rare breed.

"You have two minutes and forty-three seconds remaining," he grumbled in a tinny and grating voice. She grimaced, praying she would survive the next four weeks without pulling his plug. Judging by the gouges in his head-plating, many had tried.

She was late. The engineers she had encountered en route had been aggressive. They had demanded to know her name, her purpose for being there, who hired her, and so on. After Andrew verified her details, they let her pass.

Their caution was appreciated, but she hadn't liked the looks they had thrown at her...a young woman. She must have slept with Andrew, and therefore, had no skill sets. And if she was so free with her favors, then she might sleep her way to the top. She snorted. Top of HoSS Maintenance was a lifelong dream, but not for her.

Despite one or two staring at her breasts for the entire conversation, she had remained professional. She had to fight the urge to smack them, knowing from her years at U.P. any physical chastisement on her part would make her an outsider.

The air-seal door opened, and a short, stout man climbed through. When he saw her, he straightened, not that it helped his appearance. The pale white light from the bulkhead gleamed off his bald head. She winced when she imagined him naked. He was bald on top with a bulging belly. A tuft of hair at his shirt collar said he was hairy all over. Not that it was a bad thing, but coupled with the stench of him, it was an unpleasant image. Her nose twitched. His skin looked oily, and his eyes—she couldn't make out the color—squinted at her. She held back a shiver while his gaze roamed over her.

"You must be Oriana McKenzie." When he expelled a deep sigh, it slumped his shoulders. He expected her to mistreat him.

"Yes, I'm your new shift partner." At her confirmation, he didn't look up to meet her gaze.

"Mr. Morgan said you were on your way."

So, Andrew had at least taken the initiative—she wished he had done it to the entire team. She hadn't appreciated the delay.

"Any issues to report? Anything needing my attention?" She gestured to the engine room behind him.

The dip of his head revealed his shyness. She was a heel for being so abrupt with him. Andrew's judgement of this man had clouded hers. Persecuted by her dead uncles's teachings, she frowned.

"I tell you what, Johansson, how about showing me around the engine room? I want to know exactly what you think are problem machines and any improvisations or improvements you've made. Since you are here, it must mean Andrew thinks highly of your skill." Her kind words startled him, and his cheeks mottled.

"Uh, the belts for the...uh, water filtration systems are failing. We're running out of parts." He snuck a glance at her before lowering his gaze to the grated floor. His bio-optics glowed red, standard implants for working in the dark.

"Thank you. I know you're exhausted, but can you spare the time now?"

He opened the door, his cybernetic fingers gripping the handle with ease. She smiled; further enhancements for added strength. Evidence that Johansson loved his job in his eagerness to sacrifice organic limbs.

Hot on his heels, she stepped into the engine room, her gaze riveted by the engines she would be responsible for.

"Curious that you have a sec-cyb," he said as waited for her new best friend to bend itself through the door. He slammed the door and locked the latch as the cyborg settled in the corner and "observed."

"Policy," she shrugged, returning her focus to the levels-high engine room. Larger than she expected, its eight platforms housed generators for electricity, gravity, and filtration systems for air and water. Ladders connected the metal-grated passage to each grated platform and up to the next platform. Four levels ascended the one side of the room, with staggered platforms at various heights dependent on the size of the machinery they catered for.

The dim lighting cast deep shadows throughout the perforated platforms. The machinery generated a tremendous amount of heat sweltering the room. The lighting installed was as per the standard specifications, but they burned hot in an already overheated room. The less lighting there was the better, temperature-wise.

She took a deep breath, inhaling the miasma of oil, engine grease, and steam. The scent brought Uncle Bos to mind.

Flicking a gaze at the sec-cyb, she tapped a few notes on her O.D.I. "What do I call you?"

"I am SC2100 dash 24590."

She sighed. "Anything shorter?"

"No," it droned.

"I shall call you Sam." She clambered up a ladder.

"Sam is acceptable," it said.

Within the first hour, she had come to one conclusion. No matter how shy Johansson was, he was good at his job. Except when it came to tightening the bolts, he didn't go as far as he could. And when he applied grease to the gaskets, he left the excess along the edges. Overall, she was happy with his work ethic. She supposed Andrew wouldn't have tolerated Johansson otherwise, so her compliments to him hadn't been far off the mark.

"Hello, my babies. Tell mama what's the matter?" she crooned and got to work familiarizing herself with the machinery in her engine room. As the hours ticked by, she spoke to Sam, stating her findings for his records. As trained, she adhered to Uncle Bos's three-step process: Annotate, Assess, Advance.

By shift end, she was more familiar with E9 than she was with her own body.

Chapter Six

Horizon Space Station (HoSS)
Orbiting Ganymede (Jupiter's moon)
Year of 2252, March
Three weeks later.

STANDING OUTSIDE HER ENGINE room, with the door sealing her out, Ori stared at her O.D.I., disbelieving the instructions.

She tilted her arm, checking the holographic words. "This is insane."

She hit the comm button, needing to speak to her boss, Andrew. It didn't take long for him to accept her communication request and under the circumstances, she didn't bother with a cordial hello.

"Mechanics are underappreciated, underpaid, and overstressed and you just assigned me to that department. What do you mean by new species? Who's taking my shift? For how long?"

Andrew's face flickered in the image as he hurried around his desk. "An unknown ship and species limped into the docks. Eighty percent of our mechanics are down with Vemys-49, and the remaining few still standing don't know how to work with Maloidian steel."

Her heart leaped into her throat, strangling her voice. Of course, she knew how to work with it but only because of Uncle Bos.

"I overheard you mention how much better your repairs would be if you could get your hands on Maloidian steel. I didn't just put my neck out for nothing, Ori, did I? You can work with it, right?"

"Relax, Andrew. I'm on my way to the docks now. Who's my contact?" With her coffee in hand, she hurried to the elevator pods that would take her to the docks.

The yellow stripes lining the metal bucket enhanced the miasma of sweat and strange foods, churning her hastily eaten protein bar. A steel hand slapped the thick door, stopping it from closing. The glow of red preceded Sam with the other occupants shuffling out of his way.

"Penderson, docking bay 12Y."

With a cry of dismay, she ended the comm and punched in level twelve. As soon as the doors opened, she trashed her unfinished coffee and broke into a sprint, not bothering to activate her boots on the causeway. Y meant all the way at the end of the bays. Her thighs and calves burned, screaming her failure to maintain her fitness level. Working at Bodacious should have covered that, but fighting had done nothing to improve her stamina.

Stretched before her like splayed fingers were the causeways. Alongside a few were various ships "docked," as in clamped in place. There was nothing above, below, and beyond but the wide-open expanse of the outer reaches of space. A shimmer showed the dome activated, trapping what gravity the station generated. Blinking lights in the dome marked the gates in different sizes to accommodate all ships. A dome pulsed nearer to the causeways, keeping precious oxygen within the station. Each docking level had the same layout. The lowest bays were for the bigger ships. The higher docks held the cruisers, junkets, couriers, and hoppers.

When she spotted the sleek, dark silver scimitar-class ship, she fell into a dazed amble, gasping at the beautiful lines and its shape, that of an elongated water droplet. Closer to its engines to the rear of the ship was a gaping hole. The twisted metal reaching outward like tentacles implied an internal explosion and not from an asteroid as she had initially thought. A mechanic in a bright orange jumpsuit waited at the station ten meters from the lowered ramp where two Etterian warriors guarded.

Forget about the ship, these males were as beautiful. Tall, bronze-skinned with striking features and black braids to their heels. They earned the right to wear their hair long based on their performance in battle and in service. Super long braids meant they were elite.

Each had a blaster strapped to their military-black pants and their bulging arms folded across their massive chests. In her world, it was rare for men to be so masculine. Not an expression crossed their faces, but their indigo gazes darted everywhere, suspicious of everything.

"McKenzie?" The mechanic coughed into her elbow, her curls bouncing. "Here is my toolkit, my access card." And with a swipe of her arm across Ori's O.D.I., she spun to leave. "That's the location of the parts store. I'm due in quarantine."

Ori stared after her, only now seeing the sweat beading her pale skin and the purple of her lips. She wasn't worried about contracting the virus, having renewed her vaccinations just last month. Red lights flickered off the station's metallic floor. With a huff, she faced Sam.

"Glad you could make it." She grinned. He was a self-learning sec-cyb, and perhaps if she had years with him and permission to tamper with his coding, he could laugh with her.

"Your human humor is wasted on me, but I thank you for the sentiment."

Ignoring him, she marched over to the Etterians, struggling to remember how to address them. Uncle Gayn had taught her about them, which she suspected he had learned from an old Durn they had befriended, his blue-skinned face and white hair coming to mind. When she halted in front of the Etterians, they peered at her, assessing her from the caps of her boots to her hair.

"Greetings, warriors et Etteria." To at last meet an Etterian, she grinned, bouncing on her toes. "I'm here to repair your ship."

"A female?" The left Etterian arched a black-winged brow.

"Your assistance is not needed, female. We require the parts to perform the repairs ourselves." The right Etterian's tone implied she couldn't repair a torn sheet of paper.

They wanting to do their own repairs didn't surprise her since they trained in all aspects of Etterian life. She had always liked their culture.

"Understood. What parts do you need?" She activated her O. D.I., waiting to type in the list of parts.

They hesitated, shooting glances at each other as if neither knew the answer. Their stunned silence was comical, but she didn't laugh, not wanting to offend them.

"As I've seen so far, something exploded. Has the cause been attended to, or is there a chance of further explosions?" She deactivated her O.D.I. and used her hands to mimic an explosion.

"We have addressed the issue," Left Etterian said, pinching his lips into a disapproving line.

"I'll tell you what. Let me examine the damage, then I'll recommend the best approach." She gestured to the hydraulic H-lift locked to the causeway. They spun as one to look at it, but when they faced her again, their gazes fell on Sam who loomed over her.

"Why do you have a mechanical Earthian guarding you?"

She smiled, disbelieving she was in this situation. Revealing that Sam was to ensure she wasn't a threat to the station would be unwise. They wouldn't let her near their ship if they considered her untrustworthy, and the chance to work with Maloidian steel was too much of a temptation for her to risk with ill-chosen words.

"I am considered beautiful and precious." She dipped her chin, pretending to be shy. Pursing her lips, she swallowed her laughter, needing them to believe her. Her answer was one they would accept considering their protectiveness of females.

"You *are* small, and your coloring *is* unusual." The right Etterian ran a bold appraisal over her body again.

"Thank you. Now, the H-lift?"

He held up a palm, asking her to wait as he activated his O.D. I. "Supreme Commander, the Earthian engineer needs to assess the damage."

"Why is this so difficult for them to understand this simple repair?" A deep voice rumbled over her nerves. Her insides pooled at the sound, and she shivered at the tingling sliding from her neck to her fingertips.

She crowded the Etterian and grabbed his arm, holding his O.D.I. to her mouth. "If the explosion happened from within, then the damage is extensive. I must manufacture what parts the ship needs since no one but Etterians cater for scimitar-class ships. All I am requesting is the opportunity to assess the damage. I don't need to enter your ship." She flicked her gaze to the Etterian warrior and winced at his glower. "Supreme Commander." She tacked that on, just in case. Pissing off Etterians would land her and Andrew on the first shuttle off HoSS.

"Permission granted."

She tossed a smile as consolation for her highhandedness before tugging on a disposable mechanic suit designed for short trips into the vacuum of outer space. It hung on her frame, and the helmet shifted when she swung her head from side-to-side, but it served its purpose. She had to unravel her bun to slide it on. That high up, the H-lift would penetrate the oxygen seal so without the suit, she would bleed out through her eyes.

She flipped the visor down and leaped across the gap between causeway and the H-lift, which tilted to the left. Its hydraulics were failing. Mechanics suffered from the same lack of parts as engineering did. Red spots circled her vision. It would be wise to calm the anger burning through her oxygen. Her nostrils flared, and she muttered curses at Governor Granntt and his unfulfilled promises. HoSS was a bustling port, so it shouldn't be struggling for funding. There had to be other reasons why Granntt didn't approve their critical requisitions.

On the unreliable H-lift, she chose not to activate her magnetic boots to its pockmarked surface. While manipulating the joystick, she urged the platform to rise. Leaning over the console, she glided a gloved hand across the smooth exterior panels of the ship in reverence. The dark silver of the steel shone in the weak lighting and didn't detract from its beauty.

The blast had torn through several layers of steel and bulk-head—the damage was larger than she had expected. She would need a few sheets to repair this. There, peering at her through the hole, was another Etterian male. She gasped, jerking back, not only startled by his presence but the sheer magnetism in his gaze.

Something about that tempted her to run her lips across his bronze skin. An unusual reaction from her, to be sure. Her vision swirled, and she calmed her breathing. Perhaps she had contracted Vemys-49. Perhaps it was the way his suit clung to him.

He was six-feet-five or so, and bulky—his chest was huge with his biceps strong and thick. What truly snatched her breath was the self-discipline it had taken to mold his physique. His stomach was taut, each indent enhanced by the shimmering armor he wore. Her fingers twitched with the temptation to graze his rippling abdomen.

His narrow hips blended into impressive thighs, and his backside should be the inspiration for future sculptors. He also had a pleasant face, bold forehead, slashing and thick eyebrows, beautiful and long lashes. They fluttered over his indigo eyes. His strong nose flowed into sensual lips.

He mouthed something at her. In the vacuum of space, sound wasn't possible. She activated her O.D.I. through the suit's transparent sleeve, selected the shared comm function, and stuck her arm through the hole. He hesitated before scanning his forearm over hers.

"What do we need?" His voice was sexy as sin—dark, tempting, authoritative. No one opposed him.

Holy shit, he was gorgeous.

Her heart leaped into her throat. Heat radiated from her face outward, distracting her from the task. Dazed, she studied him, lingering on his square jaw. His lips in a thin line didn't deter from their sensuality. Something delicious, almost sinful coiled in her belly, throbbed and ached. This was...desire? Amazement and hope flowed with the excitement raising the hairs on her arms, sending ice down her spine. She shivered.

When he repeated the question, she hurried to clear her throat, hoping to sound normal and not breathless. "Quite a few sheets of Maloidian steel, along with rivets, and the ability to puncture the steel. Once you seal the outside, rebuilding the bulkhead layers can be done on your way home." She ran her gaze along the jagged fingers of the hole. "The powers-that-be are still in trade negotiations with Maloid. Until we receive our first order of Maloidian steel and the tools to work with it, HoSS doesn't have anything strong enough to penetrate your steel."

"Neither do we. Whoever placed the explosive device also removed parts and critical tools."

"Shit." She chewed on her lip as she considered other alternatives. This might be a think-out-the-box scenario. "If you have schematics of the parts needed, I might be able to manufacture something temporary. You're two weeks from Etteria. I don't know if our materials would hold out that long."

"I apologize for the misunderstanding. The parts are not priority, sealing the hole is. We have rivets but not the tool you require."

Double shit. She brushed her hand along the outer frame as she ran through her options. The steel was so beautiful, she couldn't resist touching it and wished she could do it without her glove on. "If we heat a Maloidian dagger, we might be able to stab holes, twisting the blade to form circles." She flicked her gaze to meet his. "Do you have daggers onboard that match the diameter of the rivets?"

A small smile curled his upper lip. That hint of emotion defined his age. He was young enough to enjoy moments of happiness, and yet Etteria had made him a supreme commander. Huh. How had he earned that position when there were no wars she knew of and nothing on the buzz requiring heroic feats?

"I'll send the rivets and what daggers we have."

Assuming the conversation was over, she gave him a respectful salute and tugged on the joystick to lower the H-lift. It did with violent jerks. She yelped, gripped the railing, and activated her magnetic boots. If the H-lift fell from under her, she would throw herself at the scimitar and walk along it to the ramp.

Nausea churned her stomach, her breathing coming in gasps. Beneath her feet, the H-lift whined. In slow motion, she spotted Sam, safe on the edge of the causeway, staring at her seconds before her impending death. A few meters below her position was the oxygen seal, and beneath that were kilometers of space peppered with docked ships. She *would* die, either by fired engines as she plummeted through their jet streams, ejection into outer space, or, if she was lucky, splattering on a docked ship below like bird droppings.

Sam's stiff lips moved, but this far away, she couldn't hear him. He activated his boots, launching himself off the causeway to catch her. Aw, she didn't know he cared.

The H-lift creaked, then dropped two meters. She hit the floor hard with stars dancing in her vision. Staggering to her feet, she leaped the short distance to the ship, locking her heels to the metal paneling as the H-lift squealed and plummeted, leaving its mangled arm behind.

Crowds gathered, maintenance and emergency staff included, but she fixed her gaze on the supreme commander now on the ramp. He tugged on a slick spacesuit ignoring the male yelling at him. The urge to panic gripped her, but with a few calming breaths, she took the first step. For that second, when only one boot held her to the ship, her body trembled until her foot touched down and locked her in place.

"Are you well?" His sinful voice drenched her with warmth, and she smiled, finding the calm she needed. He tugged on his helmet and flipped the visor down.

"I'm wonderful. Thanks for asking." She chuckled. "I don't need rescuing."

He ignored her, activated his boots, and launched himself onto the side of the ship, taking large strides to reach her.

Sam landed under her, locking onto the ship, perhaps to catch her if she fell. His presence eased the tension between her shoulder blades, and she took another step.

Her foot slipped, not locking onto the surface, and the momentum swung her leg outward. She smothered the panic blurring her thoughts as she tucked her leg behind the other. Time slowed with her heartbeat thumping in her ears, her lungs seizing. Inch by inch, her heel holding her to the ship peeled off the steel, unable to bear all her weight. With a scream, she fell, sliding down the steel, past Sam who grabbed at her splaying limbs.

"Catch me, you idiot." Yelling at the useless sec-cyb was a pointless endeavor, costing her air. A tug tore through her, jerked her hard, and she whip-corded. Pain burned from the grip Sam had on her wrist. Any harder and it would snap off.

"Sam, I take it back, I adore you." She laughed even though she wasn't out of danger yet.

But hanging here like a limp noodle couldn't go on indefinitely. Her arm trembled; painful shards rippled down from Sam's grip. If he didn't return her feet to ground soon, she didn't know how long she could smother the whimpering.

Hands slid around her waist and yanked her against a solid chest. Sam released her, and a scream lodged in her throat.

"I have you." She had never heard a sweeter voice.

The supreme commander's solid embrace imparted the belief she would live. With great gulps of air, she forced her body to go limp and not hinder his movement.

He spun her, fearless, like he couldn't drop her, and crushed her to his chest once more. Visor to visor, she had nowhere else to look but at him. She gasped and blinked at the Etterian male. The cerulean flecks in his eyes glowed.

"Thank you." She gripped his biceps, the strength of them wiping away the last vestiges of fear lingering in the recesses of her mind.

He grinned. "Do you adore me too?" He must have heard her saying that to Sam.

"For rescuing me, I just might." She smiled. "Mate with me, and we'll live on a farm, raising kreso under Etteria's two suns."

He jerked back, his brow arching. Its darkness contrasting against his bronze skin tempted her to run a fingertip along it. Good thing he wore a helmet.

"It was a joke." Dipping her face to hide her embarrassment, she imagined Andrew's mottled features when he heard she had fondled the "unknown" species.

Sam jumped to the ramp first. The supreme commander tightened his hold on her before launching off the side of the ship. His blasters lowered him with grace. He touched down with the barest of tremors.

She flipped her visor up and grinned. The crowd broke into applause, but his scowl reminded her why she was there in his arms. "Do you have the daggers?"

He grunted, loosening his hold but crowded her, forcing her to raise her gaze to maintain eye contact. He studied her face for a while, his lips clenching white then relaxing. "Follow me."

Enyl marveled at the female meeting his gaze without fear. Her pale skin and deep red eyebrows were striking, reminiscent of Etteria's oceans. But like the bold green of Ferusi crystals, her eyes were breathtaking. His heart had beaten an erratic rhythm when she fell. Malo had tried to hold him back, but Enyl had blasted his way onto the side of the *Kevol* to save her.

She had thought she would not need his help, but when she had realized it was him holding her, she relaxed, trusting him. He clenched his jaw, quelling the frustration rising within him where his restlessness usually hovered. There was something fascinating about this Earthian. Her manner was bold, arrogant for a species so vulnerable.

Her smaller stature roused his protective instincts, which was non-sensical.

She saw a problem she could fix and focused all her energy and life on it. Never had Enyl experienced the potent emotion tightening his chest when she slipped out of his sight. It had consumed him, darkening his thoughts, rushing his blood through his veins. Such intensity had to have hastened the encroaching void. To feel is to fail.

She swished as she trailed him into the *Kevol*. The ill-fitting suit hid her curves from him, intriguing him. The helmet hid her hair, and his fingers twitched to remove it. Her hair color would match her eyebrows, and the eagerness to confirm this almost had him demanding she strip.

He did not go far, pausing in the common in front of a wall of weapons. The public room was at the center of an Etterian vessel. Many males sat at the benches and tables. Others were using the exercise equipment available in the corner. A sparring mat dominated the middle of the room. The medical area was a sensible inclusion with the number of sparring injuries occurring. His males shifted to the side to let her pass, their curiosity mimicking his own. Except for Malo, glaring his disapproval.

Enyl gestured to the wall. "Would any of these suit?"

She gasped, slipping around him to admire the assortment. He waited, anticipating she might want to stroke a blade. Maloidian steel's sharpness was lethal. She did not touch the blades but reached for a spear. Unclipping it and with a firm grip on the haft, she spun it with surprising skill, testing its balance.

"Heat this to 4773 kelvin and pierce the sheets." She tapped the butt of the spear.

"How do you know its diameter is sufficient for the rivets?" Enyl found her eyes mesmerizing. She said so much with them. If only he could read those emotions. Like *damu*, these Earthians were expressive in their responses.

She gestured to the rivets on the replicator, and a slow smile formed. "Why can't you replicate the tool?"

He shook his head. "The replicated tools are not strong enough to penetrate the steel." He reached for the spear.

She hesitated, then spun it once more to offer him the butt. This simple technique validated her familiarity with the weapon. An aspect of her life had warranted weapons training. He studied her, wondering if she was a warrior, then shook his head at the impossible thought.

"Rivet then weld for double the longevity. Since you do the repairs yourself, you don't need me now." She headed for the ramp.

Ice pinched his chest, and the urge to call her back tore through him. It was illogical to experience a connection to an Earthian female without the tests confirming their compatibility.

Malo joined in watching her stroll away. When Enyl lost sight of her, he hurried to the door, pausing to scan the dwindling crowds. Spotting her mechanical companion first, he settled his gaze on her as she tugged off her helmet. She had braided her crimson hair and tucked it inside her suit. He held his breath, hoping she would remove the loose garment hiding her form from him. She did not and did not face him as she listened to an Earthian male swinging his arms in wild gestures. There was softness in the male's expression like he cared for her.

Enyl scowled, focusing his hearing to listen in on their conversation. Malo grunted beside him, reminding him in his subtle way that what Enyl did was dishonorable.

"Trust you to almost kill yourself doing the simplest of tasks," the Earthian male said.

"Simple?" She snorted, dismissing his comment with a flick of her wrist before weaving her way through the spectators. Her Sam thumped after her, shielding her from the boisterous crowd. Enyl doubted she noticed the onlookers or Sam's actions.

"I came as soon as I saw the vids. They're playing it in looped slow-mo." The Earthian male grabbed her arm halting her. "Stand still, let me scan you." Without waiting for permission, he ran a hand-held device over her.

"Quit fussing, Liam. I don't need a medic, I'm fine." She threw her arms into the air, halting the med-scan. "I'm off to see Andrew, and Lord willing, take a nap. Oh, the luxury of it." Her voice filled with longing and her deep sigh with exhaustion.

The urge to keep her near, as he had done when he had rescued her, gripped Enyl. He trembled with restraint.

Malo spoke first, bringing him back to the moment, and the weight of his duties rested on his shoulders once more. "This species might be compatible. They have similar features to Etterians."

Enyl regretted not asking for her name. He hurried to rectify that. "Deploy the tests here, and find out who she is." He scanned the crowd, not seeing her white-encased form. "Have her tested."

"Fine, but not a word about her until we have the results." Malo met and held Enyl's gaze until he nodded. "It is best to complete the repairs as soon as possible. I do not wish to interact with that

Maloidian, Granntt, although his presence proves the Maloidians have visited this sector." Malo huffed.

"We must share our navigational charts, but they do not reciprocate." Enyl shook his head. "Unless those on the station are a few escaping justice and Queen Alllero knows nothing?"

"You may be correct, my prince."

"My prince? I preferred supreme commander." Enyl forced a smile. Assuming the highest rank was easier without the pomp and circumstance that accompanied royalty. "Task a battleship to scan this system."

"That would be wise if these Earthians prove to be compatible." Malo hovered at his elbow but didn't hesitate to speak. "What about her intrigues you?"

Enyl frowned, unable to summarize what she invoked within him. "It is nothing of importance." He grimaced. "Perhaps she alleviates my boredom?" She had entertained him, and in her presence, the restlessness had settled, granting him temporary peace.

"Enyl." Malo leveled his legendary interrogation stare on him, his narrowed eyes and looming posture promising endless agony. Enyl knew that look well.

"Alodon's balls, Malo. If you must know, her manner was fearless, her confidence breathtaking, and did you see her eyes?" He sucked in a sharp breath and spun on his heel, returning to the common. His exuberant response must have satisfied his protector since he chose to change the subject.

"Regarding the sabotage, it has set us off course by eleven days. When a trip to Gikaet might have taken a week, this added diversion will delay our arrival." Malo gestured to their males to begin the repairs. "I am investigating who was behind this. The navigational misalignment happened at the Global Council since no one boarded the Kevol. The explosive device was among the council's gifts. I would recommend we return to the GC, deploy one of my males via shuttle then head for Gikaet."

"Do as you see fit, Malo. This is your area of expertise, but next time we attend a GC summit, we will go in better prepared."

Malo grunted his agreement. "I admire their audacity, but another daring strike may afford us the opportunity to display our full might."

Enyl snuck a glance, his lip curling into a smirk. There was longing in Malo's voice, one Enyl understood. A war would be the perfect time for a warrior to throw caution to the wind, to battle his way to honor and the all-consuming void. "Catching the culprit may grant us the opportunity sooner. Recall Vytus. I assume he's in a brothel on the station?"

Malo sighed and tapped on his O.D.I. "Her name is McKenzie." With that said, he abandoned Enyl to his inner turmoil now laced with tendrils of hope.

Chapter Seven

Horizon Space Station (HoSS)
Orbiting Ganymede (Jupiter's moon)
Year of 2252, April

ORIANA SHOOK HER HEAD, dispelling the image of an Etterian Supreme Commander who had no business haunting her. He did so in her sleep, and due to her exhaustion, when she was awake too. Like now. She could recall the light shimmering off his skin, the piercing intensity in his gaze. She would awaken, drenched in sweat having relived her close call. Yet, what sent tremors through her was his arms crushing her to his hard chest and the deep timbre of his voice.

She hadn't wanted to walk away, had wanted to work with the steel or see them do it. The unknown yet fiery emotions rattling her body and nerves sending ice along her spine had driven her to run. What would've happened had she been braver, if she had chosen to remain until they escorted her off their scimitar? A two-hundred-pound pissed-off drunkard didn't inspire much fear in her but lingering on the curve of the supreme commander's lips had sparked a flight response. Before she could regret her retreat, she had updated Andrew on the status, and returned to her shift, wishing for something she could never have.

That was two weeks ago.

She winced as her twinging back yanked her from her thoughts. At twenty-two, she shouldn't experience muscles spasms or have this many scars. She did climb over and under all the hardware keeping this blasted space station operational. Where she had a taut stomach, other women had soft and spongy bellies. Where her legs were strong and muscled, others were supple. Grumbling, she pushed her insecurities aside.

She greeted Bob when she entered the packed Bodacious Saloon.

"Ori," he said without inflection.

As she scanned the crowded tables, she leaned her elbows on the counter. "Had any trouble so far?"

"No."

She accepted the coffee he slid across, then faced the room while she savored the hot, bitter liquid. It was at times like this she was truly alone.

Denying the sorrow was becoming difficult. She had promised herself only when she was safe. Not once in the six years at U.P., living in suites with thin walls, not connecting with colleagues, had she found a moment to mourn. Often, she would awaken with tears on her cheeks. If she didn't deal with it soon, the time to grieve would be decided for her. At her next off-time?

Her shoulders slumped before she gathered her strength and straightened them. Now wasn't the time either. When then? She couldn't continue like this. The thought of releasing her emotional control had her trembling, fear sliding its icy fingers down her neck. Opening the floodgates would weaken that boundary, and once crossed, she would be an emotion ticking bomb, blubbering over a pet-cyb salesman's kittens.

Shifting on her throbbing feet, she shuffled trying to find a comfortable stance. Yup, she was in a good state: aching feet, numb hand, and knee-weakening exhaustion. The saloon's double doors opened to two men in full black ceremonial dress with gold tassels. She sighed, happy for the distraction. Tassels never threatened anyone.

Because the Etterian had been on her mind, she imagined bronzed skin glimmering in the dim saloon light. They had thick, black, fish-tail braids hanging to their heels. What carved asses they had—she licked her dry lips. Her gaze flew to their braids, and she gaped.

Etterians on HoSS again? She eyed the males, hoping they didn't spell trouble. The anesthetic was wearing off with a dull sting twitching her fingers. She would prefer if they were looking for companionship instead. Although, if she wasn't so tired, sparring with them and testing her Hatimaye against theirs would be exhilarating.

She tried not to stare at them or drool. Forcing herself to look away, she swept the crowd as expected of her, checking for signs of possible violence.

The crowd had stilled, their gazes trailing the two Etterians to the bar. She wished she could do the same. It wasn't every day such perfect masculine specimens crossed her path. In another sweep of the room, she glanced their way where they "conversed" with Bob. Wishing they would face her, she huffed and scanned the bar again.

"Oriana McKenzie?" A masculine rumble pierced the saloon's din and snagged her focus.

She sliced a nervous glance between the males, not sure which one addressed her. "Yes?"

"Coldar et Hendar at your service, milady."

"Myan et Phyan at your service, milady."

She switched her attention to the other man and sighed. "What may I assist you with, warriors et Etteria?"

Myan shot a glance at Coldar at her formal greeting. She hadn't said anything wrong.

"We are on a mission for our king, for Etteria. We seek compatible females to undergo various tests in the hopes of a pairing." Coldar kept his posture rigid.

She blinked at him, her mind trying to register his formal words. "I beg your pardon. Did you say pairing?"

Their expressions remained guarded, showing caution. They expected her to run away screaming. She smiled at the idea of it, understanding their wording and requirement. Uncle Gayn had shared his knowledge of many cultures and species with her, including the intricacies of Etterian life.

"You are looking outside of Etteria, hoping to spark the Ethera in females of another species? I would expect King Xeus to focus on high-grade planets and not us mere humans."

Coldar's eyebrow arched, but that was all he revealed. She smothered a chuckle, enjoying tweaking them.

"Your blood is in the system and has matched our compatibility matrix. Our king is not concerned with your planet's grading," Coldar said, his educated words were as provided by his O.D.I., but his formal tone was all him.

"Are these tests on Etteria?" She frowned when they nodded in unison. "It takes two weeks to reach your planet. King Xeus should make this easier rather than inconveniencing females across the galaxies." She released a frustrated sigh, understanding their need for commitment or contentment. "I'm more than willing to undergo your tests, warriors, but I can't afford to lose my jobs for such a long trip."

Myan smiled. "Your employers have approved your absence for the six weeks needed. They have been well-compensated for the inconvenience."

She gaped. "You paid them off?" Their need for females must be at a desperate level for Etteria to throw their vast resources at this.

"As will you be for your time. Your choice of recompense is a paid education, Ferusi crystals, or tokens." Coldar was so stiff, she wanted to ask him if he knew what a carrot was.

She shook her head to focus on them, even as she calculated her options. "I don't have that much off-time saved up." Although, time away would be a welcome reprieve.

"It is all in order. Supreme Commander Enyl tasked us to await your compatibility results. He was wise to do so." Myan scanned the room with his assessing gaze lingering on the other women in the bar.

Delicious warmth uncoiled in Ori's belly. Supreme Commander Enyl? She hoped he was the same male who haunted her.

"When did he task you?" The timeline would reveal if this Enyl was the male whose embrace she missed.

"Six days ago, after you advised on the Kevol's repairs. I was in the common when you wore your ill-fitting garment." Myan ran an appraising gaze over her revealing uniform, lingering on her exposed belly and cleavage. "This is better."

She fought the urge to fold her arms across her breasts. "The scimitar is large enough to carry a kuta shuttle, and they can't do long distances."

"True, it is why I spent six days in a housing unit awaiting Coldar's arrival. The nearest battleship was the *Kushin*. Coldar brought one of their scimitars and arrived an hour ago."

"Six days?" She gasped.

"Your vids are educational, if not entertaining." Myan grinned.

She dropped her forehead into her palm. What had he seen? Then winced, remembering the number of porn channels available.

The more time she spoke to them, the more the six weeks tempted her, but she was wise to fate's ploy. When things were too good to be true, they turned out worse for her. "Are you escorting me to Enyl?"

Coldar shook his head, dispelling her hope as swiftly. What had she expected? That the connection between her and Enyl wasn't imaginary? At least, she had made some sort of impression on him or her sliding down his scimitar was what he remembered. As a euphemism, that was a good one. She smirked.

"He is on Gikaet. We are ready to leave," Coldar said in his gruff voice.

She didn't doubt his word since the majority of Etterians never lied—they considered it dishonorable. "One minute." She raised her hand to silence him, her fingers almost touching his lips. Darting across to Bob, she leaned over the counter to catch his attention. "Did you—?"

"Yes," he said before turning to a customer.

Bouncing on her toes, she faced the two Etterians and activated her O.D.I. The comm request summoned a pixelated face.

"What is it, Ori? What happened?" Andrew's hair stood up in all directions. She had never seen him this disheveled.

"Did you receive a travel request from—?"

"Yes, enjoy," he said, seconds before his image disappeared. She could've sworn she saw a man's hand run along his shoulder. She headed back to Coldar in a daze.

"Do I have to go?" Her reluctance arched his brows, as if her disinterest had startled him.

"The destination is Resia Cay, the eastern beaches. You would not want to soak up sunlight, swim in crystal red pools, and sip fruity beverages?"

She graced him with a genuine smile at the images he painted. "They're called cocktails, and I would love to, but all my hard work will be undone."

"All the more reason to go. Your employers will have a better appreciation for your skills when you return, milady," Myan said.

Taking a deep breath, she took a leap of faith. "All right." The disappearing red glow of Sam confirmed Andrew's approval. She faced Coldar. "Let me pack."

"We have catered for all your needs, and yes, your unit awaits your return as assured by the Algri."

They had thought of everything, but something wasn't right.

From her O.D.I., she placed her services on hold—laundry, and heating for now. "Final question, do you have coffee on board?"

"We are Etterian, milady. Our vessels are state of the art, including our rehydrators and replicators." Myan flashed a breathtaking smile, bright against his bronze skin. "We have scanned a variety of popular

Earthian meals and uploaded them. Anything you need will be available to you."

"Before we depart, milady, what would your choice of recompense be?" Coldar activated his O.D.I. and waited for her response.

"Tokens, please." She beamed with the joy of excitement rushing over her. "Lead the way, Coldar. I'm all yours."

Chapter Eight

MYAN AND COLDAR LED Ori to their waiting scimitar. Two strapping males striding through HoSS attracted attention, and no one noticed her behind them. She laughed when a few women fanned themselves. But when the scimitar, with its silver metallic panels—streamline and expensive—came into view, it snagged Ori's breath. Moaning at the sight of it, she bounded over, too excited to stroll along the causeway. After all, she was about to travel on the most beautiful ship in the galaxy.

As expected, the warriors remained unmoved by her enthusiasm. They strived to be unemotional unless under duress, or so Uncle Gayn had said. It made her wonder if sex would fall under an extreme circumstance. The idea of losing her virginity to an unemotional yet gorgeous male didn't appeal to her, no matter how sexually naïve and desperate she was. She wanted him to care, to participate, and to share an intimate moment with her. Not do her like she were a sex-cyb.

The scimitar craft had a capacity for a crew of eleven. The pristine engine room and the single-bunk crew quarters were the first areas she passed. They assigned the officer's quarters to her as well as full use of the well-stocked recreational room they called the common. She surveyed her new quarters and stifled a squeal. Now this was five-star accommodation with no soul-sucking lights anywhere. The bulkheads were in metallic gray or white and in one corner sat the "kitchen" with black surfaces indicating the replicator and rehydrator. Three white chairs dominated the seating area, and by the design of them, she would bet her life they adjusted to her ass. The cleansing room held a shower and a waste receptacle. Three buttons adorned one wall.

The lack of a basin wasn't odd for Etterians. The water they showered in could shampoo, condition, and clean their teeth. She took the requisite time to admire the cleansing room, the seating area, and the bed large enough to handle two Etterian males.

In the communications room, their departure from HoSS showed on the massive vids. The comm room held all the controls and navigational diagnostics to pilot such a fast, fuel-efficient, and breathtaking ship. She ran a finger along the edge of the door, also constructed of Maloidian steel. When Coldar's voice filled the room, she snatched her hand back like he had caught her doing something illicit.

"HBA, requesting departure for scimitar HD451, confirm?" Coldar communicated with the station's Bay Authorities as per protocol.

The human man's crisp voice on the comm system proved the quality of the craft. The Etterians had spared no expense. "Scimitar HD451 *Misaia*, you have permission to depart through bay door 29E."

Coldar nodded. "Confirmed for bay door 29E."

With a steady whine, the docking clamps released without disruption. He maneuvered the craft through the bay door with a skill born from hours of training. The hum of the engines vibrated into the soles of her boots, pulsing excitement through her. Massive bay doors for the bulkier ships remained shut. The scimitar shot through the meters thick outer wall and into the dark, inky black and starlit outer space dominating the huge vid screen. A vid displayed the receding Horizon and the moon Ganymede behind it.

"It makes me realize how insignificant we are," she whispered to no one in particular.

"There are many things that cannot be explained," Myan agreed with her statement, "yet all mimic the same pattern or sequence."

Coldar's shoulder stiffened as if he disapproved of her presence in the comm room. "Destination is set for Etteria. Please inform us should you require anything, milady."

Well, that was a dismissal. Without saying a word or offering a polite smile since they weren't looking anyway, she wandered to her quarters. Unused to free time, she browsed the replicator and rehydrator to check if she needed tokens. They had stated Etteria would take care of everything, but trust was hard for her. All the items listed had no cost attached to them. She could order food and clothing at her leisure without paying. With a frown at the incredulity of her situation, she ordered a bottle of water and a chicken sandwich.

What she hoped to do was work with Maloidian steel sometime during the two-week trip. And if she could test out the variety of weapons she had seen mounted to the common's wall, that would be a plus.

The whole situation was bizarre. King Xeus must have given this deviation from protocol much thought. It didn't surprise her that her blood was compatible. Humans looked like Etterians except for their skin tone, and of course, the presence of the Ethera. Should a human summon it in an Etterian, would their eye color change too? What she wanted to know the most was whether she could bear their children. Without confirmation, compatible blood made no difference to the decline of Etteria.

Shit. She wasn't sure how she felt about that. Taking the time to consider what they needed her for would have been wise. She could go from being single to married within a blink of an eye. Well, two eyes, if the male's eye color changed upon seeing her. That was the defining factor for them, and according to their law, she would be bound to him.

She tutted at her silliness. It was no use panicking about something that may not happen.

Seated in an adjusting chair known as a comfy, she hummed as she finished her sandwich which tasted like the real deal. She couldn't remember when she had last enjoyed a meal. Authenticity was one of the pleasures of a state-of-the-art rehydrator. Her booted feet registered a slight bump, unexpected and unusual. She stilled, but no further oddities occurred, so she drained the last sip of her water.

At another bump, she frowned. She placed the bottle on the table and held her ear to the door which was silly since the bulkheads absorbed sound. If she didn't know better, she would say a tether caused the jarring. Waving the door open, she crept into the passage. Her boots clunked on the grated metal floor, keeping her attached. They had activated the magnetic flooring.

She stiffened and listened, tilting her head as nervous energy pulsed through her body and raised the hairs on her scalp. There were no space anomalies this close to HoSS, so no unexpected power surges, no waves of radiation, nothing to determine this level of caution. It could mean only one thing.

"Milady." Myan thudded along the passage toward her. "It is an unauthorized boarding." He fired his blaster at someone behind her.

She spun in that direction, as a Yithian collapsed with a gaping hole in his chest, oozing blue-black blood.

"Shit." Sharp pangs from her nails digging into her palms forced her to unfurl her fists. "Where's Coldar?" She peered around Myan's great bulk at the comm room.

"He is attempting to send a distress signal. They may have dampened all transmissions."

"Give me a weapon." She held out her hand, expecting his compliance. When her palm remained empty, her gaze swung from the dead Yithian to Myan. "Myan, give me a weapon."

He glowered, his cheeks darkening with his jaw clenching. "You imply I cannot protect you."

"I would never question your honor, but we don't have time to debate this. Give me a weapon, or I'll use my hands to fight." She raised her palms, delicate compared to his, and his blue gaze focused on her neo-band.

His nostrils flared. He hesitated, warring with his training before he offered her his spare blaster. His gaze switched between the blaster and her, and she expected him to snatch it away.

"Do not shoot me in the back," he muttered before he rushed along the passage toward the dead Yithian. When Coldar barreled along the passage, she threw herself against the bulkhead.

"Could not send a signal." He hefted his weapon with one hand before staring at her blaster.

"Don't start. You would swear I asked Myan for his hair." She jogged after Myan's fast disappearing form, with Coldar behind her.

He shoved past her, and with a flick of his head indicated she was to remain behind him. Damn males. With a cry of outrage, she shadowed him, shielded by his great bulk. He was a typical Etterian male, tall with too-wide shoulders.

She ducked to peek under his elbow into the recreational room that also held the craft's exterior door. She bit the inside of her cheek to smother a gasp. Myan lay on the floor with a blaster wound in his shoulder. Five Yithian males crushed into the narrow space around his body, shuffling in impatience as they awaited further instructions.

Coldar motioned to her to return down the passage. He opened her quarters and ushered her in. "Alodon's balls. Five Yithians." He shook his head, disbelief and anger shifting across his face.

"With more in the tether." She hoped the Yithians waiting to board wouldn't get the opportunity.

"Why would they attack us? This makes no sense." He ran a hand over his face, his blaster grasped in the other hand, the weight of it not a factor for him.

"Do you think Myan's...?" Myan must be his battle brother.

Coldar paused and sadness lightened his eyes for half a second. "Yes. Prepare for the worst..."

Lowering her gaze, she gave him time to bolster his control. She checked her blaster was set to red—in other words, kill.

"But hope for the best," she said by rote, catching his arched eyebrow. Yes, she knew the code. "So, what's the plan? Kill as many as possible as soon as that door opens?"

"Yes." His face was grim before he offered a stiff smile. "Our apologies for our failure to escort you to Etteria, milady."

"Through no fault of your own." She shrugged, unable to blame them for this. After all, Yithians were untrustworthy, unpredictable, greedy, unmerciful, and lacking honor. Who knew why they did the things they did? Her uncles hadn't had dealings with that species, their distrust blatant, their teachings less detailed.

Coldar activated the display vid, flicking through the menu until he located the folder 'Aesthetics.' On a digital plan of the quarters, he relocated two comfys to bar the door and the remaining two as a bunker for cover. In silence, they slid on the floor on their magnetic bases.

"If we make it by some miracle, the first cocktail is on you." She crouched behind the makeshift bunker.

His brief smile was a genuine one. "Agreed."

The door opened, and they fired their blasters, taking down two Yithians. More burst into the room, and as they fired, killing two at a time, more entered. As the Yithians rushed in, they split into two paths, left and right of the bunker. She fired with accuracy, but no matter how many times she and Coldar fired, more would appear. They swarmed Coldar, taking him to the floor, perceiving the Etterian as a greater threat. He couldn't fire on so many. She couldn't take the time to help since she wasn't killing her side fast enough either. Her glance at Coldar was the distraction they needed.

A Yithian knocked the blaster out of her hand, and her training kicked in. Diving away from the bunker, she spun to kneed him in the groin then elbowed him in the neck after he doubled over. Rolling over his back, she swung her legs to kick another in his chest, launching him into the bulkhead. She struck one in the throat who dropped to the floor gasping for air. Throwing herself onto her knees, she slid along the smooth flooring to uppercut another in the groin. When she leaped to hammerfist him in the neck, she tried to avoid his teeth.

"Stop or I'll kill him," a skinny Yithian hissed in Galactic as he entered the quarters.

She froze then dodged the three-fingered punch of the Yithian she had struck. Coldar on the floor, with Yithians towering around him, curled the cold fingers of fear around her spine. Besides where he clutched his ribs with one arm, his face was bloody on the right side.

"What do you want?" She leveled her gaze on the speaker's black eyes.

"You, of course." His hissing laugh crawled spidery tingles across her shoulders. "Your two-move defeat of a scout has intrigued our Great and Illustrious King Urio. He is most eager to test your skill in our arena." The speaker admired hers and Coldar's handiwork—nine dead Yithians and twelve wounded. "He will be most pleased with your attempts to resist."

"How many did you bring with you?" She hoped escape was possible for her and Coldar. He was pale under his bronze skin and needed urgent medical attention.

"A full compliment."

Shit. Her heart leaped, forcing her to suck in a calming breath. To bring fifty soldiers was a rare excursion for Yithia when less than half the contingent was the protocol. There was no getting out of this alive. Not if they continued to fight. These aliens had come prepared; their obvious need for her far outweighed their intrinsic frugality.

"I'll agree to go with you on one condition." She met the Yithian's gaze, hiding her anger and fear, needing him to see her threat as a possibility. Painting on a smug smirk, she masked the hatred burning her lungs and pumping adrenaline through her veins.

"You cannot bargain with me, female." He hissed a laugh again.

She smirked. "Of course I can."

Her confidence should worry him, and hopefully, morph his laugh into a frown. Of course, the idiots didn't have the knowledge of human physiology.

"You want me alive, don't you?" She studied a torn fingernail.

The thought of dying in an alien arena triggered her flight response. Struggling to keep her casual stance, she steadied her breathing. She did rock once on the balls of her feet before she smothered the tremors. Uncle Diso couldn't have anticipated this or trained her for it, but failing wasn't an option. Only survival mattered.

"How would you bargain with your life when I have you surrounded?"

Sighing, she threw out her hand to hit a nearby Yithian in his chest, striking with two fingers in two places. The male jerked back, but a second later, slumped to the floor, lifeless. She arched a brow at the skinny male. The dead soldier at her feet proved her ability to continue to fight, surrounded or not.

The Yithian paled at the sight of the dead male, anger and disbelief twisting his features into that of a demonic shark.

"I will fight you until you have to kill me to save yourself. Informing your king of your failure won't be beneficial to you or your estuuba." Playing on their greed might work because bringing her in would earn a tidy profit for him or his family, if not influence with King Urio.

He narrowed his solid-black eyes. "I do not bargain with lesser species." His lips curled downward. "What is this condition?"

"That Yithia will never harm him, and I mean never." With a nudge of her head, she gestured at Coldar, whose widened gaze shot up to hers, before warming with barely contained fury.

"I accept this bargain," the Yithian hissed, his capitulation was swifter than she liked.

She frowned, assuming he hadn't understood her demands. "He dies, I die, and many Yithians, as well. Swear on the life of your family, your estuuba."

"I understand and accept this condition on the life of my estuuba, of King Urio, and on Yithia," he lisped. He gave her a look that implied he wasn't an idiot. That was debatable. So far, he showed no signs of intelligence.

When she remained silent, two Yithians grabbed her upper arms. They used more force than was necessary. She smothered a wince at their manhandling then snorted. Like she couldn't free herself from such a hold. She pretended to struggle when they semi-dragged her toward the tether. Coldar's guards sliced glances between her and their fallen comrades, then in mutual agreement, handled him with care.

Her lips twitched when she tried to restrain a mocking smile. They believed her threats with due seriousness. Idiots. If they knew anything about humans, it was that they would fight to the end rather than sacrifice their own lives in a pointless demonstration. Regardless, she had the Yithian's assurances they wouldn't harm Coldar. The deal bought her time to plan an escape and for him to heal. His mangled face and broken ribs limited his ability to help. She had to be vigilant and strong on his behalf. Time was all they needed.

As soon as they dragged him through the tether, her "escorts" followed. She "struggled," swinging out her legs with enough effort to reach two buttons to the right of the outer door. The blue one would shut and seal the door after they had gone through it. The yellow one would send a distress beacon to a predetermined destination. She hoped it was the closest allied vessel. If she didn't have to become a killer for Yithian entertainment, she would be grateful.

They needed a rescue, and for that to happen, the Etterians had to find Myan and the Yithian corpses. She hoped the Yithians didn't blow the scimitar or destroy the distress beacon she had just deployed.

Once inside the Yithian M-class slave ship, her escorts waited while the skinny male argued with a larger-than-usual Yithian. He wore the black and yellow badge of a ship's commander.

"The craft is not destroyed, and they managed to launch a distress buoy. This will require tracking. You failed on this mission," the commander said, spittle forming on his bottom lip. His opinion of the shorter Yithian wasn't a good one.

"I did not fail. I have the contender. Leave the ship and the buoy. I want those arrogant bastards to know it was us." The speaker's black gaze shifted to Ori. An evil smirk twisted his lips, and his elongated teeth gleamed in the yellow light.

The commander crossed his arms with his focus on her, but his face remained impassive. "Is that wise?"

"You dare challenge me? Have you forgotten whom you address?" the shorter Yithian demanded.

If the commander chose to do so, he could swing his beefy arm and launch the idiot Yithian against a bulkhead. Instead, he raised a three-fingered hand to indicate compliance and strode off. She studied the glowering Yithian. Only a special forces operative outranked a commander.

With a dismissive flick from the operative, their escorts trundled them along a passage. They paused in front of an air-seal door and forced her and Coldar into a cold, dark cell. As soon as the door shut behind them, sickly yellow lights lit up the bulkhead and ceiling. She darted across to a groaning Coldar who had slithered to the floor. Ignoring her bruised, aching arms and knuckles, she feathered her fingers over his ribs, careful not to harm him further.

"Why in Alodon's hell did you ask for such a condition?" Enraged, he tried to swat her hands away with one hand.

"You want me to watch you die and still be at the mercy of these bastards?" She touched his torso until he flinched. "You have a few broken ribs. Command your suit to cinch your torso. It will act like a tight bandage."

While he tapped on his O.D.I., she stood, unzipped her jumpsuit to yank off her vest. Revealing her bra didn't matter at this point. Kneeling again, she held her balled-up vest to his face.

"Hold it there," she said, and his obedience surprised her. "Any other aches, pains?"

He shook his head. "Dazed." With a grimace, he leaned on the metal-paneled wall. "Regardless, your condition was ill-conceived. You should have bargained for your life."

She fought the urge to snort. He was being a typical male—an idiot. "They needed me alive. You, my Etterian, are the redundant one."

"I am not your anything," he said. Well, at least his rage had subsided. It hadn't seemed a wise response when he was in so much agony.

She sighed. "I beg to differ. Until we escape, we're partners."

"Partners? What does that mean? This is not a word I am familiar with and not this context."

She succumbed and huffed like an older sister having to deal with a petulant younger brother. "Teammates, battle-bonds, we share everything," she said despite his deepening frown. "Don't argue with me—it's done, you're alive, nothing else matters."

He grunted in frustration but said no more.

Raising her chin, she tried to communicate there was no point in debating this.

"Must you be so stubborn? See logic, milady."

She grinned, liking that he could read her body language. "I'm your first human?" When his brow furrowed in confusion, she gave him a pointed look. "Activate English language protocol on your O.D.I, Coldar."

He grumbled, did as she instructed, then sat in absolute stillness, trying to keep his head movements to a minimum. His dizziness had to be worse than he had let on. "No, you are not my first human. I have met your males."

"So, first female?" She chuckled. Boy, was he in for fun times.

"I have never seen anyone fight with such efficiency. I liked the way you killed the Yithian with two punches." He rumbled in approval.

"Yithians do have two hearts." She shrugged and winced from the burning between her aching shoulders.

They were alive, so any pain she endured was negligible. Even though she had said so to Coldar, she should believe it. It was surreal to sit here with him discussing fighting techniques. When the Yithians kept rushing through the door and exhaustion trembled her limbs, death seemed inevitable.

"By that reasoning, one punch should kill single-heart creatures," he said.

"Yes, and three punches for a species with three hearts. Gika have those." She peeled her T-shirt away from his eye, trying to assess the damage.

He popped open his good eye to stare at her.

"Not that they'd let anyone within punching distance. A blaster and a greatsword are far more effective." She winked.

"What and how do you know about Gika?"

She smiled, enjoying teasing him. Splaying her fingers, she ticked off her facts one by one. "Gika are a hive-minded species. They have red, oversized mandibles and razor-sharp pincers. Dismembering their eight legs is time-consuming which is why you prefer your greatsword. Their bites aren't lethal unless they inject or spit their acidic saliva."

"Are you not an engineer?" His confused expression hardened into an accusatory one, as if she'd deceived him.

"Also bar security, don't forget that." She patted his knee.

He winced. "Your inappropriate joy is annoying."

"I could wail and pound the walls if you prefer." She curled her fingers into fists and fake-pounded the air in front of her.

He grumbled something under his breath. She chose not to respond. Instead, she shifted away to give him space. Some men needed time to process—perhaps he was one of those. Or he was a big old baby when injured. Uncle Bos had been the same.

The tears threatened again. She sucked in a breath, blinking in desperation, hoping to stem the flow. No matter how hopeless the situation, she had to keep her shit together, to focus and plan.

CHAPTER NINE

Planet Gikaet
Calustrum
Etterian Ground Base
12252 years, 5th month

ENYL SWUNG HIS GREATSWORD across the exposed underbelly of a Gika. He made quick work of lancing through its hard carapace and managed to dodge the acid saliva, for the most part. Scanning the battlefield, he caught Base Commander Remi's last strikes as he took down his own Gika. Enyl grinned, the smile hidden within his visor.

The Gika soldier he had killed had stopped twitching. In a fluid motion made easy by the strength in his arms, he removed his greatsword from the creature's thorax and scooped up his discarded blaster. Gikaet had its own beauty—rolling dunes of gray sand against a burnt-orange sky. On the horizon, craggy rock formations and chasms rippled across the surface.

His black metallic-infused armor sizzled from the dead Gika's saliva. Thankfully, the Maloidian suit was saturated in acid retardant.

He loved being this side of the galaxy, fighting a war that had lasted longer than four hundred years. Gikaet had become a rite of passage for Etterian males. Upon reaching their eighteenth year, they would spend the next four years at Calustrum, the Etterian ground base north of Gikaet's equator.

This war wasn't madness, as a few older males declared. Extensive history with the Gika proved they had a hive mind and fast reproductive cycles. Unrestrained, they would consume worlds, eradicating existing planet life in the process. For this reason, the Etterians fought an endless war ensuring the Gika never returned to their former destructive power.

Whenever life as a crown prince became overwhelming, this was his escape. Out in the field, there was nothing to denote his royalty. He was a warrior as any other earning his honor. To battle Gika, to test his mettle, to hone his body, his strength, and his reactions against a true opponent was the closest to ecstasy for an Etterian without triggering the void.

To rid his armor and boots of the dead Gika's green slime, he stomped into the ground base, stirring up dust clouds. The sprays in the neutralization zone rinsed off the remaining acid on his suit. After two minutes in the zone, and with the white light giving the all-clear, he headed for the shared cleansing room.

Striding past the large crate, he dumped his blaster and greatsword, sparing a grin since it was Vytus's task to attend to them. The cleaning and prepping of these weapons for tomorrow was the task for the young recruits. It ensured optimal knowledge of all weaponry. Enyl had held the same task six years before. Vytus would return the next solar year to start his four-year service.

This training incorporated daggers, long swords, greatswords, and blasters. From a young age, Etterians learned unarmed combat to assist in the control of their emotions. Only with a female may they show affection and lust, to a certain degree. Unless of course, she was his Dar Eth, his life force.

Enyl frowned at the path his thoughts had taken. It required a miracle to find his Dar Eth. None could recall when the last Ethera pairing had occurred. It had fallen into legend, yet every male longed for the female the Maker had designed to be perfect for him.

Once satisfied he was clean, Enyl activated the air dryer, taking the time to read his message.

Malo had news about McKenzie. Remaining silent, not pestering Malo as promised had been harder than Enyl had expected. But he had agreed and had to adhere to it. He grinned, flicking through the message.

With a roar, he bolted while yanking on a wrap, sprinting along the wide passage to the common. He prayed to the Maker he'd find the older male there. Enyl skidded to a halt. Malo sat alone at a table.

When Enyl slid onto the bench, Malo scowled. "I send you a message, and this is how you react?" He shoved his uneaten kreso aside.

Enyl grinned, unable to control his excitement. His leg bounced beneath the table. He had no intention of stopping it. What Malo couldn't see, he couldn't chastise Enyl for. "Your message said 'McKenzie is compatible.' That tells me nothing, Malo."

"She has agreed to travel to the Resia Cay for testing. In two weeks, we will know whether her species will trigger the Ethera." Malo grabbed his giyua juice and rose. He paused and met Enyl's gaze. "I hoped you had forgotten her."

Enyl pinched his lips. Forget McKenzie? His memories had intensified, fixating on her green eyes, or the light reflecting off her red hair, or the dusting of spots across her nose. He'd liked the way she spoke to him, as if they had known each other for years, like they were battle-bonds.

Malo stomped off.

His reaction didn't bother Enyl, not after one of his prayers was answered. McKenzie was compatible. He grinned as he ordered his meal from the rehydrator. This day was a good one.

THE BUILDING SHUDDERED, AS several explosions boomed, startling Enyl awake. It took him a moment to shake off his dream. He relived hearing McKenzie's voice for the first time, when he slid his arms around her waist, and when she flipped her visor back to reveal her Ferusi green eyes. His groin throbbed as it did every morning. He grunted, ran a hand over his face before he swung his legs off the side of the bed, struggling to recall what awoke him.

An explosion quaked the floor beneath his bare feet. He grabbed his armor, clipped it into place, then raced into the passage filled with males running in both directions. Many boots thumped on the grated floor and echoed off the bulkheads. They knew the drill—to assume their allocated positions.

Enyl was visiting and didn't have a position to assume. Instead, he rushed to the communications room to find Remi. Perhaps he would assign a task to Enyl, or at least, inform him of the situation. Malo and Vytus burst in as Enyl did. He spared them a nod in greeting, then leveled a frown on Remi. No resources of value were on the planet to justify an attack. And there was no empire powerful enough to take on Etteria. The Yithians or Maloidians could try, though. Neither made sense. Etteria had a peace treaty with Yithia, and they were trading partners with Maloid.

"Gika have managed to construct fighter crafts and are bombarding Calustrum. I suspect it is a distraction while another contingent escapes off-planet," Remi offered before any of them could ask.

"Gika have done what?" Enyl pinched his lips to hide his shock.

Remi cast him an impatient look. "I have split the asteri peju into two: the first wing to keep the Gika occupied, the remaining wing to do reconnaissance."

The building shook again as missiles struck the shields. The thunder of Calustrum's programmed target-and-response cannons, or chokaar, returned fire. Their firing force had the building quaking as well. The idea of an actual battle inflamed Enyl's blood. He could thank the Gika for the excitement and energy punching through his body.

"Have we received damage reports?" He settled his focus on Malo, who analyzed the multi-lit console and panoramic display vids.

The calm male showed no reaction to this development. It took all Enyl's training and control not to bounce on his heels. For now, he relished the struggle to keep the smile from his face and hide the surging eagerness. His fingers twitched to be out there, fighting alongside his males. As a prince, doing nothing was unacceptable. As an Etterian warrior, doing nothing was unforgivable.

"Shields are at seventy percent and holding," a data officer said to the room in general.

"The king will disagree with my decision, but I have reserved two peju in Hangar B." Remi eyed Malo and Enyl. "I need more information. Why are they attacking in force? When and how did they manage to construct these vessels, and what else have they built? What is their ultimate goal?" He pointed at Vytus. "You stay here with me, youngin."

Eager to enter the fray, Enyl didn't wait for Vytus's forthcoming grumbling.

With Malo beside him, Enyl sprinted along the passages and darted around the males hurrying to their assignments. He burst into the underground hangar and chose one of the waiting two prepped combat kites. The kite's shape was a reverse elongated triangle, with the three points curved and the sides bull-nosed. The bulk of the kite waited toward the rear to cater for the pilot, navigation, propulsion, weaponry, and liquid oxygen. Molten-silver reflective panels covered the craft and were set to stealth when in flight.

When he halted below the craft, he peered through the hatch at the capsule's interior. He accepted a helmet from the ground crew, scanning the organized chaos as the ground crew prepared peju for flight. He flipped his visor over his face, cupped the edges of the door, and hoisted himself up. As soon as he was inside, its panel slid forward with the seat attached. Twitching with impatience, he slipped into the seat as the panel locked beneath him. The design of the panel and seat were for easier ejection during an emergency.

The multi-lit console wrapped around him as seat belts secured him in place. The activated panoramic display vids showed Malo disappearing into his own peju.

As Enyl ran through the pre-flight checklist, his visuals skimmed from infra-red to motion sensors to normal. "Command, this is Alpha-45, requesting permission for immediate departure."

"Alpha-45, request granted." Remi's voice was crisp through the peju's comm system. "Return without harm, Enyl."

"Instruction received." He grinned before powering up the engine with a flick of a finger over the left console. Excitement burned through him as the kite lurched. The intuitive tether detached, and the peju hovered in anticipation. He rolled it toward the large exit doors in a smooth glide.

With a forward thrust of his hand, he increased the propulsion percentage and dropped the inertia dampener. The peju shot through the bay doors—the momentum thrust him back into his seat. He roared with laughter at the adrenaline rush and the view of the star-filled sky. Banking to the right over the ground units, a sense of pride blossomed and swelled within him at the sight of his valiant males fighting. The flashes from blasters and light glinting off many greatswords were mesmerizing to behold.

Remi was correct. From this vantage point, the Gika lured his males to the east. Other peju engaged the Gika crafts, attempting to steer them away from their ground forces. A crashed craft could kill many of their males. Enyl zoomed the display vids on a few Gika ships.

"Their construct looks weak. I am surprised they are capable of flight." Malo's voice filled the peju's confined space as he brought his peju in line with Enyl's.

"It is as Remi stated, a distraction. The Gika pilots must have known they go to their deaths." Enyl scanned the fighting masses. "They are steering the battle to the east."

"It is the *why* that I am interested in," Remi said, impatience in his gruff voice.

Enyl veered to the left, heading west. He flew high enough not to trigger the Gika's ground sensors but low enough to transmit good visuals to Remi. Gray dunes spread out in all directions.

"See anything?" Malo's voice came through Enyl's hood as he aligned his peju beside his. He assessed the horizon and scowled. The quiet was unnerving.

"My instinct says west." Enyl scanned the jagged lines marring the horizon.

"Mine says southwest, not far from the base." Malo's instincts would be more honed than his.

Enyl didn't doubt his statement, but the thought of the Gika's building within striking distance to Calustrum and without discovery was disturbing.

"Would they build right under our noses?" From a strategic position, it was a brilliant, decisive move.

"They could have built a nest beneath us—we would not look there." Malo's words confirmed Enyl's thoughts, to which he grunted.

"Surveying there now." Remi's anger came across the channel.

Enyl flew over the large mesa on the horizon. It scarred the dunes, standing out as a rocky formation might have. He hovered over the canyon below where an enormous chasm carved the valley floor. Large metallic doors gaped, their asymmetry indicative of a hurried opening. The debris piled around it must have aided the camouflage until today.

Their scouts had missed the massive scar. Even with the debris, the disturbance of the soil should've roused suspicion.

"Alodon's hell." Malo cursed a few more times. "That entrance is large enough for space-worthy ships."

"Return to base," Remi commanded on the general channel. "All units, air and ground, return to base immediately."

Enyl switched to their private channel. "We must take a better look, Malo."

"I agree, but we have received our orders, my prince."

Malo reminded him of his birthright, that Enyl had to set the example, to think of his father, of Etteria. Enyl scowled at his console. This was too important. If the Gika made it off-world, millions of lives would pay the ultimate cost.

He pushed on the holographic lever and dropped into the chimney to the sound of Malo's cursing. In a horizontal spin, Enyl captured as many visuals as possible. Various conduits led away from the chimney, none of them well lit. There were no Gika sentinels or soldiers. A machine must have carved the ground. This he found odd since no vibration had reached Calustrum. They couldn't have done it by hand; that would have taken them years. At the base of the chimney sat a colossal spacecraft. Powered and humming, the sound penetrated the kite's metallic frame.

"Alodon's hell." Malo seemed to share Enyl's disbelief.

Malo's unexpected emotional outburst startled Enyl into action. He launched a data bot, attaching it to the hull of the ship. He waited a few precious moments to ensure it activated. Time had never passed so slowly. He shifted his gaze across the conduits, expecting an attack.

Once the data streamed into their Etterian system, he shot up and out of the chimney.

As he returned to the base, he endured Malo's beratement. He understood from whence it came. His thoughts, however, remained on what he had discovered, not on any further chastisement he was sure to receive. Losing a foot of his hair for this was worth it. "Alpha-45 requesting permission to dock."

"Return to Hangar B—your window is thirty-three seconds—and report to me immediately." Remi clipped each word.

Enyl slid his kite into its previous slot before powering down. The seat belts released him, and as the seat withdrew, the hatch opened. He dropped through it.

"I would hate to be in your footwear." Malo flipped his visor back.

Enyl did the same and matched Malo's gait, striding to the communications room as commanded.

"Brilliant move, my prince," Remi said as soon as they entered, startling them both.

Enyl arched a brow as he snuck a glance at Malo.

"Malo's instinct was correct regarding the nest beneath us." Remi's smile faded into a scowl. "We will abandon Calustrum and detonate explosive charges, razing everything to the ground. They have been content to remain on Gika for four hundred years. The data bot you planted has delivered far more information than we have time to delve through. But a cursory scan reveals the loss of clean water is driving this exodus."

Silence deafened the room. The Gika were dying. For Gika to attempt to save their people, this was honorable. Despite knowing

Etteria would thwart their attempts to depart this world, they were willing to take the chance.

"We have a dilemma, my males." His father's voice came over the communication. "Do we steer them to Dyuqa, the nearest habitable planet, or do we wipe out an entire species?"

Having not known his father listened, Enyl's frown deepened when Malo coughed. He pointed to his boot and smirked. Enyl shook his head.

"Until we have processed all of the data, let them flee off-world. There is still time to decide their fate before they reach Dyuqa. Attach trackers to each of their spaceships and have our battleships shadow them. I want no surprises. These trackers will ensure Dyuqa is their only destination and no other colonized planets." Father paused. "In the meantime, since Calustrum has been compromised, evacuate then destroy the base and the Gika nest. We cannot have the stranded Gika acquiring our knowledge or technology." His father's sigh was heavy, hinting at exhaustion and despondency. "I will liaise with Etteria's advisers and revert with our decision. I will need your counsel, Remi. This could have far-reaching consequences for generations to come. Enyl, we will later discuss your reckless behavior and blatant disregard for command." The communication ended.

Remi faced the room. "Your thoughts?"

"As far as I see it, we have two choices." Malo tapped the vid displaying the fleeing ships. "Destroy this planet and its stranded Gika with our world taker and decimate their escaping ships. Or allow them to colonize another planet, and we relocate there, as well. The first option would change our way of life, the second could mean another four hundred years of fighting."

"There is a third option," Enyl said. "Destroy their escaping ships and force them to die out on Gikaet."

"There is a fourth." Remi surveyed the communications room before continuing. "We can give them water purification technology, then they need not leave Gikaet at all. We can debate this once we have boarded the shuttles for the northern base, Aluna." He faced the data officer. "Evacuate Calustrum. I want every male accounted for before we destroy it."

The sirens blared, and white lights flickered along the passages as they jogged to the hangars. Boots thundering on the metallic flooring rang a dirge as the base emptied in an orderly fashion. Kuta shuttles took off like swarms of insects, clouding the orange sky.

"I prefer the fourth option," Vytus said as they climbed into a shuttle. "We may even form a truce with them."

"A truce?" Remi echoed, aghast. His face contorted, pulling tight across his gaping mouth. "How do you see that agreement forming, Prince Vytus?"

"Simple," Vytus offered a cheeky grin, "They vow to never leave the planet, and we vow to only spar with their soldiers."

"In theory that would work, but what if we accidentally kill a soldier? Is the truce canceled then?" Remi frowned, squaring his shoulders.

"Either way, this means change for us." Enyl peered out the door at the mass exodus before him. As the shuttle rose with the exterior door open and the wind whipping his braid, he gripped the available handhold. They hovered, waited, until the number of launches dwindled. The impact of this moment held Enyl's tongue. Sadness warred with angry helplessness, at something so precious being ripped from his hands. He couldn't stop this from happening. And worse, he understood the Gikas' need for survival. Directing his anger at them was illogical.

Remi confirmed all Etterians had evacuated before detonating the explosives.

Soft, peppered booms reached Enyl as Calustrum exploded. Balls of fire, gas, and dust engulfed a once-beloved base. As the dust clouds diminished, in its wake lay a massive hole, deeper than it was wide. Before them, in the gray soil of Gikaet, was a crater, a visual indication of how the enemy had breached their defenses without their knowledge. It was as alarming as it was impressive.

"I have instructed all bases to implant ground sensors. It would not surprise me if we have been compromised across the board." Remi stood to the left of Enyl, one hand raised where he gripped the top of the door.

"I have never known the Gika to be proactive or strategic." Enyl frowned, acknowledging the loss darkening his soul. Calustrum had been a haven for him, for many males—some calling it their home.

"Judging from the data your bot collected, they send out punished soldiers to battle us." Remi scanned his O.D.I., shared the data link from the bot, then regripped the door's edge.

Enyl leaned against the bulkhead to free his hands. Flicking through the data on his O.D.I., he gasped as he read the findings. "They use us to mete out justice?" The thought hadn't occurred to him, and it should have. The Gika sent out soldiers to die and had done so for centuries. He had never questioned their sacrifices because he was grateful for the emotional high killing them gave him.

"It is why they fight with such fierceness," Malo said, reading the shared data, as well. "To survive a battle with us is to redeem their place in their society." He deactivated his O.D.I. and stared at the disappearing crater as the kuta shuttle carried them to their new destination. "Their complexity is surprising."

"Let us hope this data helps your father, Prince Enyl," Remi said, "for your sake."

Malo slapped Enyl on his back. "It might buy Enyl forgiveness."

"Truly, I was not in danger. We were not fired upon, there were no Gika visible, and I was in stealth." Enyl sliced a glance at Remi. "We did not even fire upon a single Gika craft."

"I apologize, I was not aware you wore Vytus's breeches today," Malo smirked.

"That would explain why they feel tight." With a sad smile, Enyl watched the flames consume the remnants of his haven, the blaze shrinking the farther they traveled.

He should look ahead, should see this as a new opportunity to serve Etteria, but he struggled to release what Calustrum had meant to him. Its destruction revealed the gaping hole in his life. He had no definitive purpose other than serving as the heir to the throne—a task he dreaded.

Drawing in a breath, he turned his back on Calustrum and scanned the faces of the males on the shuttle with him. Their expressions mimicked his inner turmoil. At that moment, they were one, suffering from the loss in unity.

"I am proud to have survived this day with you, battle-bonds." He gripped the closest warrior's forearm.

Tension eased from their shoulders and smiles broke across their soot-stained cheeks. The impact he made with his words and his presence brought home what he meant to his people. He served them, Etteria, and his sons would do the same. It was a pivotal realization. He vowed then to embrace his duty and serve them well.

Aluna

Etterian Northern Ground Base

"WHAT DO YOU MEAN the Gika are returning to Gikaet?" Enyl gripped the communication console at Aluna, his knuckles white. He tamped down on the anger burning in his chest and hardening his voice. To feel was to fail.

The data officer rechecked the scans. "I mean exactly that, my prince. All the Gika ships are traveling to Gikaet."

"Keep monitoring them." Enyl punched a key to activate a comm. "Remi, they are retreating for reasons unknown. I will keep you informed."

He answered an incoming communication request from his father. Dammit, what else had transpired? Why would they now return, having not achieved what they set out to do? This silly endeavor had cost Etteria *and* Enyl a most beloved of bases. This was all for nothing.

The rage that burst through him made him want to smash things, roar his anger, punch something. He sucked in slow, deep breaths as he fought for calm. It wouldn't do for him to face the void over this.

His father's voice sliced through Enyl's anger. "The Gikaet ruler, Tjakik, has accepted our assistance with water purification devices and any additional environment healing technology we believe is necessary."

"How did this come about, my king?" Malo's eyes widened.

"You spoke to their ruler, Father?" Enyl's voice revealed none of his inner turmoil, but he caught the flickering emotions crossing Malo's face. It calmed Enyl somewhat to realize he wasn't the only one affected by these events.

"The interaction was enlightening. Tjakik was cordial despite Etterians having killed thousands of his males."

"Deception?" Enyl distrusted anything and everything at that moment. His orderly life had flipped over. "Why would the Gika decide to flee their home now after four centuries of slaughter? They must have realized decades ago that their world was no longer viable. It would take that long to dig the chasms by hand."

"It is wise to be cautious." Father's voice broke through Enyl's circling thoughts. "Our engineers assure me that there are no components within our devices that could form weapons or improve their space-traveling abilities."

"To assist a dying species is an honorable decision, Father."

"So, we can keep killing them?" Malo teased. The full smile that played across his features was rare for him unless he was enjoying himself. The male thrived on change.

"Then I agree with this treaty, Father." Enyl leaned over the console, forcing a smile to contort his clenched lips. "At least, we retain our way of life without eradicating the Gika."

"If we remain their executioners." Malo gave him a pointed look. "The number we kill daily indicates the vast size of their populace or the stringent rules by which Tjakik governs them."

"Or their ruler is a dictator and has us kill his opposition," Enyl suggested.

"Either way, their populace remains out of control." Father broke up the debate between them. "Does Remi intend to build a new Calustrum at Aluna?"

Enyl chuckled. "He oversees the construction as we speak."

"I shall dispatch supplies," his father said.

"As you command." Adviser Cales's voice came through the connection, no doubt attending to the promised shipments.

"We appreciate your assistance, Adviser," Enyl thanked Cales, wishing he had done so more often. Without Cales, his father would've sought the void years ago. Gratitude swelled within Enyl. He scowled at the emotion, hating that he was experiencing it at this level of intensity.

It had been King Pius—his ancestor—who had approached the Durn for guidance. The superior Durn had devised their current strategy: the extensive training, the development of a fighting people into a feared and respected warrior race. They had also modified their DNA, and thus the Ethera was born. He suspected the Durn—revered for their higher intelligence and their statistical focus—hadn't anticipated the decline of the Etterian female birth rate.

"All Etteria is with you." Father ended the communication.

"Data Officer, summon me if there are comms requiring action." Enyl shifted his focus from the data officer to Malo. "What are you waiting for? We have bulkheads to construct, injured to attend to." He grinned at Malo as they sprinted out of the communications room.

As Enyl hurried to medical, he didn't bother to task Malo. He would go where he thought he could best serve. Excitement coursed through Enyl at the change of protocol. The Gika's audacity and strategy were something he admired. As remarkable as their ingenuity and their diplomacy were, he didn't trust it. The Gika king must be as plagued by naysayers as his father was. It must have taken them this long to decide on the most viable approach. It was a humbling thought.

Bursting into medical, he navigated the wounded to collect a med-gun. Attending to one injured male after another, he scanned, patched, and re-skinned. With efficient determination, he rushed males in and out in various stages of repair. It was honorable to serve Etteria as required, alongside males such as Remi and his father. He would continue to do so, whether the Maker blessed him with a Dar Eth or not.

He scowled. Yes, he wanted one, but to have thoughts of something so rare plague him, was futile. Tormenting him further was the hope that she had red hair. He couldn't live his life on such a hope, yet he couldn't abandon it either. Therein lay the true darkness—to abandon the hope—it was a darkness he wished to avoid at all costs.

The void was absent when he held McKenzie against him. Perhaps, that sense of freedom was what he liked most about her, which might have been an Earthian trait. Until he met another Earthian female, he would yearn for the peace she had brought upon him.

Chapter Ten

Enyl stepped under a cleanser and activated the spray. Gargling the water to clean his teeth, he hurried through his ablutions. Once done, he waited for the air dryer to evaporate the water droplets from his body. As he exited the cleanser, he accepted an offered wrap.

"Thank you," he said, triggering the wrap to adjust to his proportions. A male had served him, which was something he didn't tolerate on the best of days.

"Would you require further assistance, *my prince*? Perhaps you need some poor bastard to carry your *royal* balls for you?"

The sarcastic voice shot Enyl's head up in surprise. He grinned. His blood-bond, Vytus, stood before him. They grasped each other's forearm in welcome.

"Vytus, I have not seen you since the attacks on Calustrum. Do not tell me...my father commed you? Is it time to depart?"

Vytus shook his head and fell into step beside Enyl as they exited the cleansing room. "This time, it was Malo. He has dire news."

"Dire?" Enyl rubbed his face as the burden of leadership dropped onto his shoulders. It had been absent for most of his time on Gikaet. "My father is eighteen years older than me. I do not expect to assume the throne anytime soon." They strolled down the widest passage, Vytus steering them toward the docking bays.

"This has nothing to do with the growth rate or King Xeus." Vytus flashed his wrist over the craft's security console and ushered Enyl onto the docked scimitar.

Enyl hiked up the lowered ramp as soon as it touched the bay floor, relishing the slight burn in his thighs. He was in a wrap, but Etteria provided everything. He need not return to his Aluna quarters to dress.

"Maker," he grunted. Whatever this 'dire news' was, to instruct Vytus to escort Enyl was the precursor to force. If Enyl hadn't agreed to come willingly, Malo would have intervened. To Enyl, it meant he could no longer stall returning to Issneen.

Speaking of Malo, he waited at the top of the ramp. "Welcome aboard, my prince."

Enyl greeted Malo by grasping his forearm and glared a fake warning at him. "If you 'my prince' me one more time—"

"Curse it, Enyl. You have had months of no protocol. Let me adhere to it at least once this journey." Malo tapped his left forearm to activate his O.D.I., instructing Pilot Afax to commence departure protocols, the holographic letters big enough for Enyl to read.

"Poor Malo, stuck escorting royalty. What did you do to be assigned this duty in the first place?" Enyl teased as he strode through the ship's bay door, along the passage to the common.

"Did you not kidnap a Maloidian princess?" Vytus said with a twinkle in his indigo eyes.

"Lies," Malo said, "mostly."

"Mostly, he says." Enyl grinned.

"Well done, Vytus. I am pleased I did not need to drug Enyl to get him on board." Malo folded his arms across his chest, smirking at Enyl.

He winced. "No more pleased than I am, I can assure you."

"Have some respect for my skills, Enyl. I would have used the Foutas silver frog's venom and not the Uikl lizard's," Malo said with well-deserved arrogance.

"Small mercy." Enyl laughed as he removed a sword from the weapons wall in the common, swinging it to test its weight. "I like my malehood in working order, thank you very much."

He cycled through his stances, swinging his greatsword in precise movements until his arms trembled and sweat drenched his wrap. Malo had remained to watch, no doubt documenting where Enyl might need improvement. His sharp gaze didn't miss much, but he couldn't read Enyl's thoughts, know his torment. It wasn't his earlier restlessness that haunted him, but an Earthian with green eyes. He pinched his lips, once again regretting having vowed not to ask after her.

When Malo did speak, his tone was hard, his words clipped. "I bear news."

Enyl swung a few more strikes, pushing his body to the limit. "Yes, Vytus said it was dire."

"News of McKenzie."

Enyl paused and lowered the greatsword. "Status on the compatibility tests?" He broke the silence first, the hum of the engines soft and comforting. What he meant to ask was *how is she*?

"Deployed to all known species, including Lysara and Kulai." Malo's stance implied he would wait as long as needed for Enyl's undivided attention.

Enyl sighed and mounted the sword to the weapons wall. He tossed off his wrap, used it to mop the sweat off his face and chest, then strode to the replicator to order armor and boots. As he dressed, he flicked glances at Malo. "What is it?"

Malo unfolded his arms only to clasp his hands behind his back. "When I did not hear of McKenzie arriving at Resia Cay, I sent out my operatives and asked for information along my networks."

Ice chilled Enyl's shoulders then exploded across his face. "Are you saying she never arrived?"

"I received word of a male rescued by a research vessel. I sent a scimitar to retrieve him." Malo nodded his head at the warrior hovering nearby. "Warrior Myan has an alarming tale."

Enyl faced the male, excitement increasing his heart rate. McKenzie was onboard? When no female emerged, he scowled, cursing himself for being a fool. If she failed the tests, he would have to cease this obsession. Perhaps, he should have pestered Malo despite promising otherwise, then he could return to his usual restlessness and forsake his foolish hope.

"How fares the compatible female?" Enyl gestured to Myan to step forward. Vytus did so as well, with a plate in hand as he chewed his kreso, eavesdropping with blatant disregard for policy.

Myan squared his shoulders. "My prince, we collected the female and embarked on the journey home when Yithians boarded us without warning. They wounded me, then seized her and Warrior Coldar. I assumed, in error, the Yithians had killed them, but arena vids prove otherwise."

"The Yithians attacked an Etterian vessel without provocation?" Enyl's anger reverberated in his voice. He growled, taking a moment to control his reactions. "And they took hostages? She has been in Yithian hands for a month?" He paced across the common, forcing males to abandon hope of a meal. "Set course for Yithia."

"Should we not comm your father?" Vytus asked around a mouthful of kreso.

Enyl shook his head. "No time to follow protocol. Nine days to reach Yithia, and who knows what awaits us." He rubbed his brow. "I will comm Father en route."

"I suggest we comm him—"

"Am I not your prince, Operations Commander?" Enyl met Malo's gaze, standing firm. "We will rescue our male and the last possible hope we have for Etteria. Or do you have another compatible female en route to Resia Cay?" He did not wait for Malo's response. "If I need to beg my father's forgiveness after the deed is done, I shall."

"Very well, *my prince*." Malo tapped on his O.D.I.

"Test more females from her species. Send males. Collect those compatible. McKenzie cannot be the only one." Enyl gestured to the mounted display vid. "Warrior Myan, you mentioned arena vids."

Myan selected the applicable menus before navigating to the most recent. He returned to Enyl's side as a vid played. There, filling the void was a face he would never forget. She looked exhausted—shadows darkened her green eyes, and her hair was a dull brown. He dismissed his disappointment, having expected her hair to be as vibrant as he remembered. Ignoring the death-like vise squeezing his ribs, he sucked in a shuddering breath.

He would test the scimitar's limits to reach her. What did she do to need rescuing this much? Not that he complained. His heartbeat stilled...she was compatible. With that, something heavy sunk his heart. She hadn't triggered the Ethera in him, and therefore, he shouldn't form an attachment to her. Not until they knew for sure her species could pair with Etterians and, more importantly, bear females.

Surrounding her were a pack of wiry four-legged, snarling animals, mottled-brown in color. They flanked her in a beautiful, ever-vigilant dance, before striking as one or as a unit. She killed with an efficiency that bordered on the supernatural and ignored any scratches and bites she received like they were a nuisance.

"Is that Hatimaye she is using?" Malo's admiration mimicked Enyl's who gaped at the vid. Where had this skill been when she had plummeted down the side of his scimitar? This grace, this strength, and agility?

Warrior Coldar remained in the center with his hands clenched at his sides. He stumbled often, collapsing onto a knee before staggering to his feet, never assisting, or protecting the female. Enyl scowled as he observed McKenzie's efficient attacks.

She dealt with the last creature clinging to life. With tenderness and respect, she grasped the creature by its jaw, then with a sharp jerk, snapped its neck. She glowered at the viewer. Her tear-stained face filled the vid, revealing every detail.

"Her species is strangely beautiful," Malo said.

Enyl was unable to form words when his voice lodged in his throat.

"I have never seen eyes that color," Malo said.

"Did you not study her when she aided us?" Enyl folded his arms across his chest, mimicking Malo's earlier I told-you-so stance.

The older male shook his head, his mouth gaping. "I thought her weak. Now, she would be an asset to Etteria. Do you think her species—?"

"If she triggers the Ethera, Malo, then the Maker has not forsaken us." Enyl couldn't bear to hear the hope in Malo's voice nor the thought of another male pairing with her. "He has blessed us, instead."

"The Etterian male battle-bonded with this female," Vytus said to Myan, then tapped the screen where information scrolled. He bounced on his toes. "I find nothing wrong with that."

Enyl grinned. The weapon sterilization had not dimmed his blood-bond's enthusiasm.

"Is she your female?" At Vytus's question, Enyl nodded while inside his heart roared, "mine."

"I am most interested in her." Vytus laughed. "The idea that a weak species could be the arena champion fascinates me."

"McKenzie's the champion?" Enyl dropped his chin to his chest to hide his surprise, although, he had seen her fight. Still, the urge to protect her warred with the glow of pride warming his chest.

"I cannot assist in the rescue in case I am recognized," Myan said. "I am uncertain as to whether Yithians think we all look alike as we think they do. I would prefer not to jeopardize your mission."

"A wise decision, Warrior Myan. Have medical waiting should there be injuries. Please remain with us while we strategize. You know Coldar well and might guide us with the female," Malo said.

"The arena is well-guarded with a port-dampening field shielding it. We may be able to get in with purchased vouchers, but we will not be able to port out with the prisoners." Enyl massaged his temple and the ache building there. "It would mean having to escape the difficult way."

"How would we communicate to the prisoners we are willing to assist?" Malo frowned. "This is madness, my prince. We need a better plan than this. We need the might of King Xeus behind us. Let him wage war on the political side."

"I will comm my father, Malo. As to the madness of it, you are our operations commander, madness is your area of expertise." Enyl grinned, confident they would find a solution. "If prisoners need to 'escape,' then you and I are the best warriors to accomplish it."

"You are flattering me, *damu*," Malo said with a smirk. "Your sweet, encouraging words saturate my heart with happiness."

Enyl snorted. He had laid on the compliments, hoping Malo wouldn't abandon him in this.

"It would make for an interesting diversion." Malo shrugged. "It has been a while since I assisted in a rescue, especially one that will anger the Yithians."

"Well, we need a workable exit strategy." Enyl offered his battle-bonds a smile. Nothing in the universe would stop him from teleporting down to that heat-infested, dry-as-dust hell called Mascroba.

"I don't need rescuing." Her words spoken that day in her lyrical voice reverberated in his memories.

He sighed before answering his memory. *"You do, sweet McKenzie."*

WITH THE SCIMITAR AT full pulse devouring the distance between Gikaet and Yithia, Enyl faced the display vid in the officer's quarters. Malo leaned a shoulder against the bulkhead, silent as he waited.

"King Xeus et Prius," Enyl said, then cleared his throat. Time crawled past until the black vid flickered to the face of his father.

"My son, I am pleased you commed."

Enyl offered a smile in greeting. "Father."

His father's joy faded. "What is it?"

"I am not certain whether Malo informed you of our brief stay on an Earthian waystation. Regardless, I met a female, and she..." Images of McKenzie bombarded him, so emotive, he wished he could reveal them to his father. "She showed promise. I tasked Malo to deploy the tests there."

"Yes, with excellent results." His father frowned. "Malo sent two males to collect her."

The tension eased between Enyl's shoulders. At least he didn't need to waste time explaining his actions. "Yithians boarded the scimitar and captured her. She is in Mascroba as an arena contender."

Father roared, his cheeks darkening. He jumped to his feet to pace, crossing in and out of the vid. "How dare Urio allow this."

"We are en route to rescue her and the Etterian warrior with her." Enyl glanced at Malo. "Share the arena vids. See for yourself, Father. I suggest we not inform Urio of our impending rescue. I would hate to arrive and his people have relocated her to somewhere unknown."

His father's focus shifted to the side, his attention fixed on what Enyl suspected were the arena vids.

A gaping Cales appeared behind Father. "Is that Hatimaye?"

Father scowled at Enyl. "How far are you?"

"We just left Gikaet." Nine days away. *Maker, please protect her.*

Father pursed his lips. "I understand the need for stealth. I will notify Supreme Commander Xan to be on alert should you need assistance. How certain are you this female will accept the Ethera?"

"There is no guarantee, but we need her alive to test her." Enyl gritted his teeth. If he had his way, she would never be in danger again.

"True, and passing the first test for compatibility could mean her species is as viable. We need to maintain secrecy in our search for Dar Eths. If we are successful, Yithia could target the species and destroy all hope for Etteria." Father splayed his hands on his desk. "Is Malo with you?"

"Yes, my king." Malo slid beside Enyl.

"Notify all agents."

"Acknowledged, my king." Malo activated his O.D.I. and punched in commands Enyl didn't bother to read.

"Take care, Enyl. Get in and get out." Father leaned back in his chair. "And as soon as she is onboard, comm me."

The comm ended. Enyl released a long sigh, grateful for his father's support. He could have commed King Urio and complicated this. Then again, if the rescue went awry, a galactic war could result.

Malo laughed and abandoned Enyl. He didn't move, preferring to replay the arena vids. By the fourth time, he paused it and stroked his finger along the curve of her tear-stained cheek. "We are coming, McKenzie. Please...stay well."

Chapter Eleven

Yithia

City of Mascroba

Arena dungeons

Year of 2252, June

YITHIA WAS IN PERPETUAL sunlight with three weak suns. Yet despite the heat factor, oceans covered the planet with little land surface. The majority of Yithians, including their females and offspring, lived in unending cities spreading across the bottom of their oceans.

Yithians were not fond of heat and most preferred to spend their "evenings" in the underwater cities. These remained chilled throughout the year. It was due to their dislike of high temperatures that they took to space where climate control was a necessity. At least, the underground dungeons were a few degrees cooler than the surface. Ori was immensely grateful for that even as she fanned her face with the end of her braid. Much good it did.

"Did you sleep last night?" Coldar preferred to keep his eyes shut. He said it was to minimize the dizziness, and she believed him.

"I'm sorry about the nightmares, Coldar." She winced, vowing to herself and not for the last time, she wouldn't let anything disturb his sleep. "I hate the killing part. Those creatures were imprisoned, taken from their natural habitat. They don't deserve to die like that."

"You kill them with respect, Ori. That is merciful." He tilted his head to meet her gaze. "Do not think for one moment they would mourn your death."

"I know they wouldn't, Coldar. But before they die, there is terror and sadness in their eyes like they understand what I'll take from them. I don't know how many more creatures I can kill. A part of my soul dies every time."

"That is a price to pay in the taking of life, Ori. I am sorry you have to pay it for both of us."

She tapped on her O.D.I., aware his gaze was on her. The holographic keys changed colors under her nimble fingers. She wasn't reaching out for a rescue. The port-dampening generators around the arena limited the O.D.I.'s range.

"What are you doing?" He had to drop the milady since it had attracted unwanted attention from the Yithian guards and some of the arena contenders. She hadn't liked the honorific anyway.

She giggled. The mischief swelling her chest made her giddy. "Placing a wager."

"What?" He sat up with a grunt, his broken ribs still mending, but at least the bruising had faded. His movements were easier these days. "I hope you are betting on us?"

"Well, when the odds were in our favor, I saw no reason why we couldn't make a fortune on the side." She showed him how much by holding out a forefinger and thumb with an inch between them.

He grunted. She imagined, if he was a human, he would have rolled his eyes.

"I've been doing it since our first fight. And for you, you know."

He shook his head despite the possibility of dizziness.

"Hey. I will escape here, buy myself a craft one day soon, and follow in my uncles's footsteps. It's the ultimate freedom for me." She grinned, loving how she had managed to wear down his formal attitude.

He was an Etterian male stranded in an arena dungeon and now her friend. She hadn't expected such an outcome to this adventure. Nor was she displeased. She got to experience true friendship; it was something she would forever cherish.

"What if you die?" He frowned as he studied her form.

She knew what he was thinking. He had voiced his opinion at every opportunity, *you are so tiny, yet what you can do is spectacular to behold. You know moves I have yet to learn, and you combine strikes I never thought to.*

To say his opinion of her had changed would be an understatement. "Then tokens won't matter. *When* we escape, we'll need those tokens."

"How much was the initial amount?" He squeezed his eyes shut against a wave of dizziness. His lips curled into a grimace. Despite him being an Etterian male, she had learned to read his tells.

"I had about twelve thousand to start with, so I bet it all."

"Do you recommit the entire amount at every battle?" He furrowed his brow, perhaps calculating how much they had made.

"Of course. Needless to say, half of it is yours, Coldar."

He grunted. "No, they are *your* tokens, not mine."

"I disagree. We're partners." She tilted her chin expecting him to recognize her determination since she had used it on him throughout their Yithian "vacation." "It means in all things we share. Although, I'm not sharing that cocktail you owe me." She winked. "I can't wait to see you sipping something hideously pink."

She marveled at how she could remember the promise they had made to each other. So much time had passed, with the universe abandoning them at the arena. It was trivial to remember the promise of a cocktail when their lives hung in the balance. Yet she needed to look forward to something. It gave her hope, and her hope bucket wasn't bottomless, as she had come to realize.

"Since we're so good, we're not making as much as we used to." She persisted in using "we" when he hated it, claiming there had been none of him in any of their fights.

When he tried to fight, she demanded he not 'help' when his efforts served to distract her. She hadn't wanted to have to haul his ass from the fire. Regardless, he couldn't defend a female, which went against the grain, making him a failure to the code, to Etteria. She couldn't fault him for this. It was their way. As long as they survived, she would do whatever it took.

"I don't want us to throw a battle that might get us killed, not for tokens."

He said no more.

Eight Yithians marched toward their cages. Their gazes shifted and their three-fingered hands gripped their blasters to their chests. They wore the uniform of their royal guards. She frowned. They were coming for her. At least, it wasn't for Coldar. His wounds were healing, besides his dizziness.

This many guards meant the dungeon master sanctioned this. He must have advised on the requisite numbers to bring when "visiting" her. As much as they valued her skills, they feared her unpredictability. She released a tired sigh, her energy draining from her weakened body. Despite what her fans chanted, she wasn't invincible.

She deactivated her O.D.I. and positioned herself at the back of the cage in her usual defensive stance.

"Female, you have ceased to enrich Yithia. Our king has demanded you lose in the next contest. We are here to ensure you comply," the captain lisped.

His bravado stemmed from his safe position outside the cage entrance. He shifted aside to let seven Yithians rush in as soon as he opened the gate. They wore protective gear since groin strikes were a favorite of hers. So, she aimed for the knees, dropping them to the ground as fast, before hitting them in the eyes or neck. But she couldn't handle seven at once.

Coldar's roars faded into the background. He was on his feet, stomping the sand and kicking the bars as he cursed her attackers. Though she managed to incapacitate four, the last three broke a few ribs. They had done so to minimize her movements. They snapped fingers on her right hand, to reduce her ability to attack. The pummeling on the side of her face was to impair her vision. It was quite strategic for Yithians. She could appreciate that despite the agony that coursed through her body and the shivers that hindered her strikes.

While struggling to stand, she glared at the captain, who hissed in laughter. He glanced at the two holding her, and they released her. The loss of support left her swaying, as she fought her injuries' insistence she fall to her knees.

"Let's see if you can fight, you worthless Earthian."

She might have ignored him with the amount of crippling and burning pain weakening her, had he not challenged her. Straightening her spine, she gave him a withering look despite feeling like a ragged punching bag.

"I'm a human woman, you ignorant ass," she said with misplaced pride.

Ignoring the screaming pain of her broken bones and the blood dripping into her eye, she launched herself with the last of her strength. With her good hand, she hit the laughing Yithian in two spots on his chest. "And you never piss off a woman."

He crumpled to the floor, his dead mouth gaping in shock. The last two Yithians raced out of her cage, slammed the door behind them, and left the corpses with her.

Energy drained from her, like oil leaking from a busted gasket. She slumped, unable to keep herself together. In hindsight, that might not have been such a good idea. Though, to end the bastard's life, she would sacrifice much.

"Alodon's hell." Coldar's voice was hoarse. His long-fingered hands gripped the bars, revealing his frustration. "As much as I love it when you do that to them...how are you, *ensa*?"

His use of *sweetheart* cut through her resolve. She sucked in a breath as she tried to sit on the dirt floor. "I won't lie to you, Coldar. I've been better."

Moaning from the pulsing agony, she wiped the blood off her face and accepted the stinging as part of the cacophony of complaints her body made. Blood dribbled into her eye, fluttering her eyelid. If the wound didn't stop bleeding, she would have to add blood loss to her current injuries.

"Status?" he asked.

Without him, she didn't know if she would have survived this long alone. Telling him would only embarrass him when he didn't know how to handle displays of emotion.

"A busted rib, maybe more, a few fingers too, and I can't see for shit through my eye."

"You better change the bet to the other opponent." He forced a smile, spun his back to her, then slid to the ground, resting against the bars between their cages. "I do not think we will win this time, Ori."

"Oh, ye of little faith," she said. "Let me get my strength back, and I'll go through these bodies. Bound to be something on them we can use."

"How do you do it, Oriana?" His whisper penetrated the silence a few minutes later as he raised his gaze to the stone ceiling. "Keep going?"

"To lose hope is to admit defeat."

Knowing the code, he grunted at her words. It was the exact code taught to all Etterian males. At least they shared that knowledge. Puny human female had something in common with elite Etterian warrior? Sure.

"Coldar, would you mind if I had a good cry?" She battled yet another wave of pain and wailing at the world was a way to ease the emotional turmoil building within her. She had to warn him though, not wanting him to think she was malfunctioning.

He shot a glance at her in concern. She pinched her lips despite the action making her face throb. It was strange how humans believed clenching their lips helped fight pain. It made no logical sense. She hugged her waist while clasping her injured hand against her chest. Her shaking had worsened as the remnants of adrenaline faded.

"Sit beside me so I can wrap an arm around you, Ori."

Using three of her limbs, she crawled across the black dirt floor. She lowered herself into a sitting position with excruciating slowness. Everything hurt, even breathing. Her arms ached, her ribs throbbed, her fingers were on fire, and her eye burned as blood dripped into it. Worst of it all was the ache in her chest, as despair threatened to clog her airways.

She pressed against the bars, needing the warmth emanating from his body. At least she was within his reach. He slipped an arm through the bars and across her shoulders, along her collarbone. The hug, as awkward as it was, brought her an immense amount of comfort. After a sniff, a nose twitch, the floodgates opened. She wept, sucking in shallow, shaky breaths between her sobs, and ignored the tears splashing onto his forearm. Her crying dwindled into pain-inducing hiccups. Using a lock of her hair, she wiped her tear-stained cheeks.

"Better, *ensa*?" He patted her like she were a child. She found it soothing, wanting to believe his hope and affection flowed through his fingers to ease her burdens.

"Yes, though crying with broken ribs isn't easy. Uncle Diso said tears were for special occasions only. I guess he would've allowed me this." Her shoulders sagged. She tapped Coldar's forearm, indicating he could release her anytime he wanted to.

"Tell me, how did you land up in HoSS?"

"You want my life story?" This subject hadn't come up before, so it startled her that he brought it up now.

"Yes, as much as you are willing to share."

She took in a slow breath, careful not to expand her lungs to a painful degree. And spilled the beans. From the moment she stepped onto the Lunar Base to her time on Earth. "HoSS was the furthest away. I was on that station for about seven months by the time I met your supreme commander and you. I'd made friends and a life for myself."

Silence stretched before Coldar cleared his throat. "Thank you for sharing, Ori. Life has not been kind to you."

"Says the male who will return to fight Gika like he is stuck in a time loop?"

"It is fun." He shrugged then winced. "When we get out of here, you can come with me. We will kill Gika and drink cocktails."

"Now that, Coldar, is a deal." Not that they permitted females on Gikaet.

But she gave him the moment, the hope they would indeed escape. Every damn day, regret plagued her, for agreeing to accompany Coldar to Etteria. If she had chosen to stay on HOSS, Coldar wouldn't be in a Yithian cell, and Myan would still be alive.

"I'm sorry about Myan," she said, and not for the last time, her regret ran too deep to cease apologizing.

The fact they were still prisoners attested to Myan's demise. No one had found the scimitar, the beacon hadn't reached its programmed destination, and his body lay in a drifting tomb.

She snuck a glance at Coldar. They had been on Mascroba, the main city of Yithia, for thirty-two days. She fought in the arena without protest because she fought for herself and Coldar. She shrugged. If it spared him, she'd do it, regardless of his well-aerated opinions.

Some nights, between nightmares, she dreamed of her supreme commander, imagined him striding between the cages to free her. Other nights, she recalled the intensity in his eyes and the exact huskiness of his voice. When she was exhausted, those were the saddest nights. She would sleep through without nightmares, but that meant the loss of dreams.

She wiped away a stray tear. Only a fool yearned for someone she wouldn't see again, never mind form a romantic relationship with. After all, to feel is to fail, and without the Ethera, he wouldn't touch her.

"Maybe this time we'll escape." She gritted her teeth with renewed determination.

"I love your enthusiasm, Ori." An answering smile played across Coldar's lips. Just seeing it made her giddy. As a brother, a true friend, she couldn't have found anyone better.

"What? No 'you shouldn't have to fight for me' drivel? Or 'an Etterian never endangers a female' nonsense?" She failed to mimic the gruffness of an Etterian male, but she made her point.

He laughed, something he had struggled with at first. She valued each lighter moment with him.

"You would not listen to me anyway, female," he said. "Besides, I have seen what you can do—you can defend yourself. You are not Etterian, and as such, should not live by our expectations."

She blinked before giving him a huge smile. It sent fresh darts of fire to water her injured eye. Yet it was worth it for a flicker of blazing joy in the darkness of her life.

"I love it when you say sweet nothings to me." She adjusted her bra before climbing to her feet to search the corpses. Every time she bent over, her vision blurred, her world spun, and a wave of nausea rose from her churning stomach to choke her.

Their boots had been the first items to go, within the first ten days of their vacation. Coldar's ceremonial jacket was also gone, leaving him in his breeches and bare-chested. In this heat, the clothing wasn't needed. They had traded it away last week. Yesterday, they had bartered her saloon uniform for food. The stale bread had been heaven-sent. Anything was better than paste.

Her lack of covering had become less awkward for her. She wasn't self-conscious anymore about her state of undress since aliens didn't find humans attractive. Her win. In her current state, she wouldn't be attractive to humans either. It had been so long since her last cleanse, so long since she had slept on a bed, or had a cup of coffee.

She shrugged off the longing, wishing her skin didn't itch under the thin layer of sand coating her. Her hair tie had snapped, leaving her hair to hang down her back in disarray. It no longer shone red but brown from the sand and filth. She offered Coldar a neo-band for his eye, but it wouldn't help much since they weren't Etterian med-patches. Theirs contained nanotech to speed re-covery. He accepted the protein bar she thrust at him before she lowered herself to the sand, inch by excruciating inch.

"I dream of a cleanse." She ran her uninjured hand through her hair. A cloud of dust formed around her when she fluffed it. "You must be happy you need never shave. You would look like a gorilla by now."

A pale golden-red dusting of hair on her legs was more than Coldar had seen on his face his entire life. Although, they had hair on their heads and sexual organs. She squeezed her eyes shut, forcing the image away, not wanting to think about her friend's privates, even in passing.

"I would appreciate a cleanse," he said, but his tone lacked enthusiasm.

She opened her eyes, scrutinized her cell, and peeked into the other cells where the contenders prepared for their turn in the arena.

Not that she could prepare for battle like they did. Weapons, clothing, and food required she spend her hard-earned tokens when they might need them to escape. If they didn't leave soon, she would have to reveal to the prisoners she did have the funds with which to purchase food and medical aid.

Her ribs were broken. Coldar would have to wrap her fingers with one of the neo-bands she had taken off the corpses. Her eye was swollen, limiting her vision as each hour passed. It must be worse than she thought since he winced whenever he looked at her.

The dungeon master hobbled between the cages, tossing in packets of paste and water. She stared at them, where they had landed against the boots of a dead Yithian. Turning her face away, she didn't push herself off to the ground to tear open a packet and suck the bitter, white paste that made her gag. She had half-expected the Yithians to withhold both water and food. The slave-trading bastards believed an injured or weakened fighter made for better sport. Hence her injuries.

"I have a good feeling about today." She flashed Coldar a grin.

It cracked her crusted lip, causing it to bleed again.

"You always do." He chuckled but glanced away, not meeting her gaze.

Chapter Twelve

Yithia

City of Mascroba

Arena podium

12252 years, 6th month

"WHAT IN ALODON'S BALLS are you doing, Vytus?" Enyl faced his blood-bond. "You are not supposed to resemble an Etterian."

Without Vytus having to say a word, Enyl realized the absurdity of his statement. How did they hide three over-six-foot-five tall males with bulk to match? His words were unreasonable, yet irritation coursed through him. The grittiness of Mascroba didn't help.

Black stone and walls formed the massive arena. Four massive metal doors led into the sandpit below. The suns slithered through shifting shields too high up to offer much relief. Various species packed the arena, but Enyl didn't take the time to identify them—cultural studies wasn't his forte. Their excitement was deafening as the suns baked the unshielded. The Yithians love of the arena far surpassed their hatred of the heat.

"You are miserable because Mascroba is dusty, smelly, and hot." Vytus's lips twisted in amusement but not quite breaking into a smile.

Enyl grunted. Vytus wasn't far from the truth.

"When did you turn into a female?" Malo teased as he sat next to him.

Enyl scrutinized the crowds, wincing at the many curious gazes upon them. Three Etterians attracted attention, as they always did, from the sheer size of them. They were in their version of a disguise, dressed as merchants, and not sporting their usual armor. Enyl patted his thigh where his blaster should have been. Lack of weaponry further irritated him.

"Wait, practice your patience, and your reward will come." Malo had to feel the same, yet the always-in-control commander showed no discomfort.

"You sound like Remi." Enyl nudged Malo with a sharp elbow, which he dodged with ease.

Enyl scanned the arena again. As a young Etterian, he had once enjoyed the atmosphere and the fights. Now, the air stank of poverty, desperation, and bloodlust, not of excitement as in his memories.

"You know the play." Malo studied the exits before sweeping his gaze over to the port-dampening generator thirteen steps behind their seating.

The crowd broke out in excitement as a familiar figure marched to the center of the arena. Enyl couldn't make out the indecipherable name they chanted. The Etterian joined her but stood in a wide stance behind her, farthest from the large gate. Enyl shifted in his seat. This male had to be Coldar, but the name the crowds chanted for McKenzie had him doubting the creature was her.

"He does appear injured." Enyl focused his far lens on the Etterian male despite the urge to look at her. He assessed the male's stance, his glazed eyes, and his hand on his stomach. "There is a familiarity to him."

Angling his lens on the Earthian brought the female into detail. He absorbed the wild flow of brown hair surrounding her like a cloak and falling to below her waist. McKenzie had a braid but of crimson hair, not this dull brown. Perhaps her species had hair that changed color depending on their health? The arena vids had revealed her features, confirming her identity. With the Etterian male present, and despite her diverted face, his leaping pulse recognized her.

"Earthians are smaller than Etterians." He admired her fine-boned hand when she finger-combed her hair like she wasn't in a Yithian arena about to battle an unknown opponent.

"Are you judging her species by her size, or is this an observation from your brief stay at the Earthian station?" Vytus said before peering through his own lens. "She lacks armor. What is that sash across her chest? It does not grant her much protection."

Enyl tightened his grip on the lens. He raised it to study her once more. Strips of white hugged the top half of her body, conforming to her breasts. Her waist indented to where the indigo fabric covered her hips and backside. Her bare legs scored with muscle to her bootless feet showed how similar Earthians physiology was to Etterians.

"The female Earthian requires it for modesty," a gruff voice gurgled.

Enyl faced the elderly Algri who had squelched into a seat next to Vytus.

"So, it is true? She fights?" Enyl hoped his sincere interest would help him to extract as much information from the Algri as possible.

"She is quite remarkable." The Algri's admiration was palpable despite his toneless voice.

"What is wrong with the Etterian?" Malo slid into the seat between the Algri and Enyl.

"He has a head injury if you can believe the buzz. She fights to keep him alive."

Enyl peered through his lens. He swallowed a gasp. She had raised her face and in doing so confirmed her identity again. Bold, breathless, and blazing excitement swept through him. He gripped the lens as he fought the tremors racking his body.

It was her. His McKenzie. She surveyed the arena, revealing the bruises of an abused prisoner. His vision tinted red. He squeezed his gritty eyes shut to calm his fury.

"Breathe." Malo leaned in. "We will save her this day."

Enyl willed himself to calm before opening his eyes. She would need medical assistance. Where she cradled her hand against her chest, her fingers twisted in unnatural angles. She held herself immobile with her breathing shallow.

"Alodon's balls." He wished he could breathe for her, but his lungs had seized. "I want to burn this arena to the ground."

"As a species, she is not a pretty thing with the one side of her face beaten," Vytus said.

"She has not fared well. The Yithians need her weakened. They have staked a large fortune on her losing today," the Algri droned.

Enyl grunted. The Yithians could end their lives, and by the justice of the arena. And his father taking Yithia to task for the death of an Etterian warrior would be met with insincere apologies. What happened in the area was beyond Urio's control, or so Urio would claim. Her death-by-opponent would earn Yithia millions of tokens. The cost of an apology would be negligible.

With his lens fixed on her, Enyl caught her glancing at the exits and around the arena.

"She is looking to escape." Malo nudged him, his words in a low whisper only Etterians and those with acute hearing could discern.

"That is good." Enyl almost rubbed his palms together. "We need her to run toward us."

The massive metal gate opened as an image popped up on the enormous vids surrounding the arena. It enlarged her face and body to gargantuan proportions. He slipped his lens into a cloak pocket. With her features in detail, he searched for the female he had first met. But her image this large only highlighted her injuries. The extent of the damage to her face was alarming, with her bruised eye sealed shut. Her jaw sported another bruise, and her mouth was swollen and bleeding.

He didn't need to see her green eyes to replicate his reaction to her. The warmth pulsing in his chest and spreading to his extremities heated his body until sweat formed under the layer of black dust coating his skin. Her chest rose and fell with every painful breath. Her breasts were large for her frame, but he didn't know Earthian physiology to say whether that was normal. They tested the strips' ability to contain their bounty.

He frowned. What she was wearing shouldn't have intrigued him. Her space suit had engulfed her, hiding her physical attributes from him. He had yearned to see all of her. Now that she was overly exposed, it wasn't lust that dominated his senses, though that did tease the edges of his control. Concern, a need to heal her, save her, care for her drove him to ignore logic and leap the boundary wall to reach her.

A hush broke out across the crowd as a drumbeat vibrated through the arena saving him from succumbing to the suicidal urge. The crowds were eager to know what creature would challenge their favored champion. It wasn't anticipation that coiled something solid in the pit of his stomach.

A distinctive gurgling roar reverberated from behind the metal doors. The crowd gasped before their cheering tore the silence. They bolted out of their seats with an energy that was intoxicating. A wilanegy burst through the metal gates, bending one and near ripping it off its hinges as it charged into the arena. It paused on its knuckles, sniffed the air, then altered direction, galumphing toward her.

Feared for their bloodlust and incredible strength, these beasts, with their blue, foot-long spikes, were invincible. The more they smelled fear or blood, the more they went berserk. It *would* smell blood—the Yithians had seen to that. By wilanegy standards, it wasn't a large one, six feet tall and as wide, but it could still kill with ease.

He focused on McKenzie as Coldar spoke to her. Enyl couldn't hear their words through the din of the arena. She nodded once but didn't remove her focus from the wilanegy stomping toward her, having set its sights on her. As the beast neared her, she didn't shift, twitch, or show any sign of fear or nervousness. She stared down her opponent in absolute stoicism.

As it was about to pounce, Coldar knelt in front of her. It happened so unexpectedly Enyl thought he had collapsed. She used his position to launch herself in the air, swinging her left arm to strike across the wilanegy's throat. The weak spot was its neck, but she couldn't have known this. Wilanegy were native to Lysara, far from her solar system.

McKenzie landed on the ground with a roll that had to have been excruciating. The wilanegy doubled over, gurgling in distress. She dashed around it and hit it with her elbow in a smooth downward stroke, at the precise spot on its neck. Within two moves, she had brought the creature crumpling to the floor, immobilized but breathing.

He sucked in a sharp breath, digging his fingers into his knees where he gripped them. His shoulders jerked with each demonstration of her startling skill. Hers was such a vulnerable species rich with hidden talent.

The crowd went wild. Their jumping, cheering, and chanting shook the foundations of the arena. Using his skills, Malo merged with the shadows, with the raucous crowd to execute his part of the plan.

One large display vid replayed the action in slow motion. Torn between watching her do it again or battle four armed Yithian soldiers, Enyl focused on her. The soldiers had run out in full regalia, not underestimating her. Armed with pikes since using stun lasers or blasters might kill her, they attempted to incapacitate her.

Despite having cost the Yithians a fortune by paralyzing the wilanegy and winning the challenge, they were unwilling to harm her in front of her fans since death-not-by-opponent meant double the payout. The crowd jeered at this turn of events, defending their favorite arena champion.

When the guards reached her, she swung her leg, sliding sideways, forward, but never backward. Her kicks and punches landed with precision. Before the last guard hit the ground, she and Coldar sprinted toward Enyl. He swung his gaze to meet Vytus's in disbelief for both her abilities and their choice of direction.

Vytus jumped up. "You would think they would go for the exits."

"They must have seen us. Well, that makes our part easier." Enyl leaned over the wall as she lunged first and scrambled up.

The three meters didn't hinder her in the slightest, although her grunts of agony said otherwise. Her injured arm must have been painful, yet she used it regardless. Coldar was behind her. She hadn't spared Enyl a glance, instead, once she reached the top, she turned to assist Coldar if needed. How she could be of use with her one hand once again cradled to her chest, was beyond Enyl's comprehension.

The green of her healthy eye mesmerized him. Peace descended as per their first meeting, yet pulsing through his veins was this inexplicable fiery excitement. He had no more doubts she was McKenzie with the green exquisite in her dirty face. The bright smile she bestowed upon him eradicated his calm and stuttered his heart before it settled into an unsteady rhythm.

"Greetings, Supreme Commander. I hoped you'd find me. Silly, I know."

She hadn't forgotten him and had expected him to save her? He couldn't smother a smile. Despite the years of warrior training behind him, her faith in him disarmed him. He stepped toward her.

Coldar slipped around her, saluted like an elite guard—a fist held to his chest—before crumpling to the floor. She cried out and rushed to the unconscious male's side. Her touches to his temple and cheek were gentle, caring. She met Enyl's gaze with her one eye pleading for his assistance.

In his peripheral vision, a Yithian soldier raised his blaster. Enyl dove behind her, shielding her body with his. He had to, for a blaster shot might kill her. Iced fire lanced through his shoulder. He grunted as he slid along the stone, then jarred to a stop when he slammed into a step. Ignoring his throbbing wound, he clambered up and hefted the fallen Etterian male over his other shoulder.

Enyl swerved through the crowds, bounding up the stairs to where Malo worked on the port-dampening generator. She followed Enyl, her presence registering on his senses. A backward glance revealed the crowds forming behind her, protecting her from further blaster shots. They cheered encouragement, patted her shoulders, and stroked her hair with reverence.

"Blue wire," she said in a pained gasp as she caught herself on the railing with her good hand. "It's the blue one."

Malo growled his frustration, yanked out the blue, and the humming of the field wound down.

"Five to port," Vytus said into his O.D.I., then gripped her shoulder and Malo's while Enyl grasped Vytus's arm. Nothing happened. "Five to port." He growled when they remained on Yithia, shooting a glare at them.

"Alodon's balls, I thought it went too well." Malo searched the arena for another escape route.

"We are going to have to do this the hard way." Enyl squared his shoulders, winced from the fire lancing across his back, but was still determined to proceed with the extraction.

With a quick note of her pale cheeks, he vowed to let the Yithians capture him rather than forsake her. As he shifted the male's weight into a better position, he glanced across the podium steps.

"Let me go first." She darted in front of them. "They don't want to kill me. I'll form a barrier."

He stared, stunned at her suggestion. Allow a female to defend them? Place a female in harm's way? Never. Who she was, and what she meant to Etteria, to…him, made it more imperative she survive.

"No." Enyl appraised her wounded body. "Malo take point. Vytus guard our backs. We move swiftly, and we move now."

"Let me take him." Malo gestured to Coldar.

Enyl shook his head. "We need you free to defend. Clear us a path."

"Are you always this stubborn? Domineering?" Her warmth teased his back as she pressed against him. He shot her an annoyed look, not needing her to distract him. "Then again, you ignored me on HoSS when I told you I didn't need rescuing." She blessed him with an unrepentant smile, so bright and dazzling against her dirty face. He blinked. "I'm grateful, for then and now."

"Here they come." Malo bolted across the top steps, choosing their path.

Enyl stayed on his heels. Her footsteps confirmed she obeyed him, with Vytus securing the rear. As the Yithians attacked, Malo incapacitated them before they could fire. Their blasters flickered red—that wasn't a good sign. If she had been in front, she would have died. Although, they had switched the blaster settings as soon as Malo charged them. Any sane male would have.

As a skilled assassin or operative, he had attacks and weapon knowledge that hadn't formed part of Enyl's warrior training. It was a mesmerizing sight as the infamous Malo battled. His unarmed strikes were swift and lethal. Enyl wished he could take the time to admire his battle-bond's skills in action.

Fists hitting flesh and bodies dropping behind him meant Vytus had ensured she remained unharmed. Enyl couldn't afford to confirm this. They needed to escape the arena and reach higher ground. With suitable altitude and distance, they might be able to port. He didn't wish to spend a "night" on Yithia. They had failed to plan this mission for success. A second option would have been wise, to ensure Vytus and their cargo made it out alive. Enyl hoped he didn't lose a foot of honor for this idiocy.

He broke through the main gate and glanced back. All were with him, but Vytus's eyes were wide. McKenzie's lips were pinched white, and her skin had paled. Enyl would request details later.

Malo steered them north where black mountains stretched out on the horizon. From there, they would contact the Kevol or the battleship *Gladio* which had lagged the faster ship.

As they sprinted along the various alleyways, Yithians scattered in fright. Etterians running toward them was a rare sight. Enyl grunted, increased his speed, and maintained his vigilance, despite each thundering step jarring his shoulder.

The soldiers had to find them soon. Yithia was not this incompetent, this unprepared. So far, they hadn't met with one, not even a city guard. The alarm had to have sounded. At any second, an influx of soldiers should engulf them. Malo targeted a point in the city's wall—lower in height than the rest. Enyl sighed. An escape route.

Malo clasped hands, and Vytus went over first. Enyl handed Coldar to the youngin's outstretched arms, before Malo hoisted Enyl up. Instead of going over the wall, Enyl re-positioned himself on the top of it as Vytus had done, extending his arms to McKenzie. She ignored his offered hand and, instead, scampered up the wall and vaulted over.

Enyl growled. He widened then narrowed his eyes. Doing careless actions like that worsened her injuries. Malo grabbed Enyl's outstretched arms, and he tugged them both over. Before Enyl could reach Coldar slumped against the wall, Malo threw the male over his shoulder.

Enyl grunted his gratitude—the wound's burning had spread down his arm. As he peered at the distant mountains, McKenzie's face snagged his attention. In his line of sight, he lingered on her pain and her pride as she forced herself to stand upright. She slumped then sucked in a breath before straightening.

The three suns beat down without mercy. Malo set a steady pace. She panted but said nothing. Whenever Enyl snuck a glance, her face had grown paler and her cheeks rosier. He pinched his lips against his own pulsing agony. Up ahead, Malo growled. This mission had gone worse than they had expected.

"Pilot Afax, acknowledge," Vytus said into his O.D.I. with no response.

In silence, Malo pointed to the top of a hill. Vytus tapped the female on her arm. When he gestured to his shoulder, she hesitated before nodding. She clambered onto his back when he knelt in front of her. He grasped a hand around her forearm, then rose and fell in line behind Malo.

By the time they reached the hill, Vytus stumbled more often as time marched on. He had yet to train as a warrior, but he did have the Etterian pride of one. He refused to show his waning strength. At last, he lowered McKenzie to the ground. He slumped with exhaustion, yet he still saw to her care, taking the time to steady her with a hand on her hip.

As soon as she stepped away, he tapped his O.D.I. and received crackling noises for his effort. He scanned the surrounding lands for another high point, then gestured to a hill, glancing between Enyl and Malo.

Malo faced their new target and strode on. Enyl hoped it was the final one. The weight of the unconscious Coldar must be tiring the commander. Smiling, he imagined Malo's gruff response if he mentioned this.

"Come, milady." Enyl held out his arms to her.

She flashed a smile. "I can walk for a while."

"It will be like the last time I carried you, or are you scared of me?" he teased, surprised that he could.

She laughed before holding out her good hand. With a swift and fluid movement, he swung her onto his back. Grasping his uninjured shoulder, she wrapped her legs around his hips and the forearm of her broken hand around his throat. When he grunted, she shifted her weight, trying not to put pressure on his wounded shoulder. He appreciated her consideration. Blood had soaked through his coat and tunic, sticking the garments to his skin.

"You are being silly." Her hot breath on the back of his neck raised the hairs there. He tried to suppress the shiver but doubted he was successful.

"Silly?" Humor rose in delicate swells and engulfed his chest. He let it flow into his voice. The joy was unexpected, and he relished it.

"You're as injured as I am. Is it your Etterian pride that dictates you don't succumb?"

"Pride and determination to get you home." He tightened his grip on her thighs vowing not to drop her no matter how injured he was.

"Acknowledged." She lay her forehead on his shoulder.

He assumed she was too exhausted to hold up her head, and with no one to see her, she didn't need to be strong. Vytus attempted to contact their ship again, but Enyl wasn't focused on that. For a few minutes, having her on his back brought him peace—the same as on HoSS. The irritation, that had been his constant companion in the recent months, was absent. She wiped it away with her presence. He needed to know how she did that.

Vytus and Malo had widened the distance. Enyl would have to exert himself to catch up but found he was resistant to do so, relishing this private moment with her. He slowed his pace despite not wanting to be in the baking suns for longer than was necessary.

A jagged rock outcrop cast shadows and offered a too-tempting reprieve from the unbearable heat. He took it and gently lowered her. Her head lulled to the side when he leaned her against the cool rocky surface. She didn't awaken. He dropped beside her and tugged out his med-gun, running it over her hand and her torso, not knowing which side had injuries. She mumbled. He raised his gaze, admiring the fall of brown hair cushioning her back.

She stilled, and her eyelid fluttered open. Maker, her eye color was magnificent. Her wide smile split her lip and blood dewed. He scanned her there, ignored his trembling hand, and hoped she hadn't noticed how much she unnerved him.

"Thank you." She held out her palm.

He blinked and placed the med-gun onto it. Tingles surged up his arm when his fingertips tested the softness of her skin. He lowered himself onto his backside to help her reach his shoulder, wringing his hands to ease the strange reaction.

"I'll scan it, but I'm not sure it will heal well." Her voice was as he remembered, husky and confident.

He sucked in a sharp breath as her fingers fluttered around his wound. The constant ache in his shoulder and arm lessoned bringing awareness of her gentle touch.

Blaster shots fired over the boulder, aimed at Vytus and Malo's disappearing figures. Four Yithians rushed past them where they huddled in the shade. Enyl took the med-gun from her and slid it into his pocket. In silence, he gathered her hand in his and led her around the boulder and down the cliff toward crashing waves.

A strip of black sand met a green ocean. On the beach, he scurried from shade to shade in the direction Vytus had gone. If they headed in the same direction, when they were no longer pursued, they could reunite. He snuck glances behind him, and despite her keeping pace with his long strides, she was in agony—her lips pinched white. Not a sound had escaped her. Alodon's hell, the female kept impressing him.

The salty, tangy scent of sea meeting baked sand permeated the air—thicker and hotter this near to the water. At the far end of the beach was a cave, promising shade, and a possible hiding point. It worried him they were out in the open, visible to an observant soldier.

"The cave, can you run for it?"

She studied their destination, then met his gaze. At her nod, they sprinted along the shore, keeping to the waves to hide their footprints. When they reached the cave's blessed coolness, she threw herself against a wall of rock. When she slid down and tilted her head back, he crossed the cave to join her. He punched their location into his O.D.I. and hoped Malo or Vytus would receive his comm.

"Do you think we're safe?" She splayed her hands on the rock, rising. Her injured fingers jutted out at odd angles. A proper scan would repair them.

"For now." He gestured to her to remain seated.

Time passed in comfortable silence. She didn't overwhelm him with questions but dozed. She mumbled mid-dream, but when he placed a hand on her knee, she jerked then quietened, falling into a deeper sleep.

He left the cave to comm a message to Vytus, not wanting his voice to disturb her. This time the response was immediate. The rock surrounding them must have dampened the signal.

After scanning the beach, Enyl strolled into the cave and slid down next to her waking form. "I reached Vytus. Malo took care of the Yithians, and they're searching for the cave."

"It will serve as a shelter if we can't return to your ship," she said.

"How are you?" Enyl swept a brown curl off her temple. Her temperature was mild, but since he didn't know Earthian physiology, he had to assume she was well. The bruises on her face were fading, as were the ones on her straightened fingers.

"Better. Thank you for this." She met and held his gaze.

Her sincerity touched a chord in him, one linked to his heart if his breathlessness was an indication. Not knowing how to respond, he sat in silence, watching the waves crash against the rocks. She lay her head on his shoulder when she fell asleep again. It worried him that she was this exhausted. Perhaps there were deeper medical reasons the med-gun couldn't heal.

"At last." A Yithian operative slithered into the cave, his shadow preceding him. Behind him, queued more soldiers, their blasters aimed and flickering red.

Enyl scowled and nudged her awake. He rose then helped McKenzie to her feet, needing her ready should he decide on the next course of action. The soldiers shifted as one, keeping their blasters pointed at her. They feared her more than an Etterian warrior. Darkness trickled from his chest into his stomach, that she was in danger, that he might not be able to save her. He trembled, as energy tore through him demanding he act.

He lunged in front of her and cut off their line of sight. They shifted again, their nervousness ramping now that he shielded her and made her unpredictable.

"You are free to go, Etterian, but the Earthian remains." The operative threw out a three-fingered hand to appease him. "We have no quarrel with Etteria."

Enyl grunted. If they knew he was the prince, perhaps they would grant her free passage. Or they could kill him, leaving her unprotected. "I am an Etterian warrior. I cannot release an injured female into your care. Not when it was under your protection she suffered, and when you have every intention of harming her again."

The operative hissed. "She is Yithian property."

"She was Etterian property first but that did not stop you."

"I'll go with them." McKenzie gripped his elbow, her touch burning him through his coat.

Enyl stilled, denying the effect she had on him and that he might have to let her go to resave her. There weren't many options open to them. He could fight his way through had there been a few Yithians but not eleven. He settled his gaze on her. With her injured, he didn't want to endanger her when a stray blaster shot could kill her. "Where she goes, I go."

Gasping, she tightened her fingers. "No." She darted around him, peering up at him with her green eyes pleading as she had done for Coldar. "Please, if you're free, then they have no leverage over me."

The operative hiss-laughed. "The warrior will join you...as leverage." He gestured with his fingers for them to follow.

She didn't, glaring at Enyl instead, before giving him her back as she faced the firing squad. Her shoulders stiffened with exaggerated confidence filling her voice.

"You have hounded and degraded me. At some point, you must realize your life is in my hands." She chuckled, the husky sound raising the hairs on Enyl's neck and pooling heat in his groin. "As you must know, I have killed many Yithians with my bare hands, Operative."

Operative? How did she know the Yithian's rank? Enyl arched a brow, vowing to ask her later.

Regardless, the Yithian's skin darkened. He sliced nervous glances at his soldiers. "I am not afraid of you, Earthian." His soldiers shifted, distancing themselves from their leader.

Wind and sand blasted the cave, and Enyl wrapped his body around her, his back taking the brunt of it. The whir of engines meant a shuttle had landed on the beach. All hope of Malo saving the day drained from Enyl.

He cupped her face, forcing her to meet his gaze. The swelling had lessened, and her injured eye was no longer squeezed shut. Despite the pain she must have endured, the kaleidoscope of colors on her skin enhanced the bright green. For a moment, he lost his train of thought.

"Fight or leave with them?" He wanted to battle his way to freedom, buying Malo time.

Enyl's focus was compromised with her under his protection. Something intense—weighing on his lungs, his senses—compelled him to save her, no matter the cost. He obeyed the instinct, adjusting his planning accordingly.

"They might have reinforcements on that shuttle, but if I can steal a blaster?" She grinned, snatching his breath.

Maker, her courage, resilience, and determination were admirable. Patting him on the chest—her touch sent out shards of need like a sunburst—she slipped around him and dipped her head, appearing meek. "He stays, and I'll come with you."

"No—" The operative died, his mouth gaping in death.

A blaster wound burned where one of his hearts used to be. As chaos erupted while she took down the nearest soldiers with blurred movements, Malo and Vytus fired from behind. Enyl charged, throwing punches and kicks while the sounds of blaster shots and fists hitting flesh ricocheted off the cave walls.

"Is this where you two are hiding?" Vytus met his gaze across the corpses.

Behind him, a kuta shuttle had landed on the black beach. Etterian warriors hovered at the open door to the compartment. Others surrounded the shuttle with blasters raised.

"What took you so long?" Enyl chuckled, thankful for their rescue anyway. He fixed his gaze on a smiling McKenzie, then strode toward her to lace his fingers through hers.

"I cycled through the known frequencies hoping Afax monitored them all." Vytus rattled on as Enyl tugged her into the shuttle. "When

I mentioned you were missing, he deployed a kuta for immediate extraction."

As his males boarded, Enyl lowered her into a seat and strapped her in, sweeping a curl off her temple. Medic Aldur knelt beside an unconscious Coldar, running the med-gun over him. Malo entered the compartment last. The door sealed, and the shuttle shot upward. Enyl slid into the seat beside her, lacing his fingers through hers again, marveling at how much he enjoyed touching her.

She blessed him with a smile and leaned her head on his shoulder. Within seconds, she slept.

He ran a fingertip across her cheek. "My thanks, Malo."

Malo scrubbed his face with his hands. "Worst mission I have been on in decades, Enyl. Either I am losing my abilities, or they knew we were coming."

"A traitor among our males?" Enyl scoffed, though how else could they explain it. Malo was too good at his skills for this to reflect on his record. "Have a data officer scan all communications since the Yithians took McKenzie."

Malo typed on his O.D.I. "Done."

She slipped her hand between his elbow and ribs to tug him closer. The coolness of the kuta in contrast to the heat of Yithia brought on shivers, and she snuggled against him. Enyl raised his arm and looped it around her, bringing her into his warmth. She sighed but didn't awaken.

Malo draped a blanket over them, one he must have requested from the kuta's replicator. Enyl nodded his thanks, taking the time to ensure she was well-covered.

"Her inner strength makes her species appealing." Malo furrowed his brow, his gaze studying her upturned face as Enyl had done seconds ago. "Since you find her intriguing, she is yours to care for, to protect until we deliver her to Resia Cay."

The Ethera tests—Enyl grunted as he tightened his arm, almost crushing her against him. They needed to confirm her compatibility, but he didn't want to think about letting her go. Since the Ethera hadn't struck him down, that would mean she wasn't his, or Coldar's, or any male's on the shuttle.

Part of Enyl wanted her to trigger the Ethera, another part didn't want to lose sight of her. Despite these warring emotions, he would choose Etteria and what she could mean to his people. Maker, he hated being a prince and an honorable warrior. If he wasn't, he would keep her. Losing his soul to the void was more than worth it.

Chapter Thirteen

Etterian Battleship, Gladio
Cloaked and en route to Etteria.
12252 years, 6th month

As Etterian warriors disembarked the kuta, Medic Aldur escorted Coldar off the shuttle with a promise to visit Enyl as soon as he could. Enyl rubbed her shoulder, trying to wake McKenzie. When she didn't, he rose, gathered her in his arms, and carried her. She placed her hand on his chest and slept on.

"I best inform your father before he hears from another source." Malo removed the beige merchant's cloak and tossed it at a waiting warrior before storming off.

Vytus trailed behind Malo, shaking his head.

Enyl scowled. They had abandoned McKenzie, brushed her off as his responsibility. He understood why since he had been with her the longest, had saved her twice. As the prince, they expected him to act as the diplomat. If only they knew whatever roiled within him wasn't the slightest bit polite.

Her fingers fluttered as she stirred. "His name is Coldar et Hendar. His battle-bond died during the breach. Please honor Myan et Phyan as having died in battle." She peered at him, her cheek against his shoulder. "They're elite guards judging by the ceremonial dress they used to wear." She forced a polite smile, cracking her dry lips, which didn't bleed. "I've thanked you for the rescue, but I can't express how grateful I am, Supreme Commander."

Enyl bowed. Revealing who he was would have to wait. As well as Myan's good health. If she saw the male, she might find it easier to believe.

"I am Enyl. May we see to your needs, milady?" His polite offer of aid slumped her shoulders.

She rubbed her forehead with dirty fingers. "Yes, please." With a wriggle, she made silent demands for him to lower her. He was resistant to do so, not finding her weight taxing. "I can walk."

He ignored her until he stood before the door to his quarters. It was the most suitable for a female and the only officer quarters onboard. He entered and guided her to the waiting comfy. She winced as the chair adjusted to her shape. The door chime distracted him from going to her, though what he would've done he didn't know.

"Greetings, Aldur. Please see to milady. We've healed each other with the med-gun but may have missed a few injuries."

The medic hurried across to her. "Greetings, milady. I will perform an assessment."

She nodded, and her wide-eyed gaze didn't waver from Aldur, who scanned her with his forearm. His O.D.I. device flashed green, blue, and white—green for assessing, blue for diagnosis and repairing, and white for completion.

He punched a few holographic keys. "Milady has dehydration and malnutrition. I have adjusted the cleansing room to cater for this." He focused his wrist on her face, her right eye, and over certain parts of her body that had taken the brunt of her misadventure.

Her abuse angered Enyl. He marveled at the intense emotion burning in his chest, tensing his muscles as if he prepared for battle.

"You had extensive bruising throughout your body. A broken rib, two cracked ones, two broken fingers with a bruised and swollen face. All are healing well." Aldur withdrew a med-gun and scanned her ribs again.

"The bones have knitted well." He ran the gun over her face. "The swelling and bruising should fade by the time you finish your cleanse. I should not have to tell you to minimize movement. A long cleanse will speed the healing. Would you like an anesthetic added to the water?"

"Yes, thank you, Medic Aldur." She blessed the elderly male with a gentle smile. "How's Coldar?"

"His eye was a swift repair. He had a burst eardrum, which caused his imbalance and nausea. I have placed him in hibernation to ensure his ribs heal well."

"I'm happy to hear this. He can be stubborn." The wider, brighter smile she flashed Aldur made Enyl uncomfortable.

It was one of gratitude, but it implied a deeper relationship with Coldar. Why the thought of it bothered Enyl, he couldn't say. He shifted in his seat, trying to ease the restlessness plaguing him. Her presence hadn't silenced it. He frowned and gripped his bouncing knee—a sign of his charged energy and irritation.

"Would you like to cleanse first or eat something?" His offer of a cleanse gained her immediate attention. He gestured to the cleansing room.

With aching care, she rose from the chair, gasping when the door slid open. "It's the size of my unit on HoSS," she whispered as the door shut behind her.

Curious about Earthian females and this one, in particular, he was tempted to remove the wall's opacity, to watch her undress. In the end, he respected her privacy. Aldur waited as Enyl fought the temptation and his moral code.

"The Yithians horrendous treatment of such a creature is unacceptable." Enyl assumed a comfy. "I have never seen a female in such a condition. Did you see the bruises on her arms, as well?"

Aldur nodded with a disgusted expression twisting his face. "The buzz says she is the arena champion?"

Enyl grunted his response before stilling, letting Aldur work. He removed his ruined cloak and shirt when requested to do so, granting Aldur access to the wound on his shoulder. The synthetic skin adhered to his existing flesh and pulled tight, as it formed a barrier to prevent scarring and further blood loss.

"She must be part of the elite guard on her homeworld."

Enyl met Aldur's inquiring gaze. "She is an engineer, as far as I can recall. I do not think long hair means the same thing in her culture; although she does deserve that honor in ours." He glanced at the cleansing room's door then at the old medic. "It was remarkable to behold. With such grace and minimal movement, she took down a wilanegy. Two quick moves and the beast fell." He couldn't hide the awe in his voice and didn't try. Aldur's scan would reveal Enyl's spiked heart rate. It was, therefore, pointless to lie.

"It must have been amazing to witness. Your eyes are a pale blue, my prince."

Enyl scowled at the warning. "I am not emotional."

Aldur frowned as he examined Enyl again. He smacked the O.D.I. to recalibrate it, before repeating the scan.

"It is your Ethera." He gasped, glancing in McKenzie's direction. "She is your Dar Eth. Have you experienced sharp pain, weak knees, and uncontrollable lust?"

"None of those. Besides, it is a legend, Aldur. All males believe so." Enyl wanted it to be true, but he wasn't a fool. She invoked so many unknown emotions in him, and those alone might be why his eyes paled.

Aldur gave him a look that implied he was being an idiot. Enyl sighed, not willing to admit he couldn't bear to hope the elderly medic spoke the truth. He focused on the events since he'd met McKenzie. He hadn't fallen to his knees, hadn't experienced pain or visions, and his eye color hadn't permanently changed. Uncontrollable lust? He found her attractive but nothing that seared his mind with demanding baser urges. He liked touching her, though.

"As you say, my prince. Sit still," Aldur said before leaving the quarters.

Enyl closed his eyes to focus on his breathing. His new skin would take time and patience to adhere which he was far from capable of. His Dar Eth? Nonsense. Unbelievable. Absurd.

The cleansing door opened. Hearing nothing else, he peeked through one eye. She poked her head out the doorway. He admired her face, now clean of Yithian black dust. Her cheeks dimpled with her lips curling upward at a corner of her mouth, and water droplets glistened off a bare shoulder.

"Towel?"

"Blue button." He dipped his chin, seeking serenity. The bruising on her face had faded to a pale yellow with the swelling reduced. He fought the urge to shrug like her presence didn't matter.

Her squeal of laughter made him jerk but not jarring enough to disturb his shoulder. He cracked a smile at her infectious joy. A few minutes later the door sounded, so he peeked again. Her head peered around the side of the doorway, a smile breaking across her face. Her pale skin was smooth and creamy—a beautiful perske color.

"Clothing?"

"Gray button." He stared at the door. Her hair color from his memories matched her eyebrows, as he had hoped.

The lack of a prickling sensation on his shoulder meant the skin had adhered well. Rising to his feet, he paced across his quarters to stretch his back muscles, tempted to cleanse, as well. Mascroba made his skin itch—Vytus had been correct about that.

The door swished, and this time she strolled through it, wearing a thick, white wrap. It had adjusted to her curves and accentuated her form. As he ran his gaze over her, tingles burst across his face to his hairline. His hard-fought calm evaporated, and with the full view of her, cleaned and revealing, white pleasurable pain shot through him.

He fell to his knee in a smooth descent. The pain was intoxicating, like energy bursts rushing through his blood. He shuddered as he experienced a thousand bolts of ecstasy—across his skin, along his nerves, culminating in his groin. He hardened in an instant, snatching his breath, increasing his heart rate.

A vision appeared, of her on top of him, her legs spread wide to display her femininity, himself buried deep within her as she undulated her hips. He could *feel* her tighten around the length of him, the heat, her incredible softness. He could *smell* her sweet, delicious arousal, and *hear* her throaty moans and gasps.

He broke out in a sweat as the burning agony weakened him. When she knelt before him, she brought her exotic fragrance. She hovered her hands around him like she wanted to touch him but feared to do so. He was grateful she didn't. His control was non-existent.

Her face contorted with worry. "I'll get help."

He shook his head, taking deep breaths, the hot sensations lessening but not abandoning him. They lingered, roiling, and swelling, overwhelming him with emotions he couldn't identify.

"I am well." He pulled himself into the comfy, sitting still for a few minutes, and willed his heart to slow and his breathing to calm. "Are you feeling better?" His voice was hoarse and uncontrollable, as he slanted his gaze anywhere but at her. "Aldur did program the cleanse to replenish you." He forced the words past his clenched jaw.

"Oh, to be human again." She chose the comfy beside him, remaining near should he need her. The joy in her voice stole his focus—he glanced at her. Her smile was wide and unrestrained, her green eyes sparkled, yet concern for him still reflected in their depths.

"Human?" Repeating the word triggered an array of descriptions and images from his O.D.I. He hadn't experienced the same when he said "Earthian."

When the images cleared, he settled his gaze on her.

Her hair was a gorgeous red and the same color as their oceans. It cascaded down her back like a fiery waterfall. His fingers itched to run through her stagnant locks and stroke her skin—it appeared so soft and enticing, so pale and contrasting against his.

"It's what we call ourselves."

"Not Earthians?" He was aware he sounded like an idiot, but if he kept her talking, he had an excuse to stare at her.

Etterian females had bronze skin and black hair, nothing as vibrant as this. Her dazzling coloring kept his mind from exploring the pain, the kneeling. It couldn't be... She couldn't be his. A bold, breathtaking wave of hope drenched him, which he struggled to tamp down.

"Definitely not." She grinned. "Earth is our planet of origin, but we've never called ourselves Earthians."

"Hungry?" He appreciated the delight that tilted her bright eyes upward.

The ensuing hot dart to his groin was a painful pleasure. He shifted in the comfy, trying to ease it. Uncontrollable lust? Another confirmation rose from his gut, cresting with the urge to reach for her, to throw his head back and roar his happiness.

"I'm starving."

Seconds ticked by as he blinked at her, having forgotten she had answered him.

Clearing his throat, he lowered his gaze, breaking the hold she had over him. "If you could have anything, what would you want?" He bolted for the sanctuary of the replicator, careful to keep his arousal hidden from her.

"Well, assuming your replicator has human food, I would like a cheeseburger, fries, and a coffee."

He smiled through the pain, ignored his trembling fingers, and punched in her request. Within seconds, it had replicated her meal. Even her food was colorful. He gripped the plate and cup and struggled to gather his control before he faced her. Her crimson hair, pale skin, and green eyes pierced him anew, and his shoulders slumped.

Maker, please let her be his.

ORIANA STARED AT THE Etterian, running through the many facts she knew, wondering what was wrong with him. He was the image of the supreme commander she had first met. Oh, the universe had blessed her when it had sent her the very man she dreamed about.

His cerulean eyes against his bronze skin were a breathtaking combination. His smile was bright and white, and when two dimples appeared, she gasped. Hiding her reaction was harder than any of Uncle Gayn's tests. Hell, she even liked Enyl's square jawline.

She frown when she recalled his indigo eyes. According to the data annals, his pale eyes meant two things. He was feeling intense emotion. She studied the calm male and shook her head. No violent reactions on any emotional scale.

Which left a Dar Eth. Between now and when they had met, he must have found his soulmate—Uncle Gayn's term for the Ethera.

But she dismissed that as improbable, not when Etteria was desperate to find compatible females.

She pinched and released her chin. Or an illness was the cause behind the color change. She had panicked when he had fallen to the floor. Whatever it had been, it had looked painful. To fell a man so large and well-built must have been something as powerful. His whole body had given off heat and a sunbaked scent that made her insides quiver.

He hadn't wanted or needed her help and was too proud to acknowledge what had happened. No matter how much she considered talking to Aldur about this, she couldn't go around Enyl's wishes and ask for help. Who was she to determine what was best for him? The medic may very well be aware of the problem, and there was nothing to do for Enyl.

The idea that this vibrant man could be dying shot pain through her, cinching her test tight, like a vise hindering her ability to breathe. She rubbed her sternum, attempting to alleviate the pain.

She shouldn't care so much. He had saved her twice when she never accepted help. Closing her eyes, she recalled the sense of safety that engulfed her when he hugged her. That same peace had come over her when she had climbed onto his back and when he had shielded her with his body.

She glanced away from him as he ordered her food, after watching him stride with fluidity and determination. Admiring his tight ass was best hidden from him. He wouldn't catch her staring or drooling over him if she kept her attention on the plate he carried.

"Here we go, milady." He placed the meal on the table before her. The simulated aromas wrenched her deprived stomach.

As a distraction, she flexed her pre-injured hand to test the reparation, marveling at how quickly she had healed. She blinked at the play of light as it rippled across his sculpted chest. The thick-corded muscles in his arms and the splaying of his long fingers fascinated her.

"I thought all Etterians had indigo eyes." She picked up a fry and bit into it.

The salty flavor burst onto her tongue. She moaned. Knowing it wasn't a real beef hamburger and potato fries wouldn't diminish her enjoyment of it.

Used to chicken-flavored sandwiches and bitter Yithian paste, it was the texture that sent her mouth to heaven. "Yours are cerulean."

She offered a fry to him, which he accepted, more from politeness than curiosity. He shifted in his chair. Her question had made him uncomfortable. When he realized he held a fry in his hand, he popped it into his mouth and grimaced. She shrugged. As she chewed on another fry, she studied his features and waited for him to respond to her subtle inquiry.

"Most males do have indigo eyes. Sometimes it changes on a fully-grown male. It is unexpected," he said.

She tilted her head, wondering why he had been honest yet vague. He wasn't going to reveal any details, not that it mattered. He had a husky timbre—she could listen to him all day even if he chose to discuss the algri mating rituals. His voice stroked over her skin like he had run his long fingers over her. She shivered.

"Does it hurt when it happens? Are there any warnings, you know, like tingling in your extremities, numbness?" The annals didn't mention the effects of the Ethera, and since his eyes were cerulean, she would take this opportunity to assuage her curiosity. When Uncle

Gayn had first taught her about Etterians, he hadn't been able to answer all her questions.

She took a bite of her cheeseburger, savoring the melted cheese, pickles, burger, and barbecue sauce. "This is amazing, and yes, it might be the hunger talking." She gave him an apologetic smile because damn, she was starving enough to shove the whole thing into her mouth. Uncle Gayn's voice in her head stopped her from eating like a caveman.

"No, there is no warning, and yes, it is painful."

"When your eyes change color, it's usually brought on by the Ethera. Is your Dar Eth onboard?" While nibbling on her burger, she snuck glances at her coffee. It would be her dessert, one she eagerly anticipated.

His arched eyebrows meant her statement had startled him. She hid a smirk, enjoying surprising him. He must've thought her an alien creature devoid of intelligence. Or worse, a weak female needing rescuing since she had proven that true, twice.

"Yes." His hesitant response meant he lied. But lying was dishonorable and against their code. Intrigued, she took his reply at face value.

"I'd love to meet her. Etterian females are hardly seen."

His cheeks darkened, but his gaze settled on her lips.

She grinned. There was something entertaining about tweaking him. She bit into her burger and watched him, content to sit in silence for as long he would allow it. Besides, uncomfortable silences revealed much about a person's character.

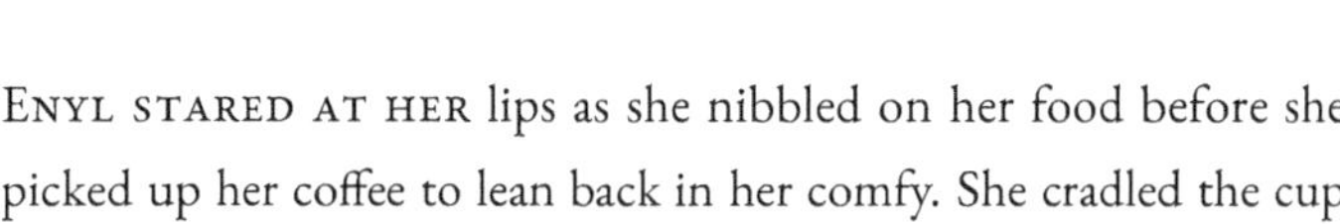

Enyl stared at her lips as she nibbled on her food before she picked up her coffee to lean back in her comfy. She cradled the cup with reverence.

"It's been decades since the last pairing, as I recall." She sniffed her beverage.

Her eyelids fluttered, and her blissful expression sent a renewed throbbing to his groin. He shifted in his comfy again. Her words pierced through the lust-filled haze. He frowned at her knowledge of pairings and the Ethera.

When he didn't answer, she settled her gaze on him and arched a brow.

"It is rare," he blurted. "The circumstances required for it to happen may vary, milady."

"Enyl, please stop with the 'milady.' My name is Oriana McKenzie." She sipped her coffee then smiled in sheer bliss. Her satisfied sigh ran through him like wildfire.

His breath caught at her unfettered responses and the way his body reacted to them. Humans lacked self-control when it came to pleasure. The memory of his earlier vision flashed through his mind, proving her responses would remain uninhibited. It was something he was eager to experience.

He rubbed his forehead when his arousal hardened to its full length. His frown formed a scowl. He never became this hard unless stimulated, but she had yet to touch him. At the thought of her doing so, his arousal throbbed in anticipation.

"What is wrong with milady? We call all females such, a verbal reflection of our respect. It is how we honor and cherish them."

Her green eyes flashed with a passion his body recognized. "I know how your culture reveres females. To me, it means you don't care enough about me, as a person, to learn my name."

He blinked, his focus turning inward as he pondered her words. She was correct, from her perspective. In their quest to cherish females they had forgotten to cherish the individual.

"Very well. May I suggest Lady Oriana?" He studied her face, aware he was staring again.

He waited for her to respond to his suggestion and didn't mind she had yet to speak. The longer she took, the more he could admire her features. Her long hair was the first thing he marveled at. It shimmered even under the artificial lighting and didn't undulate as his hair did. Her eyes were the next to endure his fascination. They were exquisite. He knew not of any species with that specific color.

Her lips appeared soft, tempting him to stroke his fingertips across them. Her skin was expressive, altering color—pale or flushing pink under his watchful gaze. He bounded up to remove her discarded plate, needing to distance himself from the temptation to touch her. Her gaze trailed him—burning into his back—as he strode toward the waste disposal. He wanted to use the replicator's reflective surface more than he needed to dispose of her meal remnants. His eyes had paled into a startling cerulean. He blinked at his reflection in disbelief.

The bright, burning joy engulfing him summoned a wide smile. He had a Dar Eth. Leaning forward until he was an inch from the surface, he widened his eyes until the cerulean pupils couldn't be denied.

"Enyl," she said as soon as he returned to his comfy. Her heated gaze traveled over his chest with as much reverence as she had held her cup. His nipples tightened under her admiration. "Are you aware you're shirtless?"

Why would she mention such a triviality?

Flustered and breathless, she rushed her next words. "Not that I mind seeing your chest bare. Etterian males are beautiful to look upon." Her cheeks glowed like an Etterian dawn sky.

He liked that she thought him, they, were beautiful, and being shirtless in front of her appealed to him.

"Does my bare chest bother you?" he teased, fighting the urge to flex his muscles under her appreciative gaze. His body's temperature rose a few degrees, but without his armor, he couldn't regulate it. He pointed to his shoulder. "I have new skin. It requires that I remain unadorned for a while."

"Oh, how rude of me." She placed her half-finished coffee on the table and rose. "Saving me cost you much, and I thanked you in passing. Uncle Gayn would be so disappointed in me." When she circled him to assess his shoulder, he frowned. "May I?"

He nodded, not sure for what she required permission. To touch him wasn't what he had expected. Their laws forbid unsanctioned physical contact between males and females, unless under specific circumstances. She must've known this since she had asked first. Her feather-like touch shot another white, pleasurable bolt of fire through his veins. He shuddered as her fingertips stroked across his back.

"Your new skin is amazing. Does it hurt?"

He struggled to shake his head, to speak. Something cinched his lungs, throat, tightened his muscles. He gripped the comfy's arms, restraining himself from lunging for her.

"It does. I'm so sorry."

He fought for control, fought the urge to pull her down to his lips, his body, his throbbing arousal. "No," he croaked.

"It does, your knuckles are white, your fists clenched."

"The skin is super-sensitive." He winced as the half-truth slipped past his pinched lips. After a few seconds of silence, he opened his eyes to find her staring at him.

"Thank you, Enyl," she whispered, cupping his cheek. His breath hitched. "For saving me and Coldar. Thank you for carrying me, as well. I don't know how much longer I could've continued."

"I will always see to your well-being, Lady Oriana," he said in a gruff voice, recalling how she had wrapped her legs around his hips with the juncture of her thighs pressed to his lower back.

He sucked in a sharp breath as the intense throbbing in his groin spiked. Mimicking that reaction was the heaviness on his heart—she was his to protect henceforth. Maker, he prayed he was up to the task.

As she assumed her seat, he was at a loss for words, with many questions on the tip of his tongue. Who was Uncle Gayn? How did she know so much about Etteria? Where had she learned to fight like that? When the door chimed, Enyl commanded it to open, grateful for the interruption. In burst his blood-bond, all energy, and excitement, as expected of a youngin.

"Greetings, Earthian." Vytus assumed the nearest comfy.

Despite laughing at his enthusiasm, she pulled her wrap tighter around her body and tucked her feet up to hide them under the fabric. Her shoulders curled forward. She hadn't done so with Enyl. This pleased him. Her alluring toes peeking out from under the wrap snared his focus.

"Lady Oriana, this is my blood-bond, Vytus. They call their species humans, *damu*."

"Humans?" Vytus tested the word out.

"Thank you for carrying me, Vytus." She offered a smile. "By blood-bond, do you mean brother, nephew, cousin?"

Enyl's eyelids fluttered as the O.D.I. rushed to explain her words. He smiled. Her language was so descriptive. "Cousin. He is the son to my father's brother."

She toyed with the hem of her wrap. "Uncle. I have always loved Etteria's simple approach to relationships. You are either a friend, as in a battle-bond, or you are family, as a blood-bond. There is no variances."

Enyl frowned. Always? How long had she known about Etteria's culture?

Vytus sniffed the room. "What is that unusual aroma?" He scanned the replicator and the quarters, then froze when he met Enyl's gaze.

He gave Vytus an almost imperceptible shake of his head, before running a trembling hand over his face, still fighting for control. Having a male, even his blood-bond, in proximity to her was killing him.

Vytus stiffened then hurried to clear his throat. "Why is your hair red?"

"What you smell is a hamburger, and my hair is this color thanks to my mother's genetics." She winked at Enyl, snatching the breath from his lungs, again. He liked that she was comfortable enough with him to be playful.

Vytus tilted his head to the side. "Are you a warrior on your planet?"

She laughed. "Hell, no. I'm just an engineer who works at a bar. Nothing more."

Enyl doubted that. Here before him sat his princess. Despite her smile, her right hand trembled as she toyed with her curls falling over her breast.

"You were amazing," Vytus gushed, bouncing in his comfy.

"No, the honor is all yours, Vytus. Saving me like that, and I'm sure Coldar will express his gratitude soon."

Enyl's chest swelled. "A diplomatic response."

She met his admiring gaze, with the green of her eyes darkening to something potent, heated, stuttering his heart anew. "What I can do is self-defense—me against the wild creatures to survive. On Earth, we used to have elite warrior teams who could do far more than I ever could."

"No, you misunderstand me." Vytus shook his head. "I am referring to the Yithians who tried to stop us."

Enyl's eyebrows shot up. When the bodies dropped behind him, he had assumed Vytus defended them.

"You strike with precision and efficiency." Vytus punched the air in front of him in mock combat. "And your strategic analysis was correct. They had not wished to harm you. A few blaster shots would have incapacitated us, but they approached without firing."

She squirmed on the comfy. "I only protecte—"

"You took them down with two strikes to their chests. I have never seen anything like it." Vytus thumped his chest twice—the sound echoing through the quarters.

"If you hit a chest hard enough you can stop the heart. I told Coldar the same thing. Yithians have two hearts; Gika three." She laughed, and the sound of pure joy filled every inch of Enyl's quarters, as it did his soul. "Oh, there are a few humans I would love to punch. Still, violence shouldn't be the first reaction."

"How do you know so much?" Enyl ran his gaze over her and lingered on her toes peeking out more, now that she opened to Vytus's presence.

She shrugged. "I have trained, just as you have."

Frowning at her vague answer, Enyl opened his mouth to speak but caught the mischief twinkling her eyes.

"I shall reveal more when you do." Chuckling, she slid her feet from under her and rose. "I'm tired, Vytus, if you don't mind saving the twenty-questions until later?"

"Of course." He leaped off his comfy and strode out.

"My apologies," Enyl said as soon as they were alone.

She flicked a dismissive hand. "I should apologize for assuming I can sleep now."

"You may—your bedroom is through there." He gestured to his room, amazed at how the thought of her in his bed sent sparks through his body. He wanted and needed her to be near him, to share in everything that was his.

"But I meant with Coldar—"

From flaming hot need to ice drenched agony, he blinked at her. "What? Why?"

"I need him." She chewed on her bottom lip with her white teeth. Enyl's focus snagged there as thoughts of her anywhere near Coldar boiled his blood. "I can't sleep unless he's touching my arm." She sucked in a shuddering breath. "All those lives I took haunt me." Her face paled further. "The truth is, I know why, I just don't know how to stop the memories. I'm not weak. I...sleep better when he touches me."

Enyl frowned—this courageous warrior suffered from nightmares? The death by his hands haunted him, as well. Even though they lived in a time of peace, where the only battle they saw was on Gikaet.

Hers was a different battle, where her contenders were innocent, as trapped as she was. Every night, the nightmares would reflect her internal struggle to retain her soul, the same he had seen veteran warriors endure night after night. Taking a life was never easy nor without emotional repercussions. He hated she was as tormented. He wished he had the power to eradicate her sadness, to heal the deep scars that were fingerprints of where parts of her soul were torn asunder.

"Would you like me to hold your hand until you fall asleep?" He was happy to do that. "I am concerned your touch might disturb Coldar's healing."

There was no way Enyl was going to let her touch Coldar. Enyl frowned at the direction his thoughts had taken. Her needs were paramount, not this volatile emotion replacing logic with fury.

"You would do that for me?" Her eyes were large. Was kindness a rare experience for her? He wondered at the type of life she used to have.

"Yes, Lady Oriana, anything my lady needs." He meant it, even if it caused him pain.

"Thank you, Supreme Commander." Her smile was alluring.

He led her to his bed, desperate to look anywhere but at her. She sprawled across it and placed her repaired hand on her outer thigh. When he grasped her fingers in his, she drifted to sleep with a ghost of a smile. Within minutes, her breathing deepened.

He sat alongside her, finding some comfort as he waited for her sleep to reach the delta level before he would leave her. It gave him the opportunity to study her features without the distraction of her mesmerizing eyes. While he stroked his thumb across her soft hand, he did so.

He admired her nose, upturned at the tip, her deep red lashes shadowed her cheeks sprinkled with spots. He wanted to kiss each one. Her full lips parted in her sleep. When he leaned in, her sweet breath fanned across his lips. He shuddered. Who was this female who inspired such a reaction in him?

In all his days, in all the worlds he had visited, never had he encountered any female quite so intriguing. He longed to lie beside her, to gather her within his arms, to cherish the gift she was. He had promised to hold her hand and hold it he would.

His thoughts drifted as he gazed upon her loveliness. It was a while later—he wasn't sure how much time had passed—when her fingers tightened around his to a painful degree. She was as strong as he had seen in the arena.

On a throaty whimper, she rolled onto her back, her leg slipping out of the wrap in her agitation. The sight of her muscled thigh—as beautiful and sleek as his own and yet soft—sent a sharp spike of heat to his still throbbing arousal. She tossed her head from side-to-side, cascading waves of red locks across the white of her wrap and the gray of his pillow.

"No," she begged, "no, no, I can't. Please..."

He squeezed her hand, trying to convey strength, peace, something to help her, to ease her suffering. She continued to thrash, her cries worsening in intensity. Desperate, he climbed onto the bed and pulled her into his arms. Running his hand from between her shoulders to her lower back and up again, he whispered soothing words. Pangs of guilt struck him, for holding her against him, for taking pleasure in it, and for inhaling her enthralling scent, spicy and sweet.

She quietened, burrowed deeper into his embrace, and sighed with unadulterated pleasure. He stilled at the sound despite knowing there was nothing he could do about it. He wanted her to come to him willing and aware, to embrace everything good and bad about being an Etterian princess and his Dar Eth. With a deep exhale, he settled down, anticipating a long, painful night ahead for him.

Chapter Fourteen

Etterian Battleship Gladio
En route to Etteria
Officer's quarters
Year of 2252, June

ORIANA AWOKE FROM THE best dream she had had in ages, maybe ever. A blue-eyed, bronze-skinned, black-haired Supreme Commander had held her within his protective arms. He'd crushed her against his impressive, hard length with a possessiveness she found exhilarating.

She released a contented sigh. This was what she had been seeking when she agreed to travel with Coldar. A chance to find a man worth loving even though she hadn't realized it at the time. A sense of security still lingered with her.

She tried to move but couldn't. Something trapped her. The slight snoring opened her eyes in a panic, only to widen with pleasure at the sight of Enyl fast asleep next to her.

True to his honor, he had stayed with her.

He had been a gentleman since he had helped them escape, ensuring she had everything she could need. Coldar had done the same with what they had in the dungeon. No matter how meager their possessions, their food, they had shared everything. Despite wishing it otherwise, it was an Etterian thing and not an Enyl thing. He wasn't showing her preference but acted as an Etterian male, duty-bound to attend to a female.

Of all the Etterian males she had met so far, she found him the most appealing with his intense eyes and captivating physical presence, but above all, his aura of authority. His braid reaching his heels bolstered her confidence in his abilities, that he could handle things on his own. He had when she had plummeted off the H-lift and during their arena rescue. Hell, he had carried her when it had pained him.

A pang of jealousy skewered her. She shoved it aside with a wince, wishing he didn't have a Dar Eth. Her thoughts drifted toward a life as a cherished female paired with an honorable Etterian male. She had pondered such a life when she was young and carefree. As a human, she could never have an Eth, nor experience the joys and passion of the Ethera.

That a man could not love her, and only her, made her sad with longing. She remembered when Uncle Gayn had explained the Ethera to her. He had said it wasn't something a human often experienced. She was eleven years old at that time and had savored the concept of soulmates, regardless of its rarity.

The fact she was here and safe was due to her uncles's knowledge. She had balked against their teachings, certain she would never need to know how to kill a wilanegy or other alien beasts. Her uncles had guarded her so well. What harm could ever befall her?

A memory flittered from out of the ether of her harnessed grief. It had been Uncle Gayn's two-hour session, the same one she had with him daily. He expected her to read from her tablet about alien creatures, their strengths and weaknesses. That morning, she had wanted to spend it with Uncle Diso, down in the engine room.

As an adult, looking back, Uncle Gayn must've known how she resented the time she spent with him. A tear escaped her at the desperate need within her to see him one last time. To rehear his instructions she lived by, that governed her reactions as he had predicted they would. To receive one of his frequent hugs or his smiles when she answered well.

Knowledge will guide you when your knees shake in fear. It'll guide you when your heart pounds in your ears. He had seemed so patient, trying to teach her beyond her limited world. *Knowing the weaknesses and strengths of all God's creatures will build a strong foundation. Good decisions come from a good foundation.*

She tilted her head, mimicking her memory as Uncle Gayn had leaned forward to tuck a curl behind her ear. *God's balance is in all the galaxies. Every creature has good and bad qualities. Knowing these empowers you to govern your own actions.*

Honor, respect, dignity—the three words they had drilled into her daily. When Uncle Gayn had smiled with sweetness in his eyes, it had made her happy. Her chest swelled on a crescendo of emotion.

I'll teach you respect and dignity. Uncle Diso will teach you honor, and Uncle Bos will teach you how to fix anything and everything. Uncle Gayn had frowned at her. *We'll not always be there for you, Ori. When we do join your mommy and daddy, remembering our shared knowledge means we will still be with you.*

As a child, she had hugged him—the sense of security indescribable—the same sense Enyl invoked in her.

She opened her eyes to study his sleeping form, wondering why she was at peace in his presence. He had saved her. That had to play a part. Uncle Diso would tell her to remain vigilant, not to let down her guard. Another tear escaped and dripped into the linen, and her nose twitched. Oh, how she missed them. Another tear followed. Panicking, she struggled to stem the flood. She blinked her eyes, forcing the pain down, as she had been doing since she first heard the terrible news.

The piercing pain refused to stay back. It hadn't reared its head when Enyl had saved her on HoSS, but after the killing, the heat, and the constant fear in Mascroba, this time, his rescue meant more to her. He had ruthlessly breached her walls.

With a wrenching sob, she buried her face against his chest, trying to muffle it. As tears poured down her cheeks unhindered, she choked on a huff at her futile attempts. Rubbing her nose across his shirt, she inhaled his woodsy masculine scent while she embedded her fingers in the fabric. There was no hint of Mascroba on his person, which meant he had cleansed at some point and donned a shirt.

As distracting as he was, it didn't stop the dam from breaking. Great sobs racked her body. But when he stirred and tightened his arms around her, she stilled. Even as his embrace comforted her, it flushed her with embarrassment. The poor male, going from asleep to having to deal with a blubbering woman. He stroked her spine with a familiarity she liked, muttering nonsensical words in a beautiful language she didn't recognize.

As her sobs dwindled to sniffles, he cupped her hip. During the night, her leg had come free of the wrap and had nestled between his strong muscled thighs. The weight of his crushed hers but in a good way. She refused to move. Lying beside him was incredible and comforting...arousing. She hoped he hadn't noticed. On top of everything, she had drenched his shirt with her tears.

"Thank you, Enyl, for staying with me." Her blocked nose muffled her words. "I...I was never safe enough to grieve, until now."

He placed a rough finger under her chin and tilted her face to meet his gaze. She wanted to hide her puffy eyes and her red nose, but the strength and determination in his touch insisted. Fighting him would be futile.

At his arched brow, she gave him a sad smile. "My three uncles raised and molded me into who I am. Pirates killed them six years ago."

"Pirates?" His deep voice vibrated through her.

After her emotional release, she struggled to breathe through her blocked nose. She didn't want to explain her breakdown, but he wouldn't remain ignorant for long. After all, Etterians had preternatural senses. He might have picked up her increased heartbeat and the spike in her temperature.

"Your uncles taught you to fight?" His morning voice made her knees tremble. She wanted to outlaw the male, mark him as lethal to all women. Since he had a Dar Eth, he was off the market. He shouldn't have stayed with her when he had a female waiting for him. *And* in Ori's bed.

"Uncle Diso taught me Hatimaye from when I could walk." She tried not to focus on Enyl's touch.

With a tenderness she found breathtaking, he wiped her tear-stained cheeks using the pads of his thumbs. Burying his fingers in her hair was such a comforting gesture but also an intimate one. Did she mention it was sensual too? He touched her like he had the right to.

"Diso? That's an unusual name." He studied her face, his eyes hooded and intense. "Your other uncles?"

He shifted, and the hard edges of his legs pressed into hers. Heat from his thighs seeped into her trapped and bare one. She struggled to focus on his question, to answer him.

"Uncle Bos was our ship's engineer. He fixed everything." Glancing at her fingernails, she frowned—the mechanical grease that had become a part of her was gone. She mourned the loss. With a sad smile, she met Enyl's gaze. "Uncle Gayn taught me everything else."

"Would integrity, honor, respect be some of these values?" Enyl's unblinking, pale gaze speared through her, making her shift to ease the throbbing between her legs. He stiffened, and his nostrils flared as he inhaled deeply.

A shudder ran through him. She didn't know why. Perhaps he could scent her emotions? Her attention shifted internally as she analyzed her body's responses. Was this desire? The aching need settling deep within her sex? The tingles and heat caressing her skin and raising goosebumps? It was as she had imagined, like when he had first saved her. She hoped the sensations weren't permanent though. It made no sense for her to desire a man she couldn't have.

"Yes, how did you know?" she whispered when she realized he waited for her to respond.

"It is who you are," he said, his voice hoarser than a second ago yet his fingers were gentle where he toyed with her hair. "Would your uncles have had your ocean-red hair?"

Ocean-red? Yes, Etteria had red oceans—she had forgotten about that. She swallowed past the lump in her throat. He ensnared her with his brooding gaze, mesmerizing her by what it did to her nerves. They skittered and danced, resonating tingles outward, like a multi-tool striking metal.

"No, my uncles were my father's brothers. They had hair as black as sin...like yours."

His gaze swept over her face and lingered on her lips. "Black as sin, you say?" His voice rumbled, like distant thunder.

"Listen, Enyl, um, shouldn't you be with your Dar Eth? Etterian males can't touch another female if they've endured the Ethera. Your loyalty is to her, so I understand if you need to go."

He blinked at her but didn't answer. His eyes had hooded with a deeper intensity that registered with her thumping heart.

The door chimed. He squeezed his eyes shut to block out the intrusion. After extricating himself, he brushed her inner thigh when he pulled her wrap closed. Freezing in place, his fingers hovered an inch above her skin.

"Enyl." Her voice was husky, so she cleared her throat. "The door."

He jerked back, then with long strides, left the room. His pants hugged his backside so well she was content to watch him walk away from her. Yes, he did have an ass nicer than Coldar's. Enyl's boots thumped with each determined stride. Without their preternatural hearing, all she caught was mumbling and cursing. Curious, she slid off the bed, straightened the wrap, then left the bedroom.

Enyl's glower surprised her as she neared him. It faded when he stared at her bare toes. She fought the urge to tuck one foot behind a calf.

She sliced her attention between him and Aldur. "What's wrong?"

"Morning, milady." Aldur hovered in the doorway. Enyl hadn't denied him entry. He just didn't want Aldur to reveal why he was there.

"Morning, Medic Aldur." Oriana smiled. She stood beside Enyl who tried not to stare at her, mesmerized by the way her untamed hair cocooned her.

He ran a hand up her back, relishing her body's heat through the wrap. Her silken curls twirled around his fingers, caressing him. Even her hair seduced. Her eyes glistened from her shed tears, and her cheeks glowed the dark pink of an Etterian dusk sky. He fought the urge to run his fingers across her skin, wishing to test the promise of warmth.

"Warrior Coldar has asked for you," Aldur said.

Her eyes widened with joy, stabbing Enyl like a serrated dagger to the heart. "Perhaps a cleanse first, a meal, and something more suitable to wear?" Anything to delay the inevitable.

Her gaze met his with such pleasure, he was tempted to shove Aldur out the door and her onto the floor.

"I can cleanse again?" Her struggle to contain her emotions amazed him—so expressive on her beautiful face. "Never mind, I wish to visit him now, please. He's seen me in less." She swept her hand down the length of her.

Enyl grimaced at the reminder of those blue and white strips. "My males have not."

Her eyebrows rose in surprise, like the idea that males would find her attractive was a novel one.

"The replicator can make anything for you." He flicked his gaze at it, seeing it as his salvation.

"I cleanse, you choose?" She gripped his forearm, her touch spiking his temperature.

He cupped her fingers, trapping her. No female he knew would let a male dress her. "You would trust me with this?"

"I'm in a rush. I'm hoping your Dar Eth will understand." She smiled at Enyl then Aldur. "Thank you for letting me know. Supreme Commander Enyl and I will be there shortly."

Aldur glanced between her and Enyl then left, shaking his head.

Enyl frowned. Did she even realize what she had done? Of course, she had, which is why she had mentioned his Dar Eth. Judging by her nonchalant disappearance into the cleansing room, she expected him to clothe her. To defer to a male and allow him to choose her garments was to state her willingness to pair with him.

The breath he released was shaky. He would need to have a talk with her. Going around Etteria and permitting males to dress her was out of the question. She had better not. He had to make her understand that she was *his* Dar Eth, curse it. He fumed as he stormed to the replicator and punched in numbers, making his selection without thought.

When the indigo-and-gold gown appeared, he gritted his teeth in dismay. Unfocused on the task, he had chosen his family's ceremonial dress. Etterian females wore their bloodline colors when among other males. It stated to any interested male to which house she belonged. Although Enyl had yet to inform Oriana of her changed status, he did need his males to know she was his.

He held the gown before him, wondering if the color would suit her hair, skin...her eyes. At the sound of the air dryer, he would find out soon enough.

"Enyl?" When she popped her head out, he handed her the gown. "Thank you," she whispered, accepting the bundle from him. The door slid shut on her gasp, deepening his concern. His choice may have been unwise.

"This is exquisite," she said from the doorway.

With one glance, he threw his hand out to smack the wall, to steady himself. He managed to make it look casual even though his knees weakened with the urge to drop him as the Ethera had done. White, hot need pulsed around the edges of his control. He sucked in long, calming breaths.

The rich blue color made her skin glow, her eyes bolder, and her hair brighter. The design of the gown wrapped around her with an intimacy that spiked his heart rate. He had also punched in her height and weight estimations, so the gown reached the floor. It was at the correct length, hiding her bare feet. He frowned and tapped in another set of numbers.

When he offered her the blue slippers, she sat on a comfy, bared creamy, well-toned calves to his hungry gaze, and slipped on the footwear. They reacted to the warmth of her skin and adjusted to her feet, remaining that size henceforth.

"Thank you so much for this. I've never worn anything quite so beautiful, but aren't these the Etterian royal colors?"

Of course, she knew about the Etterian bloodline colors. Maker.

Instead of answering her, he opened the door of their quarters and waited for her. She braided her hair as she approached him, but he stopped her, holding his fingers to hers.

"Leave it down, please." The intensity in his gaze must have conveyed his desperation when she unraveled it. "Thank you."

He loved her unmoving hair. And unbraided and wild served no purpose than for his admiration. Leading her along the passages, they made many turns before striding into the common. At her entrance, his males fell silent.

When confronted by a crowd, her expressions slipped into her arena face. It hid all her emotions, made her unapproachable, and her actions unpredictable. Not liking her withdrawal especially from him, Enyl glowered at his males but couldn't deny them their curiosity.

Running an appreciative gaze over her delicate face and exquisite waterfall of hair, his chest puffed out. She was *his* female, *his* salvation.

Despite the trouble she brought, he shouldn't forget he was a blessed male.

Chapter Fifteen

Etterian Battleship Gladio
En route to Etteria
The common
Year of 2252, June

Under the watchful gazes of twenty-plus Etterian males, Ori shifted closer to Enyl, seeking his...what? Protection? She snorted. Like she needed a bodyguard. He wasn't her anything, and since no male rushed toward her, that meant neither were any of those present. She may or may not spark the Ethera. The quicker she reached Resia Cay, endured the tests, the quicker she could go home.

When she snuck a glance at a tense Enyl, fresh tears stung her eyes. She would miss him and Coldar. At least, they had shown her she was more than ready for a romantic relationship with someone. Scanning the array of viable males in the common, her shoulders slumped. The chances of finding a human man looking like them were slim to none. It was time she returned to Earth and widened her sample pool.

"Ori?" A male stumbled forward then paused, his eyes wide in his face.

She studied his stance, his hair, his eyes, and when he broke into a grin, she ran, throwing herself into his open arms. He crushed her to him, lifting her off her feet to bury his face in her hair. The happiness warming her from her toes to her burning cheeks was indescribable.

"Coldar." She laughed—her tears fell unhindered, as she wrapped her arms around his neck.

"Do not cry, Ori, please." He hugged her tighter. "The champion of the arena does not cry."

She grumbled something derogatory regarding his malehood but mumbled it into his neck. It had the desired effect since he laughed aloud. It was a sound she cherished for they were free and well.

"Aldur fixed you? Everything?" She shuffled back after he lowered her feet to the floor, to search his face, his eyes, and watch him flex his muscles to prove his fitness. "Your scars are gone. I kind of liked them, you know." She grinned, wiped her cheeks then blinked at the tears on her fingertips. Since she had mourned her uncles's deaths, the tear ducts remained open. "Can he put them back?"

"I doubt it." Coldar's hands cupped her elbows to keep her near.

"We'll have to do something about that." She gestured to the wall of weapons.

He shook his head. "Alodon's hell, no. You will not be touching those."

She gasped, and fury flushed her body. "Like I need a weapon." With a quick placement of her foot and a sharp shove, she slammed him to the floor. Her sole focus was on his stunned expression. She laughed, her shoulders shaking as she granted the joy free rein.

"You cesu, why did you have to go and do something like that?" He grinned, folding his arms across his chest as he stared at her from his position on the floor.

"Don't tell me what I can or cannot touch, Coldar. You're healed and can fight back." She held her fists in front of her, assuming a practiced fighting stance.

"I do not spar with females."

"That's not what your last lover said. I suspect you had to wrestle with her to get her to lie still," she teased him, then offered him her good hand, which he accepted.

"I do not appreciate such a remark, Ori. You above all people understand what we go through to find a pairing."

Her eyes widened at his admonishment, and her cheeks burned in embarrassment. She did know how much they sought their pairings. Her presence here was evidence enough. Frowning, she studied his features and the darkness in his eyes. "I'm sorry, Coldar. You're right. It was cruel of me to say that."

He offered her a smile. "You look good, Ori." He made a show of studying her, turning her from side-to-side.

She slapped his hands away. "I'm well, Coldar. Want to look at my teeth, take a blood sample?"

"When we reach Resia Cay." He beamed, then his humor faded. "Thank you for requesting Etteria honor Myan for his death."

She blinked in surprise, having not expected nor needed his gratitude. "I wanted his sacrifice remembered." She placed her hand on his shoulder in an affectionate gesture often used by battle-bonds.

"We submit requests for the remembrance of honor to our elders." At the deep, sensual voice behind her, she shivered. Pure desire pooled in her, dampening her thighs. "But this time, I did not. Myan et Phyan lives. He brought your predicament to my attention on Gikaet."

"Myan lives?" She gripped Enyl's forearm, peering at him in disbelief. "Coldar?"

"It is true, Ori. He was at my side when I awoke."

"This is wonderful news." She bounced on her toes, scanning the males surrounding them, although, she doubted she would recognize Myan if he stood before her. "I hoped if I..." She didn't want to reveal her last-minute attempts when the Yithians had dragged her from the scimitar.

Coldar laughed as he tucked a curl behind her ear. "I am told my deployment of a beacon and the sealing of the breach are what saved him."

She dipped her head, praying he said no more. "That was excellent planning, Coldar, saving Myan after negotiating with the Yithians." She offered him a cheesy grin. "That condition was ill-conceived." She tossed his words back at him.

"You cesu. It was, and I stand by my assessment." Coldar faced Enyl and bowed. "My thanks for the rescue."

She glanced between Enyl and Coldar. "Why are you bowing to a supreme commander?" She frowned in puzzlement, recalling her studies. Uncle Gayn hadn't mentioned males bowing in the Etterian culture unless it was to royalty. She stroked the gown's collar. Enyl couldn't be royalty. No, that wasn't possible. No matter his rank on a ship, his males would address him as "my prince."

"It is my vessel." Enyl glared at Coldar.

Enyl's warning look made no sense, neither did his words. Etteria owned everything and provided what Etterians needed. She gritted her teeth, hating that he and Coldar hid things from her.

"That's not protocol." She rested her hands on her hips.

"Warrior Coldar and Lady Oriana, come, we have much to discuss." Enyl stormed off, his back stiff and his movements jerky.

When she arched a brow at Coldar, he avoided her gaze. The urge to stomp her foot gripped her. What the hell? Casting one last glance at the wall of weapons, she trailed the two males along various passages, into a communications room sans pilot. Enyl stared at the display vid reflecting the passing stars—the massive vid loomed over the multi-lit console.

"Start from the beginning," he commanded without facing them.

Since he couldn't see her with his back to them, she took the time to admire his physique. Her breath hitched. Liking the look of him, she gave herself the freedom to traverse his many angles, the way his sleep pants hugged his ass and muscled thighs. His eyelashes fluttered, and heat burst across her cheeks. Her reflection was on the surfaces of the display vids.

She met his gaze in the mirror image, and the intensity and fury in his eyes riveted her. Pinned under his unyielding stare, she couldn't look away. He had watched her ogle him. Despite her stinging cheeks, she flashed an unrepentant smile.

"Warrior Myan waited on Horizon Space Station for Ori's compatibility results. I was en route with a scimitar to escort her to Resia Cay."

Coldar's voice gave her an excuse to break Enyl's locked gaze. She snuck her friend a grateful look.

"You had such confidence in my compatibility you deployed two warriors." After sitting in a comfy placed against the back wall, she sighed, leaned her head back against the panel, and closed her eyes. "Because of my injuries, my DNA markers were in the system."

"Injuries? Who would dare harm a female?" Enyl spun to run an assessing gaze over her, his concern for her in his tense and scowling features.

She frowned at his uncharacteristic behavior. The man had a Dar Eth. He didn't have the right to worry about her.

"Many human males dared." She glanced at her scarred palm and shrugged.

Bringing up Bodacious or the explosive device was futile. And the mystery remained, someone had tried to bomb HoSS. Ice slithered down her spine. Or the target was her. If that was the case, someone out there hated her enough to kill her. She would find out soon enough when she returned to H.o.S.S.

Coldar spread his legs in a wide stance, clasping his hands behind his back. "We managed to convince Ori—"

"Lady Oriana." Enyl narrowed his eyes and faced the display vid again, his knuckles white where he gripped the console. His stance tensed, and his muscles rippled. She replayed Coldar's words, looking for the cause of Enyl's fury.

She focused on his back, shock burning through her and stiffening her posture. His audacity and arrogance amazed her. He had no right to determine her and Coldar's relationship. She didn't care that Enyl's gaze was vigilant and her anger apparent. It didn't matter.

"It's Ori." She ignored Coldar's attempts to quieten her. "Calling me milady got me into trouble. After all we've been through—he's earned the right to call me anything he damn well wants to."

"Please." He touched her elbow, and with a huff, she flopped into the comfy. "Once we were onboard and cleared for launch, we set our course for Resia Cay." He paused to run his hand over his face. "It was an ambush—no warning, no alarms, nothing that could have alerted us to a possible breach. The Yithian slave traders wounded Myan and captured us."

"After they injured you when we fought them."

He nodded at her, thanking her for her assistance in the telling. Then he leveled his indigo gaze on her. "With my supreme commander present, let me reiterate my stance. I still disagree with the deal you made, Ori."

She flinched like he slapped her, having not expected him to raise his displeasure yet again. "Why are you so stubborn? It was *my* fault they targeted us. Myan almost dying was on me. I had to do something, Coldar." She fumed at having to explain her reasons for the hundredth time. Curling her nails into the comfy's edges, she fought the urge to punch something. "It's done. I refuse to speak of this, do you hear me, Coldar? Never again."

"How was it your fault? What deal?" Enyl faced them, his anger fading.

"The Yithian I took down at the bar was an arena scout." She shrugged to indicate it wasn't a big issue. Judging by Coldar's words, her negotiating had driven a wedge between them he still simmered over. She didn't understand why he couldn't let it go.

"Supreme Commander, she sacrificed her freedom if Yithia promised to never harm me," Coldar said to Enyl before facing her again. "You were reckless to make that deal. I could have—"

"Done what? Tell me? They had 'killed' Myan, injured you, and had me surrounded. Tell me what you could've done, Coldar?" She was inches from his face, yelling at him with her body vibrating with emotion. Grabbing his hands, she sucked in a calming breath before continuing in a softer tone. "I know you need to protect me, but please understand, we had to survive. We protect each other, it's what partners do."

"Partners?" Enyl scowled, with his fists clenched at his sides.

For an Etterian, he was showing an extensive range of emotions. Only Eths displayed this much and at this intensity. Since he had found his Dar Eth, his responses were acceptable. Yet having spent the last two months with Coldar had preconditioned her to expect the minimum.

"Your word would be battle-bonds." She slumped in the comfy. Enyl's relieved sigh furrowed her brow.

Coldar wrestled with his anger then pushed on. "Since that day, we have looked out for each other and tried to stay alive."

Enyl unfurled his fists, his lips thinned, and he met her gaze in the reflection. Time slowed as he perused her face, then with a curt nod, as if he'd decided something, he raised his wrist to his chin.

"Vytus, comm room," Enyl muttered into his O.D.I. then stood there with his back to them again.

They waited in silence, but the air thickened with the palpable tension oozing off him. She shifted in her seat, craving something alcoholic. Every time she opened her mouth to speak, Coldar shook his head.

Keeping quiet wasn't her forte. Unable to bear another moment, she leaped to her feet.

Vytus burst into the room and halted—his unwavering gaze landed on Enyl.

He didn't look at Vytus or her. Her heart pounded against her ribs, like her body knew Enyl was going to do something she wouldn't like, like she'd somehow for some unknown reason pissed him off. "Escort Lady Oriana to her quarters."

Huh. She blinked a few times, confused, having not expected a dismissal. What could he possibly want Coldar alone for? And if he meant to harm her partner...? She took a menacing step toward Enyl, but Coldar's hand on her arm stilled her. He glared at her and nudged his head at Vytus, his message clear. She nodded but folded her arms across her chest, letting him know she wasn't happy about this.

As soon as she stepped through the comm door, it swished shut behind her, and a loud thump startled a yelp from her.

"What the fuck?" She ignored Vytus to pound on the door until her fingers stung. He stood to the side of the passage and watched her hurl herself against Maloidian metal. "Do something." She spun on him. "Or so help me, Vytus, I'll break every bone in your body."

He threw out his hands. "I'm just the escort, milady."

She screamed and threw everything she had at the door. When nothing happened, she slumped and slid to the grating. Nothing she had done had saved Coldar from a pissed-off supreme commander. Her hands pulsed, her wrist burned, and blood dribbled from her lacerated knuckles.

"Take me to Aldur."

Chapter Sixteen

Etterian Battleship, Gladio
En route to Etteria
Communications room
12252 years, 6th month

THE ENGULFING, VIOLENT BURN of rage consumed Enyl. Never had he been so furious, so uncontrolled—the sight of her in another male's arms, her precious tears spilling down her cheeks, her happy smiles for all to see. She was his and his alone. Not Coldar's.

Reaching the communications room—without incident—amazed Enyl, but the confined space heightened his senses. It was wiser to stare into space than at the two of them, affection for one another on their faces. If he could slam his fist into the display vid he would have. He held himself strong, resolved, unbending.

As soon as she left, he lunged, slamming Coldar against the bulkhead, pinning him there with his face inches away from the male's startled one. It wasn't fair of him to do so since no male could retaliate against his prince. Yet at that moment, Enyl was an Eth making demands.

"What is Oriana to you? Speak truth or die," he growled, his voice no longer within his control.

"We are warriors in arms, battle-bonds like she said," Coldar whispered, his eyes wide as he stared at Enyl.

Ice blue eyes proved he had found his Eth, and Coldar's gaping mouth was no more than how Enyl had reacted—stunned, pleased, excited, lustful. The Ethera struck Enyl, and he was a ball of roiling emotions—most of them unrecognizable to him.

"She is my battle-bond. I would die for her, kill all who wish to harm her. It is not something I expected when we met, but after so many days together..."

Enyl dropped his hand and pulled away.

Coldar raised a beseeching hand. "Think over this morning, my prince. We greeted each other, pleased to be alive, then she threw me to the floor and teased me."

"Like a warrior would do." Enyl squeezed his eyes shut against this overwhelming inner turmoil. He glanced at the male, still staring at him, waiting. "Forgive me, Coldar. I am struggling..."

The poor male didn't know what to do. A prince never apologized and never asked forgiveness.

"With your Ethera, I know." He shot Enyl a smile. "I can see that, my prince."

Enyl slumped into the comfy, imagining Ori's warmth still lingering in the fabric.

"Since the Yithians attacked, she called us partners. I have attempted to dissuade her with no success. She was incredible, always hopeful, determined, and so stubborn. Her recklessness scares me, my prince, like death has no hold on her. You need to tell her soon. It is best she hears it from you." At Enyl's raised eyebrow, Coldar rushed on, "I apologize for overstepping, but if you do not tell her she is your Dar Eth and a princess, she will assume you do not want her. Her education is astounding yet she is naïve in matters of the heart. She will see your omissions as deception."

Enyl was grateful for the advice, despite Coldar offering it unsolicited. "Thank you for guarding her, when you had yet to know how precious she is."

Coldar bent his head in shame. "It was she who guarded me. I cannot accept recognition for her current well-being."

"I appreciate your honesty. Do not let her capabilities affect your self-worth. You kept her nightmares at bay and ensured she had food. In mine and Lady Oriana's eyes, your accolades are far and wide." He chuckled. "Besides, if any of my males wish to make an issue out of a warrior female keeping you alive, we will let her handle it."

Coldar's head shot up to meet Enyl's gaze. "You would let her fight?"

He understood Coldar's shock. No male allowed his Dar Eth to be in danger. "I have seen her fight, and the blow to our arrogance would be good for them." He sighed. "She knows Hatimaye. Meric must have discovered it on Earth and brought it to us. She imbues its core values—integrity, honor, respect." Enyl rose and faced him. "I would consider it an honor if you would act as Oriana's personal guard. She defers to you, and that alone should minimize the amount of trouble she will get into."

"I will guard her with my life." Coldar thumped his chest. "I owe her much."

"Report to her in the morning."

Enyl dismissed the male, and in the unmanned comm room, he took a few minutes to calm his chaotic thoughts. The thumping on the door implied Oriana had fought the return to her quarters. But he didn't rush there now, needing to prepare himself. Telling her she was his Dar Eth had to be handled well.

"What in Alodon's hell happened?" Malo stormed into the comm room. "Your males have inundated my O.D.I. with concern. The archival vids show you've lost your mind. I have never seen you behave in such a manner. Who is this female to you?" Malo strode across and thrust his face in Enyl's as he demanded answers. Both eyebrows arched, then he clasped Enyl's cheeks, and turned his head from side-to-side. "This... It is impossible."

"I said the same." Enyl grinned, his joy over this blessing too much to contain.

"She is compatible?" Malo stared into Enyl's eyes.

"We knew she was. Just not whether she would trigger the Ethera. Let us pray she is fertile too and can bear females." He hesitated.

Her extensive knowledge of their culture alarmed him. Not that he believed she was a spy of sorts. But as explained by their elders, all data archives were under strict control. A human female shouldn't know more than what they deemed acceptable. What other information had passed through their security measures?

"Congratulations, Enyl. This will delight Xeus."

"I have yet to tell him. I thought to surprise Father when we reach Issneen. I have another task for you, Malo. Review the past day's sec-vids for my quarters. Her knowledge of Etterian culture is remarkable."

Malo jerked back. "You distrust her?"

"No, but she knows Hatimaye, knew about the Ethera, and asked after my Dar Eth." When Enyl told her the truth, he hoped she would react with delight, throw her arms around his neck and kiss him. He shook the absurd image free, even as he relished the burn of lust pulsing through him.

"She doesn't know she is your life force?" The confusion on Malo's face meant he had never considered a Dar Eth might not know what she was.

"Not yet. I will inform her soon."

"I will report my findings." Malo scanned the empty comm room. "Now, to call my males back to their duties. You do realize without Afax in this room, this battleship is on reflex mode?"

Enyl made his escape to his quarters, wondering what awaited him there. Oriana hadn't looked pleased when she had left. The door opened but the quarters' common room was in darkness. Scowling, he quieted his thoughts to listen but heard nothing, no breathing, and no tell-tale whisper of fabric. Had Vytus escorted her elsewhere?

Tapping into his O.D.I., Enyl sent a message to his blood-bond. The response was immediate. He had left Oriana in their quarters, alone. It wasn't an acceptable procedure to be with a Dar Eth without her Eth present. At least someone knew the protocol. Enyl wasn't being fair to Coldar, but their close relationship still irked him.

Realizing he stood in the passage, he stumbled into his quarters, the door sealing shut behind him. Before he could go farther, a blow to his midriff bent him over, leaving him gasping for air. A strike to the back of his neck collapsed him to the ground, darkening his vision. Within seconds, she was on his back, holding him to the floor with his arm in hand ready to hammerlock him.

"What's your problem with Coldar?" She weighed him down and tightened her grip on his arm to whisper into his ear.

He shivered, as her lips whispered across his skin. "He's too familiar with you."

His words muffled against the paneled flooring, so he turned his head to the side to admire the fiery waterfall of her hair pooling beside him. A fruity scent rose from the silken depths. He breathed it in, needing it more than he cared to admit.

"This is none of your fucking business, Supreme Commander. Coldar's my friend, the best one I've ever had." She leaned down harder, and the weight of her breasts crushed against his back.

He groaned. She was trying to kill him. He flipped on his side, threw her off, then wrapped his legs around her to pin her in place. She fell with a grunt, and her angry growl filled the room.

"That was well done, Enyl," she said in a breathless voice.

He stared at her, with her glorious curls beneath her, her bright-green eyes fiery and full of passion. With a kick of her bare legs, she was astride him, holding his hands next to his ears. Her hair draped around them like a curtain. He could stretch his neck and taste her lips.

"Are you planning on answering me? Or are you stalling while you think of reasons to explain your behavior?" Her anger vibrated her body and summoned an answering resonance in his.

He chuckled. "Rolling around sounds like an appealing way to spend the afternoon."

"All right, now I know you're up to something. Where's your Dar Eth? Because I can promise you, Enyl, I cannot stomach infidelity."

"She is near." With a thrust of his hips, he flipped her over and trapped her beneath him again, holding her hands by her ears.

"Get off me." She bucked her body to dislodge him but nestled him deeper between her thighs instead.

A shiver shot through him. Relishing the thrill, he dipped to dust his lips across her cheek. She stilled, and her breath hitched. A tangy fragrance tickled his nose. "Alcohol? Giyua?"

"One tequila does not make me drunk. Get off me."

Oriana as a temptation tore him apart. He could taste her, bury his face in her neck, kiss the pulse there. Yet his instinct warned him that to succumb and kiss her wouldn't aid his courtship. In one smooth motion, he pulled her to her feet.

She jerked away from him and dusted herself off. "Are you're done cheating on your Dar Eth?"

"In what way have I done so?" He marveled at the color splashing across her cheeks and the fire of unclaimed desire in her eyes.

"Wrestling with me and rubbing your aroused body against mine. I'm not that naïve that I don't recognize attraction." The pink on her cheeks spread down her throat.

He laughed, pleased he flustered her. "The grappling on the floor, you started. I see it as a battle of wills."

"Battle of...?" With renewed anger, she ran her trembling fingers along her jaw. "You have no intention of explaining your aggressive behavior toward Coldar, nor will you return to you Dar Eth. I will speak to Coldar, perhaps he'll share his quarters with me."

As threats went, that was a good one. Enyl bolted, barring the door to prevent her departure.

"No females may enter the barracks." He wanted to roar she didn't belong to Coldar. She belonged to *him*.

"Fine, then I'll sleep in the common, and if you have an issue with that, a cargo bay will do."

He stared at her lips, wishing he could kiss her. Her body still vibrated with emotion, still called to him, seeming to fill the hollows in his soul. She was stubborn, independent but perfect for him.

"Oriana." His voice was hoarse with an emotion he didn't recognize. "Please, stay and share your tequila with me."

She paused to study him—the sweep of her gaze across his face like a caress. Releasing a shuddering breath, she turned toward the rehydrator.

"I apologize." Apologizing twice in one day? Malo would never believe it, but Enyl pushed forward. "I did not intend for you to feel unwelcome."

She slid her fingers around a short glass with transparent liquid. Facing him, she gathered the slice of giyua off the rehydrator's glass and approached him. "Will you come between Coldar and me?" She offered him the glass.

"Do you care for him so much?" Enyl held his breath, dreading her answer. To find one's Dar Eth only to have her heart belong to another? It was an unheard-of occurrence, but she wasn't Etterian. He didn't know what to expect from their union.

"I do, like you would a battle-bond. I would give my life for his."

His breath rushed out of him. As Coldar had said. Battle-bonds. Her confirmation lessened the weight crushing his chest.

She held out her hand with a pile of salt on it. "Lick this, drink that, then suck the lime."

He took the glass and lime—giyua, judging by the scent of it—from her. By jutting out his chin and his gaze fixed on the salt, he indicated he wanted to lick it off her skin. Huffing, she offered her hand, but as soon as his lips wrapped around the salt, his nostrils flared at the taste of her skin.

"Drink the tequila," she urged.

With reluctance, he released her hand and downed the liquid. She shoved the giyua into this mouth. His eyes widened and watered as the fiery bitterness burned its way to his stomach. The giyua added to the flavor coating his mouth and ended in an explosion of heat.

"There was something I wanted to talk to you about," she said like she hadn't set his insides on fire. "Are you returning me to Horizon? I need to find out if I still have my jobs and housing unit. This excursion took longer than six weeks. I can't expect Bob or Andrew to keep me on their staff, but I have to hope they did."

He studied her, memorizing every inch again and again. "You return with me to Etteria."

She curled her fingers into fists. "What? Why?"

"You agreed to compatibility testing, Oriana." *Because you're my Dar Eth*, he wanted to say.

She didn't respond but dropped her gaze. No emotion crossed her features, but her fingers relaxed. "I'm a woman of my word."

Her words made his chest swell. An honorable female was rare indeed but best of all, she was his. His wide smile was beyond his control.

"I meant after that."

He scowled. After the tests had run their course, she would expect to return, to leave Etteria, him. "You can choose where to go, and I will ensure your wishes are met." Tossing a plea heaven-ward, he prayed to the Maker she would want to stay with him. He couldn't bring himself to let her go nor to force her to accept him.

If he told her soon, bared his intentions, perhaps her honor might convince her to save him.

Chapter Seventeen

Etterian Battleship, Gladio
En route to Etteria
Officer's quarters and the common
Year of 2252, June

IT WAS DARK WHEN Oriana awoke. Her thoughts drifted to the evening spent in the common, listening in on various conversations. The males spoke about battles fought, Gika killed. She had dipped her head to hide her smile. No matter the species, the size of the kill was all that mattered.

As her surroundings penetrated her mind, she recognized the bed beneath her, and once again found herself within the comfort of Enyl's arms. Sighing in delight, she ran her fingers over his hand claiming her hip. What a remarkable male. She inhaled his sunbaked scent.

With the wrestling business, she hadn't liked him then. She had wanted to kill him—frustration, pent-up emotion, and anger warring within her. Despite her breathlessness around him and the way they had fought, this attraction intensified between them. Battle of wills, he had called it. Yes, she could admit, if only to herself, his assessment had been correct.

Frowning, she considered how addictive he was when she had no claim to him. She wished, as much as she liked being near him, that he would leave her alone and return to his Dar Eth. Falling for him wasn't an option. Her heart wouldn't be able to survive losing someone she loved, not again. Now that she cared for Coldar, considered him her dearest friend, her battle brother, her heart was already in jeopardy.

With a grimace, she extricated herself from Enyl's arms and left the room, as silent as Uncle Diso had taught her. After creeping to the rehydrator, she requested a bottle of water and drained it before ordering exercise clothes. She needed to train, to rid herself of this restlessness and this longing for a man she could never have. Her lips twisted into a rueful smile while she stared at her reflection in the replicator. She was the idiot, tackling him to the floor like that. As trained as she was, she couldn't hope to best a skilled Etterian warrior.

Blushing, she recalled her conversation with Enyl and the way his lips caressed her cheek. His plea for Tequila had weakened her resolve. Turning away from the mirror, she donned the leggings, sports bra, and vest before she left for the common, still barefoot. The routine she had planned didn't require shoes.

No warriors lingered, except for Aldur who watched her from his station in medical. Not wanting to worry him with her sudden appearance, she strode across to address him. She hadn't lost her manners despite her recent insanity. Tackling Enyl like he was an untried recruit? Her cheeks burned, again.

"Evening, Medic Aldur." Having seen him just yesterday to repair her self-inflicted injuries made him more of a friend than an acquaintance. He hadn't commented on the futility of her efforts to break down a Maloidian door with her bare hands.

"Evening. Cannot sleep?" He rose from his desk, studying her like she was unwell.

"In a way." She gestured to the sparring mat. "I thought I'd do something physical to test my healing. What keeps you awake? Is the void calling?"

His eyebrows rose in surprise. She didn't wait for him to respond. For most Etterian males, it was a sensitive subject. As Aldur aged, so would his resistance to the void weaken.

There were whispers of legendary battle-bonds who had formed more intimate relationships and together, sought the void on Gikaet, dying in each other's arms. As a young girl, she had cried for those warriors who had sacrificed themselves. Uncle Gayn had patted her shoulder and for once, hadn't chastised her for her tears. Such an end awaited Aldur.

She gripped his shoulder as a sign of affection and respect. "When the time comes, it will bring me great honor to battle at your side."

He jerked at the unexpected formal Etterian oath she had luckily remembered.

"I…" He cleared his throat, and his eyes paled for a moment. "Your presence will bring me great honor," he answered, his tone formal as he placed his hand on her shoulder.

With a nod, she crossed the common to admire the weapons wall. After removing the two matching Maloidian short swords, she gripped and released their hilts, testing the weight. Working through the motions, she assessed whether her injuries hindered her. She swung the swords around her head, shoulders, and hips with smooth, practiced strokes. Dancing to the side, dodging and sliding across the floor, she used her knees to spin her body. Pretending the center of the mat was her opponent's position, she lunged and parried the swords not caring that they were sharp enough to slice through granite.

She knew the second Enyl arrived in the common and hovered in the doorway. Her body called to his, tingling when he was near. Anger at her growing affection for him fueled her swings and strikes. She couldn't—*shouldn't*—yearn for this male. Emboldened by her reaction to him, she ramped her efforts, slashing and stabbing the swords until sweat drenched her shirt and dripped off her chin.

She wiped her face with the hem of her shirt, uncaring she had an audience. Let the cheating bastard watch.

ORI'S GRACE ENTRANCED ENYL, her skill with the blades, her lethal beauty. She timed every movement, precise and efficient. Her focus was mesmerizing with each strike slowing in his mind. She ended her routine on one knee with both hilts gripped in her hands. The sharp blades pointed away from her, stabbing imaginary opponents behind her. Her breasts rose and fell, and her pale skin shimmered with perspiration. He inhaled her scent, held it in, and savored it before exhaling. As always, he shivered with longing and anticipation.

Her weary gaze fixed on him as he strode across the common, planning to throw himself onto his knees in front of her. Need and determination drove him. Her body called to his which reacted, doing things without his consent and forethought. As he neared her, she placed the blades on the sparring mat.

One of her brows arched in query. She didn't know why he sat there on his knees or that her heat pouring off her body warmed him. Her scent crumbled his control. Intense and unknown emotions battled within him. He yearned and ached.

He ran an adoring gaze over her features while stroking her jaw. Cupping her cheeks, he buried his fingers in her hair behind her ears. She stilled, her eyes widening. He couldn't read her thoughts, didn't want to try. As he strokeded his thumb over her bottom lip, she parted her mouth. He shuddered. His breathing echoed hers. His heart thumped a parsec a second.

Shuffling closer, he dipped his head to sample her lips. When she gasped, he crushed his mouth to hers, taking advantage of her parted lips. At the first taste of her, he groaned. He wanted nothing more than to claim her on the sparring mat, to bury himself deep within her, and remain there indefinitely.

With a sweep of his tongue, he conquered the crevices of her mouth, drowning in the sheer sweetness of her. She whimpered. Her fingers fluttered where she clung to his shoulders. Her erratic pulse echoed in his ears.

Pressing her palms to his chest, burning him through his tunic, she leaned back. "Enyl, you shouldn't—"

"Kiss my Dar Eth?" He tugged her against him, careful with her ribs. Hurting her, regardless of the rate of her healing, was unacceptable.

"Your what?" she squeaked—her eyebrows arched in surprise.

She shoved his chest, and he released her, but his fingers twitched at the loss of her. Lunging away from him, she gathered the blades but paused to meet his gaze.

Her gorgeous mouth hung open. "I'm your soulmate? Your destined wife?"

"Soulmate? Wife?" His eyelids fluttered as the O.D.I. flashed images of a human male hugging a female in a white gown with *damu* at their feet.

She glared before she returned the blades to the wall. "Earth term, it means committed to you for life."

While she stood before him, she ran a hand through her sweat-dampened locks. She was too far away from him for his liking. He rose to his full height, not wanting to be at a disadvantage and needing to be nearer to her.

"Yes." Wife. Hmm, he liked that. There was a strong, possessive nuance to the word.

She rubbed her shivering arms. "Are you kidding me? Why didn't you tell me as soon as you knew? Why hide it from me?"

Coldar had been correct—she thought Enyl had deceived her. He winced at the distress in her voice, assuming the blame as was his right. "I did not believe it myself."

She sucked in a breath and pain lanced across her green eyes.

He grasped her hips, forcing her to face him. "Many years have passed since the last known Ethera—this you know. All males hope to find it, but most believe it does not exist." He pulled her against him, unable to stop himself from touching her, to keep her within the circle of his arms. His heart still pounded from that one kiss. He longed for another taste of her. "Do not ever believe you are undesirable, Oriana. I am the blessed male to have such a remarkable Dar Eth."

She studied his face, her eyes hooded. "Any other surprises?"

He sighed in relief—she was no longer angry with him, or worse, hurt by his thoughtless words.

"My rank in Etteria." He offered her a smile and gave her a shrug that was anything but nonchalant. "It is nothing I can alter since I was born to it."

Her expression deepened in thought—one he was beginning to find most adorable with the creases on her brow. His Dar Eth was an intelligent female. His chest swelled with warmth.

"Shit, are you royalty?"

He nodded and waited for her to yell at him or walk away. Neither of those reactions he knew how to address. What he didn't expect was her laughter as her head fell back and her arm clutched her ribs.

"I don't believe it."

He frowned and squared his shoulders. "I am the Crown Prince of Etteria. Do I not look princely?"

She laughed again. "I don't doubt your royal lineage, Enyl. From my perspective, this is a story told at a child's bedtime." She wiped her tear-stained cheeks. "A prince meets an underprivileged female, and they know in an instant it's forever. Then they ride off into the distant sunset for a happily-ever-after." She raised a hand and cupped his cheek—her unexpected touch melted his anger. "How's this possible? How can I be a Dar Eth? I'm human, not Etterian."

He yanked her into his arms, crushing her to him, his fingers splaying out on her back as he rubbed his chin across the crown of her head. He snuck in a kiss to her temple.

"The Ethera chose you, Oriana, my warrior female. I am grateful for this blessing and honored to stand at your side." He admired her pink-hued face and found himself rubbing his cheek across hers. The flush of her exertion warmed him.

"The king can't be happy about this." Her protestation sounded weak.

Since she hadn't abandoned him on the mat, hope that she accepted him swept through him. "My father will be most pleased. This was his idea, to look beyond our borders for a compatible species for the Ethera. Since you are human and my Dar Eth, he succeeded. Besides, he would welcome you even if you were an Algri."

She huffed against his chest. "Well, thank goodness I'm not."

He chuckled and arched his back to meet her gaze but kept her in his embrace. "Agreed. You are far more attractive than that."

"Gee, what a compliment," she teased him. "I find you attractive also, compared to an Algri, of course." She pulled away from him.

Frowning, he trailed her laughing form as she strolled to their quarters.

AFTER A QUICK CLEANSE and another bottle of water, Ori snuggled into Enyl's arms again, absorbing his warmth as she pressed her cheek to his glorious chest. He had ordered the lights to power off, and in the darkness, her mind returned to his kiss. It had been so unexpected, so amazing. His lips were soft for such a hard male, and his tongue had been hot, commanding. His taste made her insides flutter, her heart stutter, and her breath catch. She blushed at having not responded to his kiss. Not knowing what to do, she had stood there and let him kiss her.

"Enyl?" she whispered and waited—in case he had fallen asleep.

"Yes, Oriana?" His voice was dark and smooth.

"That was my first kiss," she mumbled. Silence met her revelation, and she nibbled her lip. She should've told him when she could see his reaction. The darkness served to torment her.

"Truth?" His voice was gruffer as it vibrated through his chest and against her cheek.

"Yes."

He drew in a deep breath. "I am honored, *ensa*."

She smiled into his heated chest when he tugged her closer. Not that she minded, when his presence soothed her, as if he cherished her.

Coldar inspired the same sense of safety, except she didn't have the urge to kiss him.

"Did you enjoy it?" A few minutes passed before Enyl's soft question teased her away from the tendrils of sleep.

"Oh, yes, very much so." She flattened her palms over his chest, liking the muscled density of him under her fingertips.

"Do you want me to kiss you again?"

She licked her lips and sighed. Yes, she did. "Now?"

"When I want to, consider this my request for permission." He clenched her hip before releasing it but didn't move his hand away.

"Permission granted." Tomorrow, in the bright light of "day", she would think about having a husband.

She fell asleep to the touch of his lips to her temple, to the sunbaked scent of him, to his steady heartbeat—it was a pleasant way to drift off.

Chapter Eighteen

Planet Etteria
City of Issneen
En route to the Royal Court
Year of 2252, June – July

As soon as the ramp touched down on the bay floor, Enyl and Oriana strode onto it, heading toward the waiting hover. They had not made it halfway when a beautiful Etterian female glided toward Enyl. She wore the royal colors. Due to this, Ori didn't question her approach.

But when she bowed low before them, flashing a large amount of cleavage, she received Ori's full attention. She studied her since she was the first Etterian female she had encountered. Her arms and legs had more definition than a human but lesser than an Etterian male's. Her unbound locks cascaded around her, dancing in excitement. She looked like she was underwater with the way her hair swirled.

"Prince Enyl, I am most pleased you have returned." Her husky voice accompanied a sensual scan of his body. The female rose to assume a seductive pose. The blue and gold wrap parted to reveal a bare thigh and knee.

Ori frowned, not liking how this woman threw herself at her Eth. Wasn't the Ethera revered by all Etterians? She bristled, preparing to lambaste the woman for her rudeness.

Enyl's upper lip curled in distaste. "Milady, I advise you to remove yourself from my presence—it is most unwelcome."

The woman glowered at Ori and Enyl's clasped hands. Her hair became agitated, shooting out in aggressive spikes. "Are you choosing this creature...?" Venom dripped from her voice.

"Creature?" Ori stiffened her shoulders, preparing to smack the female across the face.

"Look at my eyes, Anin." Enyl's cold tone was dismissive and drenched with authority.

Anin's eyes widened, then narrowed. She huffed and stomped off.

As fire burned in Ori, she marveled at his cool exterior. His gaze met hers, and heat shimmered in the depths of his blue eyes. He raised their clasped hands to his lips and swept his lips across her knuckles, sending shivers up her arm. Her breath caught, but before she could respond, he held her hand to his chest and led them to the landing.

"You're going to have to deal with that, Enyl," she whispered, letting the burn of anger fizzle.

He grunted. "I have made her no promises, have never offered to mount her."

"Then why is she stalking you like this?"

"She remains unclaimed and hoped to bear the next heir." He squeezed her hand. "I have experienced court my entire life, Oriana. It amazes me females like her believe me to be naïve. Now come, *minus susa*, let me show you my world."

He tugged her into a hug. She snuggled against him, uncaring that she relished his embraces.

"Look. There are the markets." He pointed them out.

Obedient for now, she gazed upon the vista. The markets had colorful tents, striped, patterned, and cheerful. Etterians bustled through the narrow streets, the females as colorful in their ceremonial dresses. The males stood out, most in warrior black.

Enyl swung his finger to the left. "The proving grounds, where I suspect you and Coldar might spend a substantial amount of time."

Gray sand circled a ring, surrounded by raised seating. The darkness of it contrasted with the white and cream stone houses. She itched to test her mettle against Coldar, and now that he was her personal guard, she would nag him until he caved.

"On the right are the royal gardens surrounding my father's court." Enyl dipped his head to smile. His love for his home shone outward. Etteria, now hers.

Breathing in the sweet-scented air, she let the thought of home and family charm her. Pink skies stretched high, bright, with two suns and white fluffy clouds. She chuckled, expecting a unicorn Pegasus with a rainbow mane to glide across the sky. Crimson waves lined the horizon, which *were* the color of her hair, as Enyl had said. As Uncle Gayn had said. The beaches were a pale gray and inviting. The royal gardens were in blues, greens, and pinks, the flora and grass in various shades of blue, with the flowers green and pink. The royal court rose in white stone, crisp, clean, and intimidating.

Enyl studied her in absolute stillness.

"It's beautiful, Enyl."

He ran a thumb along her jaw. "The mines of Fuyra would be beautiful if you were with me."

His words warmed her, snatching her breath at the unexpected poeticism and his undeniable sincerity. "Where's Vytus, Enyl?" Desperate for a distraction, she scanned the kuta shuttle that had brought them down to the planet.

"He has chosen to remain on the *Gladio*, departing to convene with the *Kushin*, another battleship."

"He left already?" She frowned, not liking having not said goodbye.

"Yes, he has, *ensa*. He is not fond of court." Enyl blessed her with a bright smile, revealing his dimples.

The sight of them scrambled her thoughts. She leaned into him, looping her arm around his waist.

"Who is fond of court?" The rhetorical question was meant for herself, but he nodded. "Enyl, I had the strangest conversation with Malo," she said, wondering how best to phrase her concerns. "He didn't imply I was a spy, but his questions were specific like he had listened to our conversations since we boarded the *Gladio*."

"I asked him to investigate your unusual knowledge of Etterian culture."

She jerked away from him. Lowering her gaze, she hid her reaction. She wanted to rant at his lack of trust. But part of her—the one that whispered in Uncle Gayn's voice—said it was logical for their suspicions. Enyl knew nothing about humans, where she knew so much about Etterians. If they reversed positions, she would be as cautious.

It stung though, his distrust. "You could've asked me." Hurt lingered in her voice. She sucked in a sharp breath, trying to erase it. He hadn't mistrusted her intentionally.

"You told me about your uncles, but not how they knew confidential information about my world."

All they knew was gleaned from a bronze and gold data cube, ancient yet functional, they had nestled in a protected alcove on their cargo ship. "On his deathbed, a Durn granted his data cube to Uncle Gayn. He said he had no one else to entrust his life's work."

"A Durn?" Enyl's eyebrow arched in surprise. She could've sworn disbelief flickered across his eyes.

Her revelation conflicted him more. She sighed. Durns *were* rare and one happening upon her uncles would raise more suspicions. "My uncles were couriers and knew our galaxy well. They discovered an ill Durn, a species they didn't know existed. Cailu stayed with them until the plague that killed his people took him."

"The plague?"

"Cailu called it Nevid, the Unseen." After her response, Enyl gaped.

"Are you telling me your uncles spent years in the company of a Durn?"

"No, just over eight months. Cailu was a passionate xenoarchaeologist, and his studies were on his data cube. Because of what he taught Uncle Bos, I understand the chemical breakdown of Maloidian steel, its strengths, and weaknesses." Tears burned at the backs of her eyes. Cailu's data and legacy were gone forever. In all these years, she hadn't realized what else the pirates had stolen from her.

Enyl's arms tightened around her, pulling her against his solid chest. "Be at peace, my Dar Eth. We have Durn archives, and perhaps Cailu's research lies within those cubes."

She must have spoken aloud. Burrowing into him, she couldn't regret it. At least, he believed her. But he had hesitated. Despite the Ethera, their relationship wasn't yet where it should be.

"Come, my father waits."

She let Enyl lead her to an awaiting hover. "What should I expect?" Assuming the seat next to him, she laced her fingers with his, needing to touch him, amazed he let her hold his hand as often as she liked.

"The court is always crowded. I never could understand why. My father has to welcome you in the presence of the court—it will go a long way to smoothing their acceptance of you."

She frowned. "They don't like humans?"

"Some do not non-Etterians, but the Ethera has chosen, no matter their opinions."

She forced a smile but couldn't find joy in it. He was stuck with her, regardless of whether he liked her or not. It smacked of arranged marriages from Earth's history. Would he even have approached her without the Ethera in their culture? Her concerns were pointless and irrational, but she didn't know how to nullify them.

Myan and Coldar climb into the hover, distracting her. As soon as they chose their seats, the hover glided forward. The cool air blew her hair wild. She had left it unbound and wore the ceremonial dress in indigo and gold as Enyl preferred. Despite the beauty surrounding her, she dipped her chin, still deep in thought.

Since the Ethera had paired them, and Enyl needed her to ward off the void, she couldn't walk away. Besides, what awaited her outside of

Etteria? No man had tempted her as he did, though that could be the Ethera talking. He had only to touch her, look at her, and she drenched her thighs. Virgin alert. As she had feared, she had formed an addiction to him, to how he made her feel.

She was at a crossroads. If she abandoned him, she would have to live with the consequences, or she could stay with him. If she chose him, she would make the best of it. This meant being the princess he needed her to be. She leaned into him to bury her face in the curve of his neck and kiss him there. She loved that he rubbed her back, pulling her against him. He was hers, and she was his. The finality of that soothed her for the time being.

The hover stopped alongside a long, vine-covered walkway leading to two golden doors. As soon as they neared them, they opened into a vast hall. Adorned in blue, gold, and white, beautiful, painted images were on the vaulted ceiling, and the floor was a polished, white stone. Many Etterians crowded the court, as Enyl had warned, but they parted, creating a path for them to reach the dais.

Someone announced the entrance of Prince Enyl and Princess Oriana. Hearing the title of princess attached to her name added a surreal quality to her spinning thoughts. Like the first time a married woman used her new title and last name. Announcing her was a fait accompli, the nail in the coffin. Royal protocol had made the decision for her, to remain with Enyl. She couldn't withdraw and shame him or doom him to die. As a girl, she had wept for those unloved yet faceless warriors. She couldn't doom Enyl, someone she knew, to such a death. Still, this was forever. This was marriage. This was her life.

"What is the meaning of this, Enyl?" A large, broad-shouldered male barreled through the crowd, parting them in fear and awe.

His facial features were an older version of Enyl's. This was King Xeus, a male who had formed part of her studies. She adored him on sight because of his paternal persona. His gaze narrowed on her, traveled over her curves, her hair, and settled on her eyes. He thought her the compatible female and must not have realized she was Enyl's soulmate.

Rocking on her heels, she couldn't contain the glee washing over her. Uncle Gayn had been an admirer, spending much of her study time on Etteria and its history.

"You are well." It wasn't a question, more a request for confirmation despite her standing in front of him whole and hearty. He glanced at Coldar and Myan, his gaze expectant, like she couldn't speak for herself.

"She is, my king. Medic Aldur tended to her injuries."

The king faced the court. "This is Oriana McKenzie, Yithian arena champion, Earthian female from Earth, and the first compatible species found."

"And my Dar Eth," Enyl said.

Xeus's head shot up. "I assumed her announcement as your princess meant...Truly?" He rushed toward his son, ignoring the shock that rippled through the court. Freezing a few steps from Enyl, he stared into his eyes. "This is—"

"Unbelievable? Wonderful?" Enyl chuckled.

The king spun to Ori, his mouth gaping. "I have a daughter?"

Stunned at having acquired a father, her smile wavered. It hadn't occurred to her. Her heart pounded an erratic beat. Her four "fathers" had died—one biological and three surrogates. What if she was the curse? She assessed the strength and authority pouring off him. The only way he could die was due to the void. His vibrancy pressed on her, and she vowed she would find his Dar Eth. She wouldn't lose another father if she had a say in the matter.

"I have a daughter." He bounced, booming his enthusiasm.

She didn't remember her father, only her uncles, and knew not what to expect from her new father. Smiling at his infectious joy, she slipped her hand in Enyl's, now insecure under all this attention, as if a thousand gazes judged her.

"Are there more females on your world?" Xeus calmed enough to speak.

"Millions," she said.

The court reacted with gasps and cheers.

"Are they all like you?" A male from the crowd called out, hope in his voice.

"No, we are unique—even if our coloring is the same, we differ personality-wise. I assume this is true for Etterians, as well."

Enyl smiled, squeezing her hand in encouragement.

"May we run our tests as arranged?" Xeus stilled with what she assumed was dread. "Fertility still needs to be determined."

"Of course, whatever you need." After all, she had given her word. She peeked at Coldar, wondering if he remembered the promised cocktail.

"Thank you, Oriana." The king smiled before turning to the court. "We have reason to hope. The Ethera has chosen an Earthian female. I will schedule the examinations and inform you of the findings."

Another male dismissed the court as Xeus held out his hand to her. "Come, my daughter, I wish to know more. Tell me, where are you from? Your life, was it a good one?"

She dropped Enyl's hand and accepted the king's. With a gentle tug, he led her to a windowed alcove.

ENYL CLASPED HIS HANDS behind his back as his Dar Eth charmed his father. Her every move captivated Enyl, her arching eyebrow, the flick of her hair, her husky laughter, the way her lips curled in amusement. By the end of their conversation, she was calling Father 'father' to his father's delight. She had taught him how to greet a *human* and had hugged him. His father had also charmed her—this brought a smile to Enyl's lips. Smiling had become second nature to him now that darkness no longer lingered in his soul.

"Come, let us get you established. Cales?" Father raised his gaze to Cales, who hovered in the background. "Oriana, this is Adviser Cales and a lifelong battle-bond. If you need anything and I am unavailable, go to him."

She grinned at Cales when he stared at her offered hand before grasping it for a shake or two. He must have paid attention when she had taught his father. The male was excellent at his position and as Father's battle-bond.

"A pleasure to meet you, Adviser Cales."

He lifted his other hand to cover their clasped hands. The sight of it didn't bother Enyl. Cales meant no disrespect. To touch a Dar Eth for longer than was necessary was unacceptable, but Oriana was a miracle many would disbelieve until meeting her.

"A pleasure to meet you, Princess Oriana," Cales said with a smile twitching his lips.

"Please call me Oriana or Ori. I trust you may since you are dear to my new father?" She bounced on her toes, her sweet smile remaining and charming Cales in the process. "Excellent, now about my quarters, may I request a private one?"

Enyl stiffened, growling in anger. He hadn't realized how sleeping with her in his arms had come to mean a great deal to him. Yet, it meant nothing to her if she wanted to sleep alone.

She gave him a pleading look, which sent concern rippling through him. "Please Enyl, I need to face my inner demons." Her eyes flashed with Ferusi green fire. "I will conquer this."

He nodded even as his shoulders slumped.

"Of course, Oriana," Adviser Cales said. "I will conduct you to your new quarters."

She trailed him through another set of gold doors and out the royal court.

"You have done well, my son," Father said, once the doors shut behind her.

Enyl blinked at the unfettered emotion on his father's face. "I cannot take credit for this."

His father grinned. "Tell me, what is she like?"

"If you asked Coldar, who has spent the most time with her, he would say she is stubborn, opinionated, fearless, reckless. I find her to be sweet, kind-hearted, affectionate, fierce in the defense of a loved one, and well-educated."

"I saw an arena vid of her, where she killed six snarling creatures. When I mentioned this to her, she became emotional." Father threw a concerned look at Enyl—he hadn't known how to deal with a tearful female. "They were wild dogs and had been extinct for decades, or so the humans believed. Finding them in a Yithian arena then having to kill them destroyed her."

"She did not tell me this and kept to herself that day, my king." Coldar's breathing shuddered. "Ori is forthcoming with her thoughts and opinions, which is why I remember the day well."

"I assume your injuries prevented you from defending her?"

"A head wound, my king," he said, dipping his head in shame. No matter what Enyl said, Coldar had yet to forgive himself.

"Then you shall be her royal guard," Father announced.

Enyl crossed his arms over his chest and grinned. "In such a role, you will appease your guilt." Even though he had tasked Coldar to guard Ori, having his father do it confirmed he was in line with his father's leadership methods. It also made the promotion official.

"Thank you, my king." Coldar accepted his "punishment" with great humility.

"Warrior Myan, you shall also serve as guard. Oriana has indicated her fondness for you, as well."

Myan bowed, accepting Coldar's arm-grip with a broad smile.

"Tell me, Father, what has occurred in my absence?" Enyl steered his father to his office, gesturing to Myan and Coldar that they had somewhere they needed to be.

Enyl hid a smile as they removed themselves with an eagerness he envied. He wished he could spend the afternoon with his Dar Eth. The concern in Cales's gaze whenever he looked at Father was something

Enyl needed to investigate. While Oriana settled in her new chambers, he would take the time to assess the political situation and what lay behind Cales's frown.

Chapter Nineteen

Planet Etteria
City of Issneen
En route to the Royal Court
Year of 2252, July

ORI INHALED AND EXHALED in an attempt to calm herself. She strolled around the gardens, enjoying the sheer luxury of the outdoors. Freedom without metal walls of any kind, and clean air, soared her soul. On her peripherals, she caught the bright skies, open and vast, missing a dome, a metallic ceiling. She forced herself to raise her face to the suns' light. It had taken months to adjust to Earth's undomed skies, although, the protective shield shimmering on the horizon helped ease her mind. Surrounding by lush vegetation and rich soil, the organic smells reminded her of Andrew. He would've loved this place.

She frowned, having not thought of him or Liam for months. Sadness settled on her, and she dipped her chin to her chest, struggling to contain the tears. She had forsaken her friends. Months had passed since she left HoSS. Surviving the arena had been her priority. Not once did she hope they could find her, rescue her, and she hadn't wanted them to, to endanger themselves. Liam would have half-cocked the rescue attempt, getting himself killed in the process. Andrew would have rallied a group of illegals to do the dirty work for him, throwing what resources he had on it.

Sighing, she pictured him wallowing in spare parts like a man drowning in money. Sassh stroked an engagement ring. Shit, Ori even missed Sam. She ran her finger along the scar on her palm, imagining it twinged. The suns split their trajectories like a cosmic clock, telling her how long she stayed in the gardens feeling sorry for herself.

A while ago, she had thought she and Coldar would never escape the arena. That her life and worse, his, would end there. She had gone from loneliness, with no prospect of a love interest to having a husband and one thrust upon her by fate's twisted strings.

When her O.D.I. vibrated up her arm, it startled her out of her depressing thoughts. She blinked at it, unable to comprehend. It had been silent these past months. She hadn't needed her alarms, nor could anyone reach her through the dampening shields. Her friends may have tried, then their concern dwindled as their lives continued. They had stopped caring.

Tapping her wrist, she read the holographic message from Enyl. Her heart skipped a beat. She smiled like a lovesick fool. He requested to dine with her at noon in her chambers. Responding immediately, lest he rescind the request, her fingers flew across the holographic keys.

She kind of liked her husband. He was tall, dark, and handsome. Her body's preference was irrational, reacting like a misfiring engine when he was near. This insane need to be with him, to touch him had to be the work of the Ethera. Not that the why mattered when the vibrant sensations were amazing.

She faced her guards. "Back we go, I'm having my midday meal with Enyl. Oh, and Coldar?" As she "bumped" her wrist over Coldar's, she beamed, bouncing on her heels. She had transferred his share of the arena winnings from her account to his without him realizing it. "I suggest you and Myan find other things to entertain yourself."

He frowned in confusion. Not elaborating, she increased her speed and length of stride to reach her chambers faster. As the door swished open, she spun to address Coldar. "Spend your tokens well, partner."

The door shut on him roaring her name.

She chuckled, loving the darkening of his face and how much fun it was to tweak him. Perhaps, if she had an older brother, this warmth inside her would have been for him. Coldar took that role, and Myan to a lesser degree.

"What are you up to, Oriana?" Enyl's deep voice feathered over her senses, tingling her skin and raising the hairs on her arms.

Sighing, she faced him. Damn, the male sure knew how to excite her. All he had to do was speak, and her heart fluttered. "Tormenting Coldar." She strode toward Enyl.

Posing like a man from a digi-mag, he leaned against a paneled wall. He straightened as she splayed her fingers across his tunic-covered chest. The texture of his muscles under her hands summoned a shudder from her. And when she rubbed his tunic, his sunbaked scent greeted her. She dipped her head to draw in a deep inhale. He caressed her lower back, then slid his hands upward to tangle in her unbound hair.

"When you said meal, did you mean actual food?" She pressed her parted lips to his erratic pulse as she rippled her fingers up and over his broad shoulders.

"Yes."

Frowning, she ignored the truth in his words, unable to resist darting her tongue out to taste his skin. Heated caramel exploded across her tastebuds. She feathered kisses to his earlobe. When she nibbled there, his arms tightened around her.

"Unless you are not hungry..."

She shivered as his gravel voice rippled along her skin, sparking goosebumps as it traveled. Before she could ask him what happened to his voice, she tightened her fingers on his chest. The sound that tore from his throat made her heart leap in anticipation.

"Alodon's balls, the meal can wait," he rasped as he grabbed her ass and lifted her to meet the hard length of him.

Her thoughts reeled, flicking between the pressure at the juncture of her thighs and the dominant way he handled her. He slipped his hand through her hair to cup the back of her head, holding her still for his plundering mouth. His taste weakened her knees, sending wave upon wave of fiery need through her. A sweep of his bold tongue beat her heart a parsec a minute. The sweet tendrils firing outward from him massaging one butt cheek claimed her ability to breathe.

She broke away from his kiss to pant, only for him to kiss the pulse at her neck. Gasping, she pulled away from him, granting him more access. Not once did she perceive movement, until the bed dipped beneath her as he laid her upon it. When she lay there for a minute, untouched, her curiosity opened her eyes.

He stared at her with such an intense expression on his features. She couldn't place the emotions roiling in his eyes. Her chest warmed with rising swells of longing, need, impatience...love?

He sprawled next to her, then ran his hand up and over her taut stomach, between her breasts to curl around her neck. With his fingers embracing her jaw, he feathered his lips across her chin, her other cheek, and her parted lips.

She blinked in awe; to inhale his breath, to share hers with him. He stroked his trembling fingers along her neck, across her collarbone to a breast. His touch burned her through her clothes. She quivered, bombarded by many sensations, with fireworks exploding her senses. Her body responded without her control. He kissed her, robbing her of breath as he thrust his tongue into her mouth, claiming and branding her.

She was his, didn't he know that?

Overwhelmed by his kiss and his tender yet firm fingers, she writhed. He cupped her breast while stroking back and forth across her pebbled nipple with his thumb. She whimpered, marveling at the strange yet addictive nature of his touch. He raised his head to glance at his hand, giving her a few seconds to catch her breath, which she did, hyperventilating by the sounds of it. Anticipation sang through her veins when he brushed his palm across her stomach and dipped a finger into her belly button, right through her ceremonial dress.

He ventured between the overlapping fabric. The sensation of his fingers on her skin was heated velvet. She settled her gaze on his features, on the determined angle of his chin. Did he know what he did to her, how his touch affected her?

His confidence soothed her, acting like an anchor amid this new experience for her. Cool air brought her to the moment as he slid lower. A dull ache, along with adrenaline, assailed her body. As his fingers breached her pulsing sex, she arched off the bed again. She cried out, exquisite pleasure teased her senses and her hips thrust upward of their own accord.

"Ori, you are ready for me, *ensa*." His voice was an octave below guttural. Though he was gruff, she understood him through his incoherent sentences. "So ready."

She couldn't form words to respond to him. A moan tore from her as he rubbed a bundle of nerves between her legs, shooting shards of white, hot need through her hypersensitive body. She shuddered, clawing his forearm, demanding something she couldn't name.

He chuckled, and her gaze flew to meet his. His expression was still as breathtaking and intense, yet it held a yearning she was beginning to understand.

"Need this?" He flicked his fingers, merciless as something potent built within her—she arched again, crying out. He released her, and his smile was sinful, revealing his dimples.

She wanted to scream for another reason.

"Not good enough, *thamani*. Give me all of you." He brought his hand back, tormenting her no more.

Her breath hitched, her muscles tightened in anticipation of what, she knew not. He stopped again and removed his fingers. She glared at him, curling her fingers into fists, ready to punch him. He returned to the epicenter of the burning need, ruthless in his attack, and this time he didn't stop. His nostrils flared, but he didn't look away from her. Something potent crossed his features, and a slow rumble took residence in his chest.

She tried to keep her gaze on him in case he thought to tease her further. Fighting and failing, her eyelids fluttered under the barrage of sensations assailing her innocent body. Every muscle tightened, trembled, and her breathing became erratic. Her heart pounded like she climbed a mountain, desperate to reach the crest. Quicker, wave after intense wave crashed through her until she froze, tilted her head back, arched her body, and screamed his name. Her world splintered into infinite pieces, with Enyl and his gifted touch consuming her focus.

He didn't break contact, and any twitch of his fingers snatched her breath, sparking renewed flashes of joy. His hooded and lust-filled eyes met hers. He lowered his body next to her to kiss her again, sipping at her lips before he plundered her mouth. She inhaled his sunbaked scent and sighed as this incredible lassitude paralyzed her.

"You are so beautiful, Oriana. I am amazed you are mine," he whispered while stroking her stomach, having parted the ceremonial dress to reveal her skin.

"That was a…?" She gasped, now understanding why humans pursued sexual interaction with an overabundance of enthusiasm.

He smiled, tracing patterns on her skin.

She grabbed his trembling hands, his touch hardening her nipples until they tingled.

"A fulfillment." He kissed her again.

So that was an orgasm? Oh, she was so glad she waited to find him. She wrapped her arms around his neck and held her quivering body to his.

He clenched his jaw, muffling a grumble.

"Do you get one?" She was eager to please him, hoping to repay him for the wonderful experience. At the first opportunity, she would research this, not wanting to fail. Before, doing so might have highlighted what she missed out on.

He held his forehead to hers and hesitated. The pain twisting his lips suggested he would like nothing more. "Mine will have to wait, *ensa*. My father has commed me." Enyl ran a hand over his face and shuddered, holding his fingers to his nose to inhale. With a sigh, he climbed off the bed and adjusted his arousal to a bearable position within his breeches. She studied him with more interest than she had given her machines.

"Later, my Oriana, I promise." He tugged her off the bed, stroked her disheveled hair, straightened her dress, and squeezed her ass one last time. Pulling away, he tapped on his O.D.I. "It must be urgent. I will see you this evening?" He leaned forward to kiss her startled mouth.

Dazed, she gaped at him as he left her chambers sporting a satisfied smile. She was the one who had soared the stars. And not attending to his need was wrong. She had seen it, the sheer size of it bulging his pants. Striding to the display vid, she searched for archives from Earth. She had time to research how best to please him.

Tonight couldn't come soon enough for her.

Chapter Twenty

HAVING STOOD OUTSIDE HIS father's office for a few minutes, Enyl fought for calm, to ease the burning of his arousal. Delighted to discover human females were similar to Etterian, a sense of accomplishment pulsed through him at gifting Ori with her first fulfillment.

Maker. Images of her arching, thrusting her breasts, writhing beneath his fingers tormented his fragile control. The urge to spin on his heels and sprint to her gripped him.

He breathed in and out, straightened his armor, and entered his father's office to find him and Cales awaiting Enyl's arrival. As soon as he strode toward the immense Fuyra-carved desk, his father rose and hurried over to the large display vid mounted on a paneled wall. He tapped his O.D.I. and an image of Supreme Commander Ulriq appeared. The male paced across the vid, stopping to peer at Father before pacing again.

Enyl blinked at Ulriq's cerulean eyes. No, it wasn't possible. His chest cinched tight enough to cut off his breathing. If Ulriq's Dar Eth was human, it meant a compatible species had been found. Enyl longed for Ori to bear his *damu* which he hoped the tests would confirm.

"Ulriq, you too?" his father barked in surprise.

"Yes, my king, Warrior Kanzo, as well. Neither of us anticipated we would find our Dar Eths within minutes of each other. As much as I would wish to supply the details, it will have to wait. I am comming with an urgent request."

Two. Enyl parted his mouth to speak, preparing to fire questions at Ulriq, but his father approached the vid, barring his line of vision.

"Speak as needed." Father grasped his hands behind his back and waited.

"The Yithians have kidnapped my Dar Eth. I request permission to retrieve her."

Enyl frowned. Like the Yithians had done with Oriana. What could they want with humans? How could they know what the females meant to Etteria when Oriana was taken before she became a Dar Eth?

Father didn't hesitate. "Permission granted."

"Even should it start a war?" Ulriq's brow furrowed. "My control is non-existent. I want to terminate the planet, and I would, without a doubt, if she was not heading for it or on it."

"Then a war they shall have."

Enyl stiffened his shoulders against the rush of adrenaline. Etterians would revert to their barbaric ways should their Dar Eths be endangered. He shivered, hating the glimpse of the void consuming his soul at the thought of Oriana harmed.

Unable to hold back his curiosity any longer, Enyl leaned in front of his father. "Tell me, Ulriq, is your Dar Eth human?"

"Yes, my prince, Kanzo's is also human." Ulriq's eyes closed for a moment. "We violated the GC laws governing mid-grade planets, but I will explain when I have her secured. I will bear whatever punishment you deem worthy."

Enyl was grateful for the warning should the Galactic Council hold his father accountable.

"Do you require assistance? We can notify the many battleships surrounding Yithia as needed." Cales tapped on his O.D.I., verifying the locations and numbers. He flicked his fingers, sharing his findings. "These are the ships and supreme commanders able to aid you."

"My thanks, Adviser. We are two days from Mascroba. We pursued as soon as we could, though I am pleased I have your support." The stressed male ran a hand over his face before meeting Father's gaze. "Medic Teric betrayed us." Ulriq's coarse voice implied a powerful reaction to Teric's betrayal, more than his words revealed.

Something deep and menacing roiled within Enyl roiled. For one of their male's to hand over his Oriana to a Yithian? He would kill with impunity; the Etterian for his audacity, for his violation of their code, and the Yithians because they dared take what was his.

"Meric's Teric?" Cales's surprise was understandable. Elite warrior Meric had sought fighting techniques from across the known universe and brought Hatimaye to Etteria.

"We will investigate from this side. May all of Etteria be with you, Ulriq." Father ended the communication, then faced Enyl and Cales.

"Vytus and Malo are on the *Gladio* and are en route to the *Kushin*," Enyl said.

"Excellent, divert them to Yithia, task the Phoenix, as well. Monitor this unfortunate situation, Cales. Task Malo to investigate Teric's involvement. He is an honorable male, and this is uncharacteristic." An unexpected grin spread across his father's face. He was too in awe at the discovery to care about controlling his emotions. "The speed at which we found a compatible species is alarming. I cannot convey how grateful I am."

"The Maker has blessed us, Father." Enyl shoved aside the memory of Oriana's first ecstasy. He had just managed to calm his throbbing arousal.

"We have three Dar Eths. Three." Father thumped his desk. "We will need a strategy. I doubt Earth would let us steal their females. Dispatch a battleship or two to guard the planet. If Yithia is intent on kidnapping females, we should be intent on stopping them."

"Consider it done." Cales punched commands on his holographic keys.

"Excellent, this evening we will celebrate." Father laughed.

"You must inform the court of this success, my king." Cales's words wiped Father's smile and replaced it with a scowl.

"They have seen the success with Oriana." Enyl grasped his father on his shoulder in a show of support.

"True, I shall notify them after the meal." He sighed and turned away as his shoulders slumped.

Enyl arched a brow at Cales, hoping for an explanation for his father's erratic behavior. Cales shook his head.

There went returning to Ori soon. But the darkness clouding Enyl's joy at discovering his salvation, drove him to find out what was going on. He needed to confirm whether his father would soon succumb to the void. The endless tasks of being king could be slumping his shoulders and weighing down his spirits. That Enyl could help with. He would explain to his Dar Eth later, and Maker willing, finally bring his Ethera vision to fruition.

Planet Etteria
The Hall
At Dinner

XEUS ROSE TO ADDRESS the packed hall. Having summoned his ambassadors, those in attendance arrived with due haste. His confidence was boundless and his bearing regal, as she expected of a king. Yet, his gestures were big, vigorous, and his smile wide, like he played a part, believing he needed to be exuberant. This outward display of joviality was an odd occurrence for an Etterian male, which was why Oriana suspected it wasn't genuine.

"My Etterians, I bring great news." The crowds stilled, eager and patient. "We have found another two Dar Eths from among the human females."

A murmur of excitement rippled through them with hope cementing their features. She empathized with them, understood their pain, and their renewed dreams. Her gaze settled on Enyl's, and she smiled with contentment. She was his dream, his joy. But the many faces in the crowd draped a heaviness across her shoulders. As princess, she would be centerstage.

"We have indeed found a compatible species. The discovery of this proves the blessing of the Maker is still upon us. He has not forsaken us." Xeus surveyed the court with a smile. "We have deployed battleships to protect the planet from troublesome Yithians while we strategize. The current approach is to send an ambassador to negotiate with the humans."

Ori winced. Etterians had honor, but humans not so much. Sending ambassadors to negotiate with Earth's politicians would be like sending a child into a viper pit.

"I will keep you informed on the status. Do not lose hope, my males—keep strong." With a dismissive gesture, Xeus concluded the announcement.

Ori marched across the hall with Enyl behind her. Without his preternatural hearing, she was unable to hear his footsteps, but his warmth at her back marked his presence. Remembering where he had put his hand earlier burned her cheeks.

Sighing, she sidled up to Xeus who, with stiff shoulders and pinched lips, debated with an ambassador wearing the same orange as Anin.

The male flicked his indigo gaze at Ori, dipped his head and wandered off.

"Father? Might I have a word?"

"Of course, my daughter." Xeus gestured.

She grinned and slipped into his arms for a hug. He crushed her to him, smashing her face against his firm chest. She smothered a laugh.

He had taken to hugging, and she didn't have the heart to inform him his hold was often too tight.

She leaned away from him, a silent request for him to free her. He obliged, and with a sigh, she struggled to form the right words. "Humans aren't trustworthy."

He frowned. "In what way?"

"They say one thing but mean another. I'd recommend you send an ambassador with the skill to read deceit. Your operations commander might suit. Also, don't offer Earth's leaders weapons technology, which I'm certain you wouldn't have anyway. They may appear to be under one government, but there are many underground factions willing to blow up anything and everything at the first opportunity. Offer environmental healing technology, trade deals, support at the Global Council..."

The king's gaze was inscrutable before he nodded. "I shall place this task in yours and Enyl's hands, my daughter. You recognize how important this is to Etteria, to all Etterian males."

"If it pleases you, Father." She smiled, though she didn't like having this responsibility on her shoulders. It was her fault for mentioning it, but her concern had driven her to. What humans needed wasn't more fighting power or better ways to kill each other.

"You do, please me," the king said and ushered her to his son. "Are you up to the challenge, Enyl?"

She glanced between the two males who were her family, her blood-bonds. Of course Enyl was up to the challenge. She frowned at Xeus, perhaps misreading the subtle reference in his question. He couldn't mean she was the challenge, could he?

"Without doubt." Enyl's voice had deepened—its gravel quality drawing her attention, like a moth to a flame.

He tugged her against him, his bearing protective, possessive, enamored. With his hand on her hip, he staked his claim in a way she would never have tolerated. More startling than her capitulation was the fact she loved his audacity in branding her, owning her, and his constant need to possess her.

She studied his handsome face, the angle of his jaw, the softness of his lips curling in a slight smile, and those piercing eyes focused on her. For someone with her level of independence, when he surrounded her with care and attentiveness fluttered her heartbeat into a mild panic.

She struggled to calm her erratic thoughts and the urge to run. Not a coward though, she laced her fingers with Enyl's and squeezed. Merging their cultures would be difficult enough without adding senseless reactions. If he crossed a boundary she was uncomfortable with, she would tell him. And she hoped he did the same with her.

Chapter Twenty-One

Planet Etteria
City of Issneen
The proving grounds
Year of 2252, July

NAUSEA CHURNED ORI'S STOMACH, and she held her hand to her stomach, vowing to never over imbibe again. She spent most of last night and the early morning with Coldar and Myan sampling an extensive selection of Earth's whisky.

Sucking in the morning air wrenched her gut, and she swallowed bile. Despite brushing her teeth and gargling, her tongue still had a furry texture. Two suns shining with their usual enthusiasm might worsen her headache, but when Enyl's message woke her, she dragged herself from her bed. The spot beside her had remained untouched, as expected since she had asked for separate chambers. She missed Enyl's warmth, scent, and arms around her. Waking to his morning voice and sharing a coffee with him, in hindsight, had become a favorite time of day.

Exhaustion had prevented another nightmare, thank the Lord for that. But despite her undisturbed sleep, exhaustion burned her nostrils and made her eyes gritty.

She chose to wear something similar to when Enyl had first kissed her. His message had mentioned the proving grounds. Clothing for easier movement meant leggings, a vest, a sports bra, plus better boots than she had ever owned. She squinted against the magnus sun breaching the horizon.

"Morning, Ori."

She jerked, having not heard him approach, and settled her gaze on Myan. A glance at Coldar revealed an angry and grumbling Etterian male. Their skin glowed with good health, no circles darkened their eyes, while her cheeks had taken on a green tinge. As well as they looked, she suffered, having not drunk herself into such a state since Uncle Gayn had taught her to appreciate cognac.

"You can't still be angry with me?" She huffed, instead of rolling her eyes like a teenager. If the suns didn't pierce her eyeballs or set them on fire, she might have succumbed.

Coldar's reaction to the receipt of his well-earned credits continued from last night's nag fest. "Ori, it is a shit ton of tokens."

Blinking at his choice of words, she smothered a chuckle with a cough. Her phrases were rubbing off on him. She flicked her hand in a dismissive manner. "Enough, Coldar. I locked my account. You can try, but you won't be able to transfer it back." She strolled to the royal court, using the glowing signs embedded in the rock to find her way. "Share it with Myan if you like. You two need to find your Dar Eths, and you may need tokens for that."

"Alodon's hell." Coldar stomped a big foot before twisting his lips into some sort of smile. "I hate it when you are logical."

She stared at him, bringing him to a standstill. "Let me look at your eyes. You've 'hated' a lot of things lately. Feeling emotional, Coldar?" she teased, and Myan laughed next to them.

"I do not appreciate your humor." Coldar glared at Myan.

The male brought up both hands to indicate a truce.

She flashed him a cheeky smile and resumed her meander to the proving grounds, happy to have won that round. Although, mentioning their future Dar Eths was fighting dirty, so not a fair win by her standards.

Enyl waited at the viewer bunkers dressed in his Etterian armor. She grimaced—it meant her kicks and punches needed to be more powerful. Scanning the sand-lined sparring grounds, she acknowledged the challenge and accepted the consequences.

"Morning, *ensa*." His gaze traveled the length of her.

Heat infused her, from her toes to the tips of her ears. Oh, how she had missed this, missed him, missed seeing that intensity in his eyes. "Morning, Enyl."

"Did you sleep well?" Concern lanced across his handsome features.

"Yes, and I'm ready for this morning." She winced, hoping she didn't spill her guts in the gray sand. "A prepared warrior is an honorable one."

Coldar mocking her readiness with exaggerated drinking actions left her torn between pride and the urge to punch him in the ribs.

"First things first..." She crossed the sand and hugged Enyl, inhaling his sunbaked scent deep within her. "I missed you," she whispered into his neck.

"And I you." He rubbed her back. "But if you think hugs are going to buy you leniency..."

She shrugged and strode to the center of the sparring ring. He assumed a fighting position a few steps away from her.

Doing this, whether she bested Enyl or failed, would prove her capabilities to these overprotective males. She didn't appreciate having to prove herself when the evidence of her skills was available on the Yithian arena vids. Spreading her legs, she balanced her weight on her front foot and raised her fists in front of her face. Time to have done with this.

He charged her.

She dodged him with ease, bouncing to the side, with her footing sure despite the shifting sands. Used to working on slippery oil when clambering the platforms, the sand didn't challenge her abilities. Enyl attacked again, forcing her to dodge, dive, and duck. He almost touched her a few times. By the time he called a halt, perspiration drenched her as she fought for breath.

"Good. Less stamina than expected but understandable when you worked as an engineer." He dusted the sand from his breeches and smiled. "Your footwork is steady and unpredictable. I am pleased, Oriana."

Her chest swelled at his compliments, and the heat engulfing her reminded her of Uncle Gayn's praise. While she savored her memories, he strode to the middle of the ring and knelt. She grumbled and did the same. Uncle Diso had assumed the same position, which meant. Enyl wasn't done. This would test her stamina, her improvisation.

He dove for her, but she dodged his grasping hands and tackled him to the ground. She grabbed his wrist with both hands and rolled him onto his stomach to hammerlock him. Well, she bluffed the position—she had no intention of following through but needed him to believe she would. Instead, she flipped him onto his back and arm-locked him. With her thighs wrapped across his chest and neck to choke him and his elbow pinned between her knees, she leaned backward. This would straighten his arm and threaten to break it.

He laughed, and she released him, hoping they were done. Her nausea had evaporated, replaced with a rumble of hunger.

Enyl lay there, a broad smile dominating his sensual lips. "Improvisation was good. You tricked me, *ensa.*"

He bounded up then shook off most of the sand before assuming a fighting stance again. She sighed and scrambled to her feet. Bouncing on her toes dislodged the sand from her clothing and hair. As soon as she brought her fists up, he charged her, swinging his fists with front kicks, giving no quarter. Standing her ground, she dodged, and blocked, throwing punches and kicks of her own.

Pain lanced through her torso where his masterful kick connected to her stomach. She flew back and landed in the sand, gasping for air, having had the wind knocked out of her. While sucking in short, agonizing breaths, she thrust up her thumb, like Uncle Diso had taught her. Still gasping, she clambered to her feet and assumed the fighting stance again.

There wasn't time to normalize her breathing or to calm her racing heartbeat. It wasn't standard Etterian protocol to attack when she was at her weakest, but he did so. For a second, she froze. A massive Etterian warrior barreling toward her sparked her fight response. Her vision funneled, her breathing slowed, and she reacted on instinct.

Dropping to her haunches, she punched him in the groin.

His eyes widened in surprise, he grunted, then collapsed on the sand, grabbing at his offended parts. Groans rippled across the Etterian males acting as spectators.

Guilt was swift to strike. She faced Enyl, nibbling on her bottom lip as she worried she may have hit him too hard.

He raised his thumb with the hand not gripping his groin.

Relief gushed out of her in a hysterical giggle, and she sprawled next to him, stretching her aching body on the lumpy gray sand. She sucked in air as she watched the white clouds float overhead while he recovered.

"You are a dirty fighter," he rasped.

She shrugged, unrepentant. "Not everyone fights with honor, Enyl. A lesson I learned the hard way."

He must have agreed with her statement when he grumbled before sitting up. Pain still darkened his eyes.

"Besides, it's wise to bring down my opponent in the quickest way possible."

He winced as he climbed to his feet. Still, she shouldn't have punched him there. It was a low blow, but in her defense, he was a well-built Etterian male battling a puny human woman. There was no contest.

"I can kiss it better later," she whispered, images of her "education" coming to mind. Heat exploded against her cooling cheeks. "Or anything else aching."

His breath hitched.

She grinned when his eyes narrowed, brooding with lust. Good, let his groin think of more pleasurable interludes. She gave him an unapologetic perusal and wrapped her arms around him in a fierce hug.

Pressing a kiss to his chin, she pulled away with an exuberant bounce. "Now for breakfast. I'm starving."

Chapter Twenty-Two

Planet Etteria
City of Issneen
Oriana's chambers
12252 years, 7ᵗʰ month

"My prince."

The voice from his O.D.I. opened Enyl's eyes in an instant. "Report."

He flopped onto his back and rubbed his face then threw out a hand, finding nothing but cool sheets where Ori should have been. Empty, like the hole in his heart. He needed her beside him, needed her scent filling his nostrils. The Ethera made demands he couldn't ignore for much longer. The next time his father invited them to share the evening meal, he would decline.

"There has been a disturbance logged for Princess Oriana's chambers. We have unlocked her door in preparation for your arrival."

Enyl sprinted, not caring that he only wore sleep pants nor that his bare feet pounded the cold stone passageways. He burst into her chambers as an ear-piercing scream came from her bedroom. The chilling sound was something he never wanted to hear again.

He gritted his teeth, tensing his muscles as he readied to strike. How dare someone enter her chambers to harm her. But she was alone and thrashing on the bed. Tears flowed down her cheeks and incoherent words tumbled from her parted lips. He climbed onto the bed and hugged her, trying to convey some level of comfort. She struggled against him, pounding his chest, but he held firm, whispering soothing words as he stroked her back.

"Please, no." She jerked awake, rose to a sitting position, and forced him to lean back. In the dark, he caressed her arm to her face to cup her cheek, tugging at her bottom lip with his thumb.

"Oriana, *thamani*, it was a dream." His voice must have soothed her for she lay down.

"Enyl?"

"It is all right, *ensa*. Security let me in. You were screaming—"

"I tried, Enyl, but I can't." She slammed her fist into her palm. "I'm not strong enough." Anger and sadness drenched her tone.

His chest swelled, cinching his ability to breathe with ease. "We will do this together, *ensa ra ensa*."

She flung out her hands, searching for him, proving her human vision wasn't as good as an Etterian's. When she found his upper arm, she feathered her fingers across his skin, sending out bolts of fire. She caressed a path along his collarbone, down to his heart, and lower to brush his nipples. He hissed at the burning need piercing him.

"Enyl, why are you shirtless?" She shifted, stroking her silky-hot palm along his chest while layering his thighs with hers.

Her touch ramped his anticipation, broke his heart's steady beat, and intensified the unassuaged agony in his groin. His breath came in shallow gasps as his arousal hardened.

"Enyl?"

He snaked his arm around her, crushing her, unable to bear the teasing shift of her thighs, the softness of her belly against his, and the rise and fall of her breasts playing havoc across his skin.

"I…" He couldn't think why—his brain refused to focus.

She pinched his nipple between her fingers.

He jerked at the sweet torment. "Oriana…"

Something wet latched onto his nipple and sucked. His body shuddered with his arousal throbbing in his baggy sleep pants. "Did you just—?"

"Yes." She paused to place a kiss above his nipple.

"Lights," Enyl called. The room illuminated.

His breath caught as he marveled at the female in his arms. Her pale skin glowed a warm cream, and her eyelashes fluttered shadows across her cheeks. Her Ferusi green eyes didn't hide her desire for him, nor did she cover her bared legs, her exposed shoulders, and a part of a lush breast.

"Oriana," he rasped in agony, his voice unrecognizable.

He cupped her cheek and held her still as he feathered her lips with his. Her sigh of pleasure mirrored his. He stroked her cheek, along her neck, to the gaping wrap. On his journey down, he gathered the fabric, exposing the round, perfect globe of a breast.

"You are breathtaking." He brought his hand up to feather over her nipple. Her gasp shot straight through him, her back arched, and she thrust her breast into his palm encouraging him.

"Enyl, remember when you said I could ask for anything." She stilled, gripping his wrist. Her chest rose and fell in her breathlessness.

"Yes," he growled, loving how she reacted to his touch. Her breast swelled, and her nipple hardened against his palm.

"Please kiss me," she begged.

His startled gaze flew to hers. "No rare gems instead?" he teased and planted a kiss on her collarbone, a few more up her neck, and along her jaw.

"A kiss from you is worth a mountain of gems."

Dazzled, he met her intense gaze again, reading her need and affection for him. He caressed his lips across hers. She tasted of something decadent she must have had at dinner and the addictive flavor that was her. He needed to consume her, to absorb her essence into his body. His tongue conquered her mouth while he raised his hands to caress her breasts, his mind seeing her through the haze of white heat. He yanked himself back, panted for air, and fought for control.

"If you don't take me, Enyl, I will hurt you." Her threat was adorable. He laughed, tucked her under him, and wedged his hard arousal at the juncture at her thighs. That contact alone sent tremors through his body.

"Feel how much I want you, Oriana. To not claim you is to deny myself."

He spread kisses along her neck, across her collarbones, to her waiting nipples. She embedded her fingers in his hair, arching her back as she mewled. The spicy and exotic scent of her arousal filled the room but not his lungs. Not to his satisfaction. He inhaled, in desperation, loving the sweet musk of her.

"This evening will never be enough." He licked and sucked a nipple into his mouth, twirling his tongue around it.

She moaned, her hips thrusting upward, her demand clear.

"All the days in the universe are not enough," he said.

She splayed her hands over his back and scraped her nails down on a soft whimper.

He growled in pleasure, stilling to enjoy the spike of pain mixing with hot desire. "Please, Oriana, I need to taste you."

"Next time, I've waited too long. I need you, Enyl."

He gasped as the fire circling his groin burned hotter, rushing him to the edge. With a flick of his hand, the wrap opened, exposing her to his hungry gaze. Ripping off his pants, his arousal bounced free with exquisite torture.

He dragged his hand up her leg, from knee to well-toned thigh—so soft. Teasing her with his fingers, he touched her but not quite. She spread her legs wider, eager for the slightest attention. When he brushed her femininity, she jerked and cried out with such longing he couldn't torment her further. He dipped a finger into her wet channel, coating the tip before rubbing her bundle of nerves—his gaze never leaving her face, marveling at her unfettered reactions.

"You are ready for me, Oriana."

As soon as her mouth parted and her eyelids fluttered, he had found the spot that would drive her wild. He rubbed the pad of his thumb across it, unflinching in his resolve. Her body thrashed, her breaths came short and fast until she froze and exploded around him. At her cries of ecstasy, his arousal dribbled with need. He gritted his teeth, forcing his touch to remain gentle as he gripped her thighs to spread them wide.

"Oh, Maker." He positioned the head of his arousal at her entrance. Anticipating twitched it when he rested it there. Swirling her hips, she gasped, pleading under her breath. He couldn't make out her words and chose to believe it was pleading, but he never knew with her. She could be cursing him. He chuckled, loving this female spread out before him like his own personal feast.

"I am sorry, *thamani*, I cannot wait."

Her smile was encouraging, yet he hesitated. He was so much larger than her, perhaps caution was the wiser strategy. Pushing forward, he slipped into her. He growled, closing his eyes as his control shattered. She was so tight, with the heat of her almost unbearable. Her hips rose to meet him, the angle pulling him deeper into her. Squeezing her backside, he struggled to hold her still. Instead, he plunged in, embedding himself in her, breaching something in the process.

At her squeak, he froze, his gaze riveted to her face, searching for an ounce of pain. When she fluttered her eyes open and smiled, he released a sigh of relief and allowed himself to *feel*.

Ripples of tingling pleasure traveled his length. He arched his back on a groan. Alodon's balls, he had died. The unceasing, fiery, sweet sensations were incredible. The heated silk of her channel held him like a glove. He had never experienced this before—this softness, then her channel pulsed, massaging him.

"Damnit, Enyl. Move." She raised her heels to clasp his backside, her hips shifting so he sank in deeper.

He pinched his lips and opened his eyes. When he withdrew, more pleasure pierced him, wave upon wave of tingling, bubbling, hot water. His breath hitched. The second thrust was better, so he withdrew and thrust in again.

"Maker, Oriana. I am in paradise." He met her gaze, hoping to convey his desire and love for her.

With a lift of her hips, she flipped him onto his back. She straddled him, with him still inside her. He scowled, anger tightening his muscles, which she ignored, choosing instead to kiss him. While she twirled her tongue around his, she ground her hips, gyrated, and repeated, stroking and pumping the length of him. Lightning and explosions blurred his vision. His gasp merged into a moan and into a full-blown groan.

She sat upright and whimpered, thrusting her breasts toward him, her movements hypnotic. It built the pleasure into a sweet intense fire. He cupped her breasts, unable to deny the benefits of this new position or the realization of his vision. She stilled as did her heartbeat then she fractured, crying out his name, her channel clenched around him and shot him over the edge.

Stunned at the intensity, he gripped her hips and thrust upward. She screamed, thrashing under his demanding pace, her hair swirling around him, tickling his knees and stomach. He wrapped his arms around her, crushing her against him, and with one final thrust, the ecstasy flung him to the stars. He roared his pleasure. As the fulfillment faded, he slumped but kept her on top of him. Ripples of the exquisite sensations and the heat flowing off her body licked along his nerve endings.

In the darkness, a pale light shimmered into existence. He jerked and ran his gaze over his Dar Eth. What in Alodon's hell...?

"Ah, Oriana, why are you glowing?"

Pressing her hands to his chest, she pushed off him and held herself up as she flicked a wide gaze between their joined bodies.

"Why are you?" A pale white light burned around them. She shifted to climb off him, still impaled on his rigidity. Any movement she made sparked a fresh display of mini-cosmic explosions.

Enyl captured her hand and tugged, sprawling her across him. "Do not move. I like you right where you are." He dusted his mouth over her kiss-swollen lips, beginning to believe he would never tire of her taste.

She snuggled into his embrace and traced his nipple with lazy circles. "Enyl, we're glowing."

They were but rushing to Aldur would change nothing. This moment, their first union, was precious to him. "We will ask Aldur later. Right now, I want to hold you, *thamani*."

Her cheeks flushed a bright perske, but she fell silent. Peace like he had never experienced before, descended upon him. There were no words in the known languages that could describe what she invoked in him.

"Tell me, *ensa*, when I thrust into you, what did I breach? Will I hurt you every time?"

She rose to look at him, cupped his cheek, and kissed his chin. "I was a virgin."

His eyelids fluttered as his O.D.I. hurried to educate him. Emotions rose in a violent crescendo and stilled his heart for a moment. "You were untouched?"

"Yes." She kissed his nose and smiled. "And no, it won't hurt again."

He was unable to voice what roiled within him, nor did he know how to reveal it to her. When she lay her head on his chest again, he cleared his throat, hoping to break through the lump there.

"Did you find fulfillment again when I was in you?"

She hummed her answer, gave up on the circles, and flicked his nipple with her fingertip.

A familiar ache began in his loins. "How...how is this possible?"

She peeked at him and shrugged. "Human women can have external and internal orgasms and multiple times."

Her revelation widened his eyes. He grinned, eager to test this. "Truly?"

"As per my research, yes." She gave him a smirk, then kissed his chest before she pulled away from him. "Come, let's cleanse and go see Aldur."

"Do we have to cleanse?" Enyl leaped off the bed and tugged her into his arms, burying his face into her neck. "I like my scent on you."

She laughed. "All right, but you have to fuck me again later."

He grumbled as he yanked on a pair of breeches. "Oriana, when you talk like that, it makes me hard."

"Good." She left the room naked, heading for the replicator. Mesmerized, he didn't remove his gaze from her as he pulled on a tunic and his boots. He lagged behind her—still smelling of their union—and took the time to admire her in her garments.

"What are you wearing?" His voice had deepened, his arousal hard again and aching.

She wore tight blue breeches that hugged her magnificent legs. A thin white shirt hugged her torso and breasts, emphasizing the shape of her nipples, and leaving her arms bare.

"Jeans and a vest." She hopped on each foot to slide her footwear on. With the white glow forming an aura, her beauty snagged his attention. Her tousled hair draped around her, swaying in a similar fashion as when she rode him.

He growled, longing to strip her bare and spread her soft thighs again. "Let us be quick."

Guiding out the room, he ushered her to the medical barracks. Not many males would be awake at this hour, except for a small evening crew. But Aldur had quarters there. Enyl would have to break with protocol and escort a female into the barracks.

He pressed the chime, his vision sharper in the dark passage, aided by their combined glows.

Aldur opened the door instead of calling for them to enter. "My prince?" He wiped the sleep from his eyes. "What is that?"

Enyl frowned while Ori chuckled. "It is why we came to you."

"My apologies, my prince." Aldur darted into the passage to run his wrist over them.

Heat engulfed his palm, and Enyl glanced at their clasped hands, his fingers laced through hers. He couldn't remember when he had taken her hand, but he didn't want to lose her touch. This need to have her near had to be the Ethera.

"Do you feel anything? Overheated? With tingling anywhere?" Aldur typed onto his O.D.I., his fingers flying over the illuminated keys.

Ori gave Enyl a lustful perusal. "I *feel* some tingling," she said in a serious tone. "As soon as you're done with your preliminary assessment, Aldur, I'd like Enyl to do a more thorough examination."

Enyl sucked in a breath, wanting to throw her over his shoulder and sprint to her chambers.

Aldur's laughter kept this madness at bay, barely. "I will take these scans to the council. You are free to do your examinations, my prince."

Aldur grinned before leaving them in the passage. Sending the scans to all the senior medics, meant this was something unusual and required the extensive knowledge of the medical council.

"To your chambers this time?" She looped her arm around Enyl's waist.

His eyebrows shot up in surprise and pleasure as an indescribable yet familiar warmth filled him. "Yes," he said, his voice hoarse. "To *our* chambers, my Dar Eth."

ENYL AWOKE WITH A start. Sometime during the night, he had sprawled onto his back and now stared at the same ceiling as always. Yet, this morning, even though his surroundings were the same, he was different. There were strong emotions in his heart, where they had long been dormant. As he lay there, with his hands tucked behind his head, he analyzed them. Hope was strong—contentment, excitement, peace, with the longing and loneliness no longer evident. He searched for those dark whisperings, prodding his soul with a mental finger, and found them muffled.

A movement to the right of him drew his focus. He admired his sleeping Dar Eth. She had drifted away during the night and migrated back to his side. Enthralled, he watched her hand slide across the bed to find him, crawling up his chest to stay there. His heart leaped with happiness, falling into a staccato he couldn't and didn't want to regulate. Unfolding an arm to cup his hand over hers, he held it to his chest, capturing it. Her skin was soft and enticing, the scent of her as intoxicating.

"Morning," she mumbled.

"Morning, Princess." He smiled. Having taken her many times throughout the night, their combined sexual fulfillments still filled the room with an incredibly rich aroma.

She grumbled and kissed the underside of his elbow. The feathering of her soft lips across his skin shot darts of heat to his groin. A familiar ache intensified and tented the blanket draped over his hips.

"Want to cleanse with me this morning?" Stretching, she raised her arms above her head, lifted her breasts to an attractive angle, and jutted out her backside. She tempted him without realizing it.

"Are we going to cleanse or...?" His breath caught.

"Both." She blew him a kiss as she scooted off the bed and sashayed to the cleansing room. As soon as the water activated, he bounded off the bed with the blanket falling to the floor.

Entering the cleansing room, he paused to admire the water pouring over her curves, the rivulets caressing where he longed to touch. As her hands traveled where the water had flowed, he burst forward to pin her back against the wall. He captured her mouth with his to snatch her breath, her will. He roamed his hands over her body with a frenzied need.

Lifting her off her feet to pin her to the wall, he raised her so his hips forced her thighs apart for his arousal to nestle at her sex. She arched in response, her fingernails embedding in his shoulders as a throaty cry escaped her. He bent to suck on a pebbled nipple and moaned. The flavor of her hot skin burst across his tongue.

"Release your braid for me, Enyl. I want to bury my fingers in your hair," she commanded.

He growled and tugged off his metal tie, tossing it on the floor. His hair unwound by itself. She sighed with pleasure, buried her fingers into its depths, and scraped his scalp. An involuntary purr escaped him.

"It's beautiful, my Eth." Her voice was hoarse with need.

His hair swirled around him and brushed her fingers. With her distracted, he kissed a path down her stomach to her curls.

She stirred in alarm.

"You promised," he mumbled into her feminine lips, as he swiped a tongue up and over her nub.

Her sweet smoky flavor tore a shudder from him. The vibration of his voice would move through her, but he hadn't known it would make her gasp. Groaning again, he tested this theory, and she responded as expected. He ran his tongue over her hardening bundle of nerves, up, and down, rubbing across her nub, between her feminine folds, and into her channel.

Within moments, she was writhing, her hips thrusting forward. He slipped a finger into her at the same time he sucked her nub into his mouth for a deep suck. She shattered on a scream. Her nipples puckered, and a shiver ran down her body to her channel which spasmed around his thick digit. Removing his finger, he kissed along her hip, up her belly, to suck on a nipple, twirling it across the flat of his tongue. He held his hot mouth to the base of her throat, positioning his arousal at her sleek entrance, and thrust once, burying himself to the hilt.

She cried out, her hands fluttering over his shoulders and arms. The sensation of her was, as always, exquisite—tight, clenching, hot, and silky. Heaven.

He withdrew and plunged in, his movements rough with need. His thrusts became frantic, forceful, slamming her back against the wall, as he chased the pure joy his Dar Eth inspired. He slipped an arm around her to protect her as he continued to pound into her...driving the sensations through his body, alive with white-hot fire as shivers racked across his senses in anticipation. With a roar, he released into her, his body shuddering under the intensity.

The tingles subsided first, then the shivers, but the sweet lassitude remained. Shifting, he held her against the wall and cupped her cheeks. He stared into her green gaze, drowning in their beauty. Maker, she was everything he had ever hoped for in a Dar Eth. He snatched a kiss, nibbling on her swollen bottom lip, and listened to her ragged yet satisfied breathing.

WAVES OF BLISS DRENCHED Ori, narrowing in on Enyl's trembling hands and his thundering heartbeat. With exquisite tenderness, he pinned her to the wall, and feathered kisses along her jaw to her parted mouth, to kiss her, staring into her eyes. He lowered her feet to the floor, held her until she steadied, then rubbed her body under the shower's spray with his touch adoring. Wanting to do the same for him, she stroked where she could reach. She marveled at the firm, velvety texture of his muscles, at the heat of him that was hotter than a human's average temperature, at how sensitive he was to her touch as yet another wave of shivers racked him.

After switching off the water, he activated the air dryer. Pulling her against him amid the full hot blast of air, he kissed her, dueling his tongue with hers as the dryer worked. She had no concept of time as he kissed her, savored the taste of her, and kept her near to him. She did notice when it was no longer his hands and the air dryer stroking her skin. His hair, as soon as it had dried, undulated over her body.

"Enyl..." She sighed, content to have his hair show her affection. "It's incredible." Tendrils of his hair circled them, pulling them together. At their insistence, she laughed. Matchmaker hair? She couldn't find anything more alien than that.

"Even your hair seduces." She rose onto her tiptoes to kiss him, entangling her fingers in his hair at his temples, caressing it at the same time.

"The battleship *Chikara* awaits our arrival. We depart for Earth soonest." He buried his face in her neck then dusted kisses along her jaw to her earlobe. "We shouldn't delay any further."

"There is still time?"

"Time for?" He met her gaze, arching his brow when she winked at him.

"For breakfast, of course." She snatched a quick kiss.

Then with an elaborate sashay, she headed for the rehydrator, planning to eat breakfast in the nude. The *Chikara* wouldn't be seeing them before lunchtime if she had her way. She was addicted to him. Her body hummed with satiated and unfulfilled need. She couldn't get enough of him.

After how he had worshiped her and without having endured the Ethera tests, in her professional opinion, their compatibility was a done deal. No matter what those tests revealed, there was no way she was letting him go.

Chapter Twenty-Three

Etterian Battleship, Chikara
Orbiting Planet Etteria
Year of 2252, August

ORI TOSSED A GRIN over her shoulder at Coldar. He was well, with no more debilitating dizziness. So everything she had needed instruction on during their Yithian "vacation," he now made it his goal to ensure she improved. Sweat drenched her shirt to her skin. A hot cleanse was in her future.

She hadn't been this exhausted since Enyl had tested her skills.

While striding down a passage from the common to her quarters, she savored her trembling limbs and the burn of a good workout. Two thumps drew her attention. She spun and gaped. Coldar and Myan lay unconscious. Four Yithian soldiers raised their blasters. A split second after the yellow buttons on their weapons flickered, she dove at their feet, ducking under their blaster fire. She rose with swinging fists, tackling the nearest soldier, slamming her fists into his chest. Four against one were insane odds, but she had to try. It wasn't in her to go willingly.

In mid-kick, blaster stuns slammed into her. Fire exploded and spasmed her muscles, and she released a strangled garble as her jaw locked. She froze then collapsed, her vision blurring as a Yithian's face stopped an inch from hers as darkness consumed her.

She waded to the surface, blinking as she broke through her fuzzy mind. Her arms twinged, and her thoughts circled, unable to settle. Her instincts screamed something was odd. That made no sense, not when she was safe on an Etterian battleship. Her dormant instincts should have remained silent. Raising her head pulsed shards of fire behind her eyes, but she pushed past the pain to grimace at the dark metallic paneled walls illuminated by yellow lighting. Dismissing the décor was easy since everyone used Maloidian steel in spaceship construction. But she couldn't ignore the stench scorching her nostrils, like rotten eggs meets tinned fish. She knew it, was more than familiar with it. Yithians.

Unable to remember why her arms hurt, she studied them. Synthetic ties cutting into her skin at her forearms restrained her. She opened her hands to clamp around the arms of the chair...metal.

"What the..." Then her nose itched, doubling the fury scorching through her.

So, the bastards had finally recaptured her. She shook her head, trying to dislodge the remnants of "fuzzy brain."

"You are awake...good," a slimy voice hissed.

She leveled a glare on the speaker. "Good for whom?" Faking a dismal groan, she leaned over to bring her lips to her wrist. "Burn."

Whispered in a specific tone activated her O.D.I. overheating it to cut through the ties on her left forearm. Whimpering at the rising heat, she watched with morbid fascination as the O.D.I. melted her skin. Aldur would have to heal that later.

"Good for Yithia. You will once again earn our king many tokens."

This was about the arena. Dammit, she should have realized this. "You haven't gotten away with this yet."

"Empty threats," the Yithian lisped.

With her itchy nose twitching, she forced a sigh. Trying to scratch her nose with her shoulder, she analyzed the scene—one soldier to the right of her and two to the left. As soon as the O.D.I. broke through the tie, she would act. She had a plan—whether it was a good one, she would find out soon enough. Until she had her arm free, she had to keep the idiot focused on her and talking.

Tears prickled at the agonizing bursts of fire and the stench of her scorched flesh filling her nostrils. She bit the inside of her cheek to smother a scream.

Closing her eyes for a second, she sucked in calming breaths before settling her gaze on the operative. "I am certain King Urio would be most pleased with your success, Yithian. Unfortunately for you, kidnapping me has started a war."

"Nonsense. Etteria would not bother with a human female from HoSS." He sneered, and his tone grated her shredded control.

She released a long sigh, wishing she could pinch her brow where a headache was beginning to form. "That may have been true if I had not become Prince Enyl's Dar Eth."

The tie snapping overshadowed her climatic announcement. She scowled, unable to savor the speaker's reaction to her words. She leaned on the chair as leverage and swung out to kick the lone soldier. He slammed against the bulkhead and slid down. Where he landed, he remained, unmoving. Spinning back, she picked up the chair and spun it in a wide arc to take out the two soldiers. One had raised his blaster, and the other had inched toward the door. The blaster went flying as the chair's legs caught them, knocking them back.

The speaker smirked, revealing more of his sabretooth fangs. "Stupid Earthian, I could still blast you. Your defense is futile." Slapping the side of his blaster, he set it to red, his threat clear. Try anything again and he would kill her.

She held her free wrist against the still-bound arm while holding the chair, legs facing outward like a shield. Her O.D.I. needed time to burn through that tie, as well. Her every nerve focused on her arm, waiting for the tell-tale heat.

"Who are you, Yithian?" She gave him a pointed look. "I assume you are new?"

His frown encouraged her to continue.

"I'm the human woman Oriana McKenzie, Yithian arena champion, Dar Eth to the Crown Prince, and Princess of Etteria." By listing her titles, she hoped to buy time or distract him. "Do you think your blaster frightens me?" She curled her lip in disdain, though suspected her dramatic expressions were wasted on him. "You're the idiot. I hold in my hand a reflective surface."

When he glanced at the chair, she lunged with its legs outward, catching him by surprise and thrusting him back with enough force to unbalance him. As he stumbled, she punched him in his throat while she guided the heavy chair to the floor with it still attached to her hand. "Shoot me now, idiot."

Gasping his last breaths, he collapsed, his blaster sliding across the metallic floor.

She faced the two remaining Yithian soldiers crouched against the wall sporting cuts and bruises. "Two down, two to go?"

An animalistic roar echoed from the passage. Heavy feet pounded on the grated flooring. Enyl. It had to be him. Joy engulfed her, and with a beaming smile, she bounced on her toes.

She shrugged at the Yithian males. "Sorry, thought I would be able to spare your lives."

Enyl charged into the room, his handsome features dark with fear and twisted with rage. Without hesitating, he blasted the last two Yithians. He crushed her to him, squeezing the air out of her and testing the strength of her bones.

"What took you so long?" she said against his chest. Damn, she loved him—every warrior inch of him.

"Could you not have left me some?" Another Etterian burst in with his blaster raised, searching for a target.

"Sorry, I was trying to survive." She flicked a gaze at him, unable to face him since Enyl had her pressed against his chest. "Are you going to let me go, Enyl?"

"Never," he muttered, tightening his arms around her.

"How did you find me?" Her words soaked into his armor as she wrapped an arm around him for comfort. She wasn't going to complain about his too-tight hug when she loved being in his arms.

"We tracked your O.D.I." He kissed the crown of her head.

"Are all humans this much trouble?" The male chuckled, taking Enyl's blaster from him so he could hug her with both arms, which he did.

She couldn't breathe. "Yes," she sighed, content to let him suffocate her. His overwhelming affection and overbearing protection had to mean he cared for her more than the Ethera inspired. Hope that he loved her was swift to rear its formidable head.

His growl was the first indication his anger hadn't yet dissipated. "Oriana, I am furious with you."

"Why? I didn't ask for this." She rubbed her itchy nose across his right pec, still trying to tamp down her hope. And even if he didn't love her, she would relish every moment he acted like a boyfriend.

"You did not? Where are your guards?" He dipped his head to glare at her.

"Why would I need guards when I'm on an *Etterian* battleship in *Etterian* air space?" Her eyes bulged. "Enyl, I *did* have guards. Coldar? Myan?" She tried to step back, needing to rush to their sides, but his tight embrace didn't weaken.

"Alodon's balls." His eyebrows shot up in alarm. "Syna?"

"I will see to it, my prince." The seven-foot-tall male stomped out of the cell, tapping on his O.D.I. in an agitated manner.

She tugged, and wiggled, wishing she could move. Growling, she stilled and raised her face to meet his gaze. She wanted to rant at Enyl to release her, to help her find Coldar, but the stubborn angle of his jaw said it was futile.

"I received word of your disappearance. I did not know they were with you." He crushed her against his chest, burying his face in her hair. She huffed at having to kiss escape goodbye. "One day you will find yourself in trouble from which I cannot save you." He shuddered.

"I didn't start this, Enyl."

"No, you did not, but you took on four soldiers, Oriana. You may have thought your life worthless without your uncles, but you have me now. You react like you are still on your own. Any one of these fools could have killed you. I...I almost lost you today, *thamani*."

Her eyes widened at his heartfelt words and at the truth ringing in his voice. He was right to take her to task. She had rushed into danger, uncaring if death took her. Looking at her life from his perspective revealed a woman facing her own kind of void. She had gone through the daily motions with a smile, believing herself content, if not happy. When she had already succumbed to the loneliness, the anger, the sadness of grief. Her time at Universal Parts and Horizon was goalless. Deep in her psyche, she had no intention of living a long and fruitful life. To get through each day had been painful. Enyl had changed that for her.

She dragged the chair, scraping its legs on the metal floor, as a not-so-subtle reminder that he had yet to free her. "Untie me."

He jerked back then snapped the tie with his bare hands. She pinched her lips on a deep sigh and wrapped her arms around his waist. "All right, Enyl, no more stupid reactions, no more thinking I'm invincible."

He studied her upturned face, a question in his cerulean eyes. "Promise me, *thamani*." His voice was gruff with emotion—the depth of it stuttered her heartbeat.

"I promise." While offering him a confident smile, she hoped he didn't notice the tears stinging her eyes. She *did* love this big male. "We need to make an announcement. They didn't know capturing me would cause a war with Etteria." She nudged the dead speaker with her toe. Stealing a princess from any culture would result in a confrontation, no matter the species.

Enyl frowned then spoke into his O.D.I. before they ported to the *Chikara*. "We shall hold a ceremony for all the worlds to see my Dar Eth."

She scowled, but her O.D.I. distracted her with a message from Syna. Myan and Coldar had recovered from the blaster stuns. At the news, air rushed out of her. They were fine, unharmed. Twice the Yithians had attacked them because of her. It might be safer for them if Enyl assigned them elsewhere.

Wondering how best to broach the subject, she glanced at Enyl reading a similar communication. Syna was efficient. She would give him that. But when she opened her mouth to voice her concerns, she hesitated. Coldar and Myan wouldn't appreciate her suggestion for new guards, and she didn't want to endanger more warriors. The best solution would be to hold this ceremony as soon as possible, thus mitigating the risk. Parading in front of all the galaxies would be her first official event. Not that she knew what the ceremony would entail. Perhaps a formal announcement or a blood oath would suffice.

"About this ceremony, do I have to—?" She paused when she sounded like a whining teenager.

"It will be the announcement you suggested," Enyl growled.

Damn, couldn't he give her more detail? "But—"

"What now? Must you argue with me about everything, Oriana?"

With a furrowed brow, she studied his angry features. He had a right to be angry, fearful, and concerned. Did she want to debate this ceremony with him? After all, it had been her idea. She didn't have to control this aspect of her life, nor was the argument worth it. It would cost her nothing to do as he needed, to trust him.

And he did *need* her to do this. "As you command, Enyl."

When he gaped at her, she smothered a grin. She should surprise him more often.

"What?" He looped an arm around her to tug her against him.

"A ceremony would be far more romantic. I assume I'll need to wear a ceremonial dress?"

He shook his head.

She frowned. According to her studies, the ceremonial dress was required for such events.

"You have to present yourself to the court and Etteria with nothing to hide."

Her eyebrows shot up as ice slithered down her spine. "I'm to do this naked?" she squeaked.

He nodded with his shoulders slumping in defeat, then they shook, and amusement burst forth from him in a bold, full-bellied laugh.

Gasping at his unexpected sense of humor, she smacked him on the arm. "Damn, I almost believed you." She grinned, loving the dimples in his cheeks, his wide grin, and his rumbling laughter.

"I would never share what is mine." His fingers splayed across her back as he buried his face in her neck, kissing her there.

Cherished, protected, with his arms around her, warmth and contentment seeped into her soul, replenishing what was once arid. She would remain like this for as long as he wanted to, absorbing nourishment that only he could provide.

Chapter Twenty-Four

Etterian Battleship, Chikara
Orbiting Planet Etteria
Their quarters
12252 years, 8th month

ENYL AWOKE ALERT. HE paused to unravel what had disturbed his slumber while cuddling Ori, needing her soft skin against his. Burying his nose in her hair, his thoughts drifted. Until one blazed across his sleep-addled mind. The door had opened.

Frowning, he stilled, enhanced his hearing, and listened. Past Ori and his hearts beating in synchronicity, there were no sounds. A thick tension lingered, and his senses sharpened. He would have ignored them had Yithians not breached the battleships shielding. Until the lima kuu and data officers figured out how, it was best to pay attention when something seemed odd. He extracted himself from Ori's tender embrace, taking a second to pull the blanket over her.

Yanking on his trousers and his boots, he crept to the bedroom door. When he leaned against the bulkhead, he whispered, "Opacity zero."

The walls became transparent revealing the intruders on the other side. Yithian soldiers waited, inches from him. With their blasters raised, they prepared to storm his room. He glanced at Ori's sleeping form. Ice drenched his scalp, then ran down his neck and spine to his clenched fists. His body trembled with restrained fury.

Why were they still trying to capture her? She was special, but this level of effort was absurd. Especially from the Yithians. Had her arena presence been that lucrative? Or was Urio pissed Enyl had stolen her from him?

Enyl considered waking her. Unarmed, they were no match against Yithians with their blasters, and perhaps other weapons. But he didn't have long before they noticed the transparent walls. Tapping his O.D.I. three consecutive times, he activated the alarm, praying assistance would be forthcoming.

The soldiers stormed in. A solid punch to the gut of the first one took him down. Enyl had to avoid punching them in the face. He couldn't afford to lacerate his knuckles against their venomous teeth. Leaving him minimal options. Taking cues from Ori's fighting techniques, he kicked groins, knees, spots over their hearts, any part that was accessible to him. But when a Yithian leveled his blaster on Ori, Enyl tackled him to the floor.

"What the hell?" She bounded off the bed in her naked beauty to assist, taking on the next soldier stupid enough to charge.

A blaster fired, loud in the confined space. Ice turned to lead and sunk into the pit of Enyl's stomach when she collapsed, her hands sliding down the chest of the Yithian she had been fighting.

Pain, fear, denial coursed through Enyl's veins in a river aflame. He roared like a wounded wilanegy. They had killed his Dar Eth. If the blaster was set to Etterian levels, her human body wouldn't survive it. But there was still time. If the blaster shot didn't kill her, she might need immediate medical treatment.

He went berserk, killing as many as he could. But as agony exploded across his chest and froze his muscles, he tossed a longing glance at Ori before he dropped to the floor. Cold fire claimed his body, but it didn't compare to the ceaseless terror growing inside him. The fading of his vision to black echoed the expanding hole in his chest where his heart used to be. Nothing mattered anymore. He gave himself over to the welcoming arms of the void and the abyss of unconsciousness.

ENYL DRIFTED AWAKE. HE assessed his body, anticipating wounds, and encountered a sense of loss, so deep and so dark it snatched his breath away.

Oriana.

He tamped down the pain lancing through him and forced himself to breathe, to open his eyes. His brow furrowed as he blinked at his surroundings. The room he was in looked like an officer's quarters on an Etterian battleship.

"Opacity zero," he called out and the walls remained solid—a replica.

The Yithians were a greedy species, still, this was far beyond their usual effort. And to construct this illusion, to kill his Dar Eth, to capture him, the crown prince would start a war with Etteria.

The door opened with a strange sucking noise, one unlike theirs. The room looked Etterian-made but lacked the nuances. Either they had not done the research, or they constructed it in haste. Regardless, he wasn't on an Etterian battleship.

A large Yithian lumbered through the door. His impressive finery in black and silver—the royal colors—announced who he was. Enyl didn't need the garments to confirm his identity, having witnessed this Yithian's discussion with his father.

"Do you know what your people are doing, Urio?" Enyl arched a mocking brow.

"Do you?" The king's lip curled in derision, revealing his elongated teeth.

"Your soldiers tried to kidnap my Oriana a few days ago." He winced as he said her name, agonizing pain crippling him, snatching his ability to breathe. Maker, let the void take him now.

Urio dismissed his outburst with a flick of his three fingers.

"What is the meaning of this?" Enyl's anger mounted as each second passed. He was a proud, arrogant Etterian, one now driven by grief, fury, and darkness with nothing to lose, to live for. Standing there semi-clothed and unarmed didn't diminish the threat that he was. As a warrior trained to protect Etteria, he knew the weaknesses of all species in the known galaxies.

"Revenge—an Etterian should understand such a concept," the king hissed.

"My Dar Eth is dead for what imagined slight?" Enyl trembled with rage, tension hardening each muscle like he was on the verge of battle.

"You will join her shortly," King Urio said.

The ship shuddered to a halt. The lighting flickered to red, indicating life support only. Urio remained unconcerned by the immobility of his ship.

"I hope this was worth your death, Urio."

His gray skin darkened. "Yada is dead by Etterian hands. My death is nothing in comparison."

"Prince Yada is dead?" Enyl jerked back. "My condolences, Urio."

"You did not know?" The king's open disbelief wasn't a farce. A Yithian couldn't fake the paling of his black eyes.

"I had not heard he had died. May your blessed Calzantu welcome his soul."

Closing his eyes for a moment, Urio acknowledged the formal Yithian address for one grieving.

"Of all your sons, he was my favorite." Enyl spared the father before him a stiff nod. "He was quick to laugh. A trait we value."

"He was my favorite too." Urio's expression turned sour, curling his lips downward, split only by his descending teeth. "Did we kill your princess?"

Enyl gritted his teeth. "She received a blaster stun meant for me."

The king sighed. "For one as small as she—"

"Yes." Discussing it, forced Enyl to confront the reality of his loss, the darkness at the edge of his consciousness.

"I believe you killed Yada, and you believe I killed your Dar Eth."

"You have killed me like a blade to the heart, Urio. You have doomed me to the void." Enyl couldn't keep the agony from his voice. It ate at him until the need to sink into its depths was a balm to his broken heart.

"Your melodrama is not appreciated, Enyl."

"An overemotional Etterian?" Enyl glared.

"Point taken." Urio raised his gaze to the ceiling as another explosion jarred the ship. "I planned to have my operatives torture you, then toss your almost lifeless corpse at Xeus's feet."

Enyl winced, imagining the pain that would contort his father's face and perhaps drive him to succumb to the void. But Enyl would not beg for his life. Nor would he suggest a weaponless battle. Hand-to-hand combat with a Yithian Urio's size might be more than Enyl could handle, never mind the political fallout should either kill the other.

But Etterians males were onboard, wreaking havoc. He need only wait. "Release me, and I will spare your life."

Urio hissed at his arrogance. "On *my* ship, surrounded by *my* soldiers? You must be held accountable for Yada's life."

Blood for blood, Enyl could understand that. "You will pay for Oriana's."

The ship shuddered again, and this time with the loss of gravity flicking the lights to blue. Enyl activated his boots, attaching him to the floor. In slippers, Urio floated toward the ceiling, glaring at Enyl who remained static.

"Your ship is crippled, Urio. You cannot hope to succeed in this foolish endeavor. Investigate whether we are involved. It is not in Etteria's best interest to kill your son." As red to blue to red of the emergency lighting painted Urio's face, Enyl grimaced. "My father is on the Global Council, and any attacks on its representatives or their families are forbidden." Not that Malo had yet to find out who had exploded a hole in Enyl's hull. He didn't care when it had led him to find Ori.

He dropped his chin to his chest, letting a tear slip free.

"Are you implying my operatives deceive me?" Shadows circled Urio's black eyes. "Who would dare?"

"I merely suggest you investigate. I will do so from my side."

Throwing out a hand to stop himself from banging into the ceiling, Urio laughed. "I must trust you when I came to kill you?"

"Killing me will not bring Yada back. A war with Etteria, is that what you want? Millions of your people dying for what, Urio?" Alodon's hell, but this male was stubborn. But in his dark eyes, sadness lurked, as it did in Enyl's heart.

The door opened to a few angry Etterians.

"My prince." Myan rushed in, aiming his blaster at the floating king. "Are you well?" His gaze ran over Enyl's length, searching for injuries.

"I am as well as expected—King Urio needed to talk." Enyl gestured a farewell.

"I mean to avenge Yada's death," Urio threatened. "This is not the end, Enyl."

"I may still blow your ship, Urio," Enyl said, his tone hard. "Your death means nothing to me, and decimating Yithia wouldn't bring me joy either. But I will do both if you test me."

"You cannot penetrate our oceans," Urio smirked, revealing a serrated tooth.

"We can destroy your suns."

Urio pinched his lips, hiding his teeth while his eyes faded to gray.

Supreme Commander Syna stormed into the room, stomping his great boots. Perhaps he could battle Urio and win, but with the energy draining from Enyl's shoulders, he wouldn't suggest the match.

"We have crippled the ship." Syna's voice boomed off the metallic walls. "Without assistance, the survival probability of the remaining Yithians is minimal."

"Have my males deactivate their teleportation engines and any cannons on board." Enyl raised his gaze to Urio's. "Return the shop to full function. Urio has an investigation to perform."

Enyl gestured to Myan to lead the way. In silence, they strode along the quiet passages to the breach and tether. When he stepped onto Etterian "soil," he faced Myan and Syna. "I assume you received my alert and tracked it?"

"Of course—Supreme Commander Syna should receive the honor for his prompt response while Coldar and I attended to Ori."

Enyl trembled at the mention of her name. "I want this investigated. Twice, Yithians have breached our shields. I want to know how."

Syna nodded. "I will comm Malo."

"And look into Urio's claim that we killed Prince Yada. I do not appreciate being held accountable for a crime I did not commit." Enyl pinched and released his brow, unable to hold back the burning pain behind his temple.

Myan gripped Enyl's forearm to force him to meet his gaze. "Ori still sleeps—Medic Cento has not been able to wake her."

Enyl froze, tilting his head to sharpen his hearing. He grabbed Myan by his shoulders to shake him. "She is not dead?"

When Myan shook his head, Enyl roared his surprise as pleasure rushed through him, hot and breathtaking. He burst into a sprint, shoving males aside in his haste to reach medical then halted at the sight of his Dar Eth on the bed. He had never known such happiness and didn't care that a tear traced a path down his cheek. With cautious steps, he circled her, fearing she might disappear.

"I believed the stun had killed her." He wrapped his trembling hand around hers, the soft warmth of her did more to appease the Ethera than the sight of her had.

"Her heart rate is good, her breathing is regular, and her brain functions are normal." Cento frowned. "Yet she does not wish to awaken, my prince. She still glows, which I believe is a good sign."

Enyl flashed a huge smile, so incongruous in the light of her condition. She was alive. Shifting closer, he leaned across her to sweep a kiss over her parted lips. He paused to inhale her breath, her soul, her scent.

"Oriana, *thamani*, I am pleased you are with me," he whispered, running his fingers through her hair. Her chest rose and fell. He had never seen anything more beautiful. Coldar or Myan had clothed her. Even in her condition, Enyl didn't want his males to see what was his—the Maker's gift to him.

"Her heart rate increased as soon as you spoke, my prince." Cento bounced, tapping on his O.D.I. with exaggerated movements. "Please, keep talking to her."

He did, for each second, every hour, and entire days. Sitting beside her, he squeezed her hand and caressed her face. Until his voice was hoarse, exhaustion slumped his shoulders and dulled his thoughts. If pressed, he couldn't recall when he had last eaten or cleansed.

"Forgive me, my prince, but as your medic, get out." Cento stormed, snapping Enyl from his dozing. "If you do not see to your own health—" The older male sucked in a sharp breath before softening his voice. "Please, my prince, cleanse, eat, and sleep, for at least an hour or two."

"May I carry her to our bed?" Asking instead of acting on a need, want or decision, as a prince would do, surprised the medic, and the male fumbled, dropping the med-gun. Enyl grunted, aware his behavior was abnormal. Yet he couldn't bring himself to care.

Cento scanned his arm across hers. "I will monitor via her O.D.I.."

Enyl scooped her off the bed and carried her to their quarters, stripping her to lay her on the bed. He cleansed, ate something, and slipped onto the bed beside her, pulling her into his arms. With them both naked, the skin-on-skin contact soothed him, despite her proximity arousing him. Moaning, he buried his nose in her hair and let sleep claim him.

Chapter Twenty-Five

Without opening his eyes, Enyl gathered Oriana close to him, engulfed by her unique and addictive scent. Her heart thumped a steady rhythm, and her breathing was gentle in sleep. Having her near infused him with peace and tension eased from his limbs. She had yet to wake, but he wouldn't stop searching for a way to bring her back to him. He would never forsake her, not when she needed him. With a sigh, he crushed her to him, wrapping his arms around her body to bury his nose in her neck.

Not used to sleeping in, he climbed off the bed, cradled her to his chest, and strolled to the cleansing room. Careful with her in his arms, he activated the water.

He washed every inch he could reach, hoping the water would rouse her, but she didn't. With an unhappy rumble, he stepped out of the water and into the path of the dryer. Her head fell back, tilting up her face. Sadness trembled his cheeks before he brushed her parted lips with his. He kissed along her jaw to her earlobe, and up to her temple. Then feathered kisses over her brow, where furrows formed when she frowned. How he would love to see her do so again.

He dusted his lips from her cheek to her neck and pressed an open-mouthed kiss there. With a flick of his tongue, he measured the rhythm of her pulse on the tip of it. Her heart skipped a beat proving she knew what he was doing. Crushing her to him, he chanted her name. He roamed his hands up her back, disappearing them beneath the silken waterfall of her hair.

With her in his arms, he strode to their bed with an idea forming. If she reacted to his kisses, maybe he would continue to torment her. Hope blossomed as he stretched out beside her, rising on one elbow to look upon her. He fitted his mouth over her parted lips, slipped in his tongue to rediscover the contours within. It was strange to kiss her when she didn't respond, didn't participate. Teasing her parted lips with his, he inhaled her breath hoping to capture a piece of her soul, and pretended to kiss her but not fully. After doing this a few times, he watched unblinking as a wave of shivers rippled across her skin.

He grinned before lowering his mouth across hers again. His eyelids fluttered against the sheer joy that burst through him. For a few minutes, he lost himself as he tasted and toyed with her lips, grimacing when he crashed back to reality. He had to remain focused on her and not the pleasure touching her aroused in him.

Leaning back, he studied her features, her parted lips, the gasps coming from her, the erratic pounding of her heart. Her tongue dipped out to lick her bottom lip. He couldn't stop his triumphant smile. With a husky chuckle, he claimed another kiss before glancing at her face again, but her eyes remained shut.

He kissed, withdrew, and teased until she whimpered her frustration. When she made no other noise and her heartbeat calmed, he began the process again—to tease her lips and run kisses along her neck. He feathered his lips across her eyelids, willing her to awaken, before slashing his mouth over hers, his tongue thrusting in, demanding a response and her participation. She sucked in a breath but didn't move otherwise.

"Ori." He roared his anger, and with much impatience, pinched a nipple between forefinger and thumb, squeezing it.

She cried out, arching into his hand.

Stunned she reacted so beautifully, he splayed out his palm. As a reward, he rubbed her breast, squeezing gently. Any movement from her was a good sign, encouraging him to be bolder.

This time, when he kissed her, she grumbled something at him, snagging his gaze and snatching his breath. But she slept on.

"Oriana, please, awaken for me," he pleaded, his voice guttural with the overwhelming desire to take her, and the emotional need for her to return to him.

She had to respond, to kiss him back. What he craved was to taste her until her moans vibrated his tongue. What he needed was for her to awaken. He had two options: to leave, calm himself, and return to try again, or to tease her, tempt her, and force her to awaken.

He didn't like her lying there and couldn't bring himself to kiss her lower than her neck, not without her participation. His arm buzzed with a message from Cento. Enyl was to repeat whatever he was doing.

He grunted at the medic's words, then punched the bed, roaring his frustration.

Sprawling over her body, he pressed his length onto hers but supported his weight on his elbows. Where her skin touched him, the heat and softness tempted him. He kissed her again, putting in as much passion as a one-sided kiss could have. Frantic, he threaded his fingers through her curls at her temple but couldn't put into words what she meant to him.

Using his lips to show his adoration, he lost himself in kissing her. He was nibbling at her nipples when reality descended. The desire and craving for her did not cease to bombard his senses. The aroused scent of her demanded he surrender to the need. The sharp, constant throbbing in his loins he would bear for eternity if it brought her back to him.

"Don't stop." Her hoarse voice immobilized him and strangled the breath in his throat.

He raised his gaze, his eyes wide with hope. "Oriana." He was too emotional to say more, so he claimed her mouth with such happiness and gratitude. When her tongue dueled with his, he groaned in satisfaction. Now, this was a kiss.

"Kiss me again, Enyl," she said into his mouth.

His body shuddered at the intensity in her voice—her need called to him. She raised her arms to drape over his shoulders gripping him against her softness.

"Please, Enyl," she begged, arching into him, rubbing her breasts against his chest.

His eyes fluttered. She was well, alive, and in his arms. The elation was beyond his ability to handle, bright waves of unadulterated joy engulfing him, trembling his limbs, snatching his breath. Slipping his arms around her, he crushed her to him, relishing the life that coursed through her.

"Welcome back, *thamani*." He kissed her, reclaimed her, and rejoiced in her passionate response.

"Welcome back?"

Her brow furrowed. Sighing, he placed a reverent kiss over the creases on her forehead. He flipped over to lie on his back, positioning her to spread across him. Her hair fell around them like a fiery curtain.

"What do you remember last, Oriana?" Unable to stop himself from touching her in some way, he threaded his fingers through her curls.

She squinted her eyes while pursing her lips. "Fighting Yithians...here, in our bedroom." She glanced around the room, finding no evidence of such an intrusion.

"You were blaster-stunned and have been asleep for days." Closing his eyes, he offered a prayer to the Maker to never let him suffer like that again. He was a strong Etterian male, capable of extreme violence, yet his Dar Eth revealed how vulnerable he was.

She gasped with her fingers digging into his chest. "I was? So, there *were* Yithians? I didn't dream it?"

"You did not." Dream? More like a nightmare, for him.

"I'm sorry." Her shoulders slumped, and she dipped her head. "With you beside me, I was untouchable." She raised her gaze to meet his, sorrow dulling her green eyes. "Was anyone harmed? Where are they now?"

"*Thamani*, do not bear this burden. They wanted me this time." He grimaced and updated her on what had happened since she lost consciousness.

"What did Xeus say?" Her gaze darted over his face, concern stiffening her body. She reached across and laced her fingers through his, giving him a squeeze.

He released a shuddering breath, having postponed informing his father his new daughter may die. Enyl hadn't given a damn about Urio and the threat of war. Etteria was no longer his priority.

"I have not commed him."

She frowned. "Why not?"

"Oriana, my Dar Eth, I thought you had died. You have been my sole focus." His arm buzzed with a message from the medic. "I will comm him now. The medic is on his way to examine you now that you are awake."

He jumped up, and under her admiring gaze, tugged on a clean pair of military pants and a fresh tunic. "Do you want a wrap, or do you plan to let the medic see you naked?"

She huffed, shook her head, and on tentative feet, shuffled to the bedroom door. Trailing her fingers along the bulkhead, she headed for the cleansing room to grab a wrap. In time, for when the door chimed, she emerged covered.

"I am pleased to see you awake, my princess." The medic hovered until she assumed a comfy, then circled her with his wrist raised and his O.D.I. flickering.

Enyl offered both his back as he commed his father.

"Enyl? Are you well? How is my daughter?" Father's booming voice pierced the room the second he accepted the communication request.

"I'm well, Father." Ori waved.

"I am pleased to hear so, Oriana. Supreme Commander Syna updated me on what has occurred." Father arched a brow at Enyl, implying he should have told him.

Enyl scowled. When his father had his Dar Eth, then he would understand. "Urio believes we killed his son." He framed it as a statement and not a question.

Ori gasped, but her attention focused on Father, her eyes widening. Enyl let his gaze linger on the gentle curve of her face and the pink in her cheeks.

"Humans did." Father's shoulders slumped. "Supreme Commander Xan encountered a Yithian slave ship reclaimed by three human females and two Durns. One of the females shot Yada with a blaster. Xan destroyed the ship in an attempt to keep the human involvement secret. If the Yithians discovered the humans killed their prince, they would target Earth."

"A war with us would be a safer alternative." Enyl nodded. The Etterians bred for war and had advanced weaponry savage enough to decimate worlds. But Earth was defenseless.

He hadn't lied, but Urio would not see it as such. If Etteria garnered Earth's trust, they would reveal the impending danger. Settling his gaze on Ori sipping coffee, with renewed determination, he tightened his jaw. He would battle the combined forces of the universe if it meant more of his males found their soul's salvation.

Chapter Twenty-Six

Etterian Battleship, Chikara
Their quarters
One week later
Halfway to Earth

ORI FOUGHT AN EYEROLL, wishing like millions of human women, she could cancel her periods. The interest her monthlies generated was downright absurd. At least, her cheeks no longer burned.

"What do you mean by this, Oriana?" Enyl ran his hands through his unbound hair, which swirled around him in agitation. With his muscular frame, it was beautiful when it undulated. "Why can I not have you now? Your scent is deeper, incredibly rich, and more tempting than before."

"I'm not punishing you, *ensa*. It's my *period*." Saying the word didn't garner an eye flutter, and the O.D.I.'s delayed instruction didn't calm Enyl. At his blank expression, she sighed. "My uterus is shedding its lining. Repeat after me—menstruation cycle."

"Menstruation cycle." His eyelids fluttered as the O.D.I. bombarded him with images and explanations. His expressions vacillated between shock and horror, yet confusion still furrowed his brow. "What does that mean?"

She leaped off the bed to show him the blood on her sani-pad as evidence.

He jerked, and his cheeks grayed. "I am summoning the medic."

She grabbed his wrist to stop him, not in the mood to explain this to yet another dense Etterian male. "Oh, hell no. Give me five days, and I'll be fine."

"You are bleeding." His bellow vibrated the bulkheads.

Wincing, she tried not to let his upset get to her. His deep concern was touching. "Come, sit." She patted the bed. "Let me explain it again."

When he hesitated, she smothered a chuckle with a cough. He sat on the edge of their bed, but his agitation remained in his twitching fingers and stiff shoulders. "Once a month, my body sheds my womb or uterus lining, hence the blood. It's not much, only looks like it. The blood shows human females that they're not pregnant."

"Pregnant?" He repeated the word and waited for his O.D.I. to provide an explanation. His eyes widened. Lessons learned. She should have introduced the subject in small amounts. "As in with *damu*?"

"Yes. If I was...with *damu*, I wouldn't bleed. My fertilized egg would've attached to my uterus lining."

"Are you're saying you are fertile every month?" He gaped, gripping her elbows to keep her still. His incredulity bothered her.

She frowned. "Well, for approximately one week a month. Why's this surprising?"

"Our females are fertile one month a year." He grinned, sliding his hands up and down her arms.

She gasped. "What? Why don't I know this?"

He squeezed and released her elbows. "Anything reflecting or impacting Etteria's decline is not documented."

"One month?" She wiped a stray tear. As much as she would have loved one period a year, it explained why Etterian females' struggled to bear children.

"Maker, Oriana, I would love to see you swollen with my son." At his emotional outburst, her mouth fell open, despite the warmth blossoming in her chest.

Tendrils of fear tightened, darkened, that she could lose another loved one. Running her gaze over the powerful male before her, she shoved those fears aside. Not only would he protect her and their children with his life, but so would all of Etteria.

"You want children? With me?" She smothered the hope he might love her, and that this might be the moment he confessed how he felt.

"Oriana, you are my Dar Eth. We are forever bound."

Stiffening as cold chilled her heart, she pulled away. Of course, the Ethera. She was nothing more than a means to an end. Or in this case, a means to a not-end. "So, if the Ethera wasn't between us, you'd feel nothing for me, Enyl?"

"What kind of a question is that? The Ethera binds us. There is no what if—"

"What I'm trying to ask…is it just the Ethera between us?" She used "between," he used "bind." To halt the burgeoning tears, she squeezed her eyes shut. She was overly emotional, but she didn't know how to make him understand she needed more from him. Her uncles had left a massive gap in her education.

"Just the Ethera?" He gaped. "Oriana…"

With a tug, she was in his arms, close enough for strands of his hair to caress her face, to bury themselves in her hair, and to curl around her arms, pulling her against him. They released her to wrap around her, cocooning them together.

"Our bodies chose each other, and the Ethera enhances the attraction. I admired you from the moment you commanded me to let you examine the damage on the Kevol. When you revealed your green eyes, Maker, the sight of them still snatches my breath. You are my life force. Without you, I cannot truly live. Without you, I choose not to live."

At his declaration, her heart pounded a tribal rhythm. What did he mean? He found her attractive, desirable, and had chosen not to live without her, not that the Ethera would let him. Was that his idea of love? And perhaps there was something to his belief that the Ethera enhanced his initial emotions.

She snuggled into his embrace, content to wait. There was bound to be misunderstandings, and if she looked back at his reactions, affection for her was in each expression and thoughtful gesture.

"Do I have to be the princess?" The responsibilities accompanying the position intimidated her. The thought of all those lives depending on her for guidance had oily fear coiling in her stomach. She didn't need nausea along with her monthly.

He chuckled, rubbing his jaw along the top of her head. "Yes, and future queen."

Releasing a shuddering breath, she went with honesty. If there was the slightest chance she could keep him without the crown... "I only want you, Enyl."

He stilled, dipped his head to meet her gaze, then growled, slashing his mouth across hers.

She whimpered, the taste of him excited her nerve endings, with wave upon wave of anticipation and desire melting her will.

"I only want you too, Oriana." His breath teased her tingling lips before he kissed her again.

Etterian Battleship, Chikara
Their quarters
Five days later and after dinner.

ORI FROWNED, NOT SURE what had set Enyl off.

"You want to do what?" he boomed, his eyebrows an inch from touching his hairline.

"Females aren't permitted on Gikaet, but I thought you'd make an exception for me. You see, Coldar and I made a promise to each other. When we escaped the arena, we would drink fruity beverages and test our mettle against a Gika."

Despite sounding patient, she was far from it. She gripped the denim of her jeans, purging the unspent energy of impatience in one gesture. Why couldn't he let her do this? Why did it matter that she was a female?

"At the same time?" His face grayed beneath his bronze skin, but it didn't detract from his crystalline blue eyes.

Seeing her chances at killing a Gika slithering out the door, she sighed. "Of course not, I'd get acid in my drink." She shook her head like he were the insane one.

Why was this so hard for him to understand? He hunted Gika. She was skilled enough to fight alongside him. Did he doubt his ability to protect her if the shit hit the fan? She pushed that silly thought aside. No way would an arrogant, skilled Etterian male doubt himself.

"No...just no." His chest rose and fell as he struggled to breathe. What mattered to him more? Her wanting to kill Gika or breaking their honored tradition of no females on Gikaet?

She wasn't prepared to give up yet. She pleaded with her partner, tossing him a sweet smile. "Coldar, please talk to him." When he shook his head, she scowled instead. "Dammit, why am I the one asking here? You made the promise too. I'm not alone in this."

"I did not think we would survive, and it is his right to protect you, *ensa*. What you ask of him goes against the code." Coldar's grin was unrepentant. He was enjoying seeing her in this situation, the idiot.

"I wasn't going to go without him." She pouted, peering up at Enyl with what she hoped was an adorable face.

He grunted but said no more and didn't tug her in his arms. For an unknown reason, he liked touching her, keeping her near him, and sneaking kisses into her hair. She preferred that side of him—a softer, grateful male who had found his Dar Eth. Him not touching her said much about the level of his fury.

"Imagine, Enyl, you and I battling Gika side by side." She pressed against him to run her hands over his shoulders and down his bare biceps. The velvet texture of him made her shiver in anticipation. Her body reacted to him like someone thrumming an ancient musical instrument. "We'll make an incredible team, and in bed at the end of a victorious day—"

"You cannot use your body as a bargaining tool," he said, but by the twisting of his lips and the intensity in his gaze, she tempted him. He buried his fingers into her hips, tugging her closer. Sighing, she hid a blissful smile in the curve of his neck.

Leaning back, she gave him a heated look that never failed to arouse him. "I'm not using mine. I'm using yours."

He gasped, his cheeks darkened, and his fingers twitched.

Now for the perfect line... "I'm addicted to you, my Eth."

He groaned and released her hip to run a hand over his face.

Myan laughed. "You are doomed, my prince."

She didn't look at him, although, mesmerized by Enyl's eyes, she'd forgotten they weren't alone.

"It is still a no. I will not allow the female I love to battle a Gika. Not for anything in all the known galaxies," Enyl roared, his chest heaving with emotion even as the hand gripping her hip remained gentle.

At her sharp inhale, he glanced at her with an arched brow. She trembled. Her ears roared, deafening her. What had he said? Shaking her head to clear her hearing, she took the opportunity to suck in controlled breaths, hoping to assuage the burning in her chest. Her face fluctuated between cold and hot as she squeezed and released his biceps.

"You love me?" she squeaked. She hurried to clear her throat. Without blinking, she didn't look away from his face. Her heartbeat paused in anticipation. Dread and excitement exploded in her belly like a thousand sparks from a multi-tool.

He frowned with his face twisting in confusion. "Yes."

Her joy burst, raining inside her with light, warmth, and the sweetest of happiness. She gave him a beaming smile before she threw herself at him, wrapped her legs around his hips, and looped her arms across his shoulders.

He caught her with ease and crushed her to his chest. Down he slid his hands to knead her ass. She smashed her lips to his, kissed him with all the intense emotions roiling within her, savored his unique flavor, and relished how it saturated her senses.

"Let's make love like there's no tomorrow," she whispered into his mouth, her erratic breathing matching his.

"And…that's our signal," Coldar said before he and Myan escaped their chambers.

The door opened and shut, but she didn't bother to watch them leave. She kept her focus on Enyl's beautiful eyes.

Leaping off him, she stripped off her boots, shirt, and jeans, sighing at the cool air on her flushed skin. She unclipped her bra and shimmied her panties off, tossing the garments to the side, not caring where they fell.

"I do not understand." He blinked, no doubt reeling from her emotional changes.

His gaze lingered on her naked body, but he hesitated. He needed to understand what she was thinking. She could read him so well. He was unable to fathom what had brought on a quickie and the hasty exodus of her guards.

"Which part?" She strode toward him, swayed her hips, and bounced her breasts for maximum effect. His breath hitched, then he released it on a growl. She grinned as his arousal hardened to its full length, bulging his military pants.

"Why the need to 'make love?' You were adamant you were going to Gikaet."

She laughed, unable to contain the happiness bubbling out of her. Cupping his cheek, she rose onto her toes to press a tender kiss to his mouth, loving the hot softness of his lips. "I love you too." When his eyes widened with joy warming their depths, she smiled.

With another growl, he yanked her to him, grabbed her ass cheeks, and lifted her to meet his kiss.

She saw stars and implosions for three hours.

"Do we have to travel to Gikaet?" Sprawled naked on their bed, he twirled a pattern around her puckered nipple, trying to hide his troubled expression.

She adored him for wanting to please her, but his need to protect her tore him up. Who knew that fearless Etterian warriors were like engine lubricant inside, soft and gooey. "No, I don't need to kill a Gika. I want to please my Eth, my husband, my love."

He claimed her mouth with a forceful kiss as he slid his hand over her stomach to her damp curls. Fire trailed his fingers, and her greedy body throbbed for more of that delicious ecstasy he roused in her.

"Besides, I'm not strong enough to lift a greatsword." Her voice broke on a long gasp as he breached her lower lips with the gentlest of touches.

"Oriana, I love you, with or without the Ethera," he said in a serious tone.

She stilled and twisted to cup his cheeks as an unbidden tear escaped her.

"How do you know exactly what to say, my Eth?" She pulled him down for a thorough kiss, slow, heated, and reverent. "How about we work on a child instead?"

He stiffened and, with a deafening roar, spread her thighs and entered her in one smooth, powerful thrust. Her head rolled back as a moan tore from her. She was going to die from the pleasure...but what a way to go.

Glossary

Etterians worship one God, one Maker, since the universes have only His fingerprint on all of it, a single golden thread through all of creation.

Tokens: intergalactic form of currency

Kliks: predetermined length of distance.

Hatimaye – To bring an end (Hutt-ee-my-ee)

Etterian

Alodon (A-low-donn): who accidentally shot his balls off with his own blaster.

Teacher: lima (lee-ma)

Great teacher: lima kuu: (lee-ma koo)

Directions: semit (semm-it)

Lemon: giyua (gee-you-a)

Young one: damu (daa-moo)

Heart: ensa (enn-sa)

Heart of my heart: ensa ra ensa (enn-sa raa enn-sa)

Beloved: thamani (ta-mar-nee)

Little joy: minus susa (mee-nas soo-sa)

Little cat: minus cesu (mee-nas sess-oo)

Large: magnus (mag-nis)

Orgasm: fulfillment/deite asteri (see stars) / released (day-ta ass-tare-ree)

Starfighter: asteri peju (ass-tare-ree pear-joo)

Collection of glass vials: virak (vee-ruck)

Scum of the galaxies: xemi (ze-mee)

Hair up: malia pa (Mar-lee-a par)

Hair down: malia pado (Mar-lee-a par-dow)

Lysaran

Visitor: kashi (Kaa-shee)

God: Kaiha (Kigh-haa)

King: Kuna (Koo-na)

Orange fleshy fruit: Lemte (Lem-ta)

White flowers: Myameru (My-a-me-roo)

Precious: Delica (Dell-ee-ka)

Sweetheart: Sali (Saa-lee)

Arum Lily-type flower: D'nastu (D-nass-too)

Love Blossom: aroa loulu (A-row-a low-loo)

Maloidian

Title of respect: lommia (Lomm-ee-a)

Stubborn, lethal tree: tewaa (Tee-wah)

Tokauri/Kulai

Blade – Sulac (soo-lack)

Bone – Ukog (you-cog) - bone from some dumb animal, probably an ukog.

Braided – Gisul (gee-sool)

Father – Danno (dan-no)

Heart – Kassu (cass-soo)

Maker – Mugbu (Mug-boo)

Mother – Manno (man-no)

Sapphires – Buha (boo-ha)

Shit – Saho (sa-ho)

Star - stuon (stoo-on)

Stupid – Ungog (oon-gog)

Vessel/ship - sakay (sa-kay)

Pronunciations

Names

Aaro - Ah-row

Adda – Ay-dah

Aldur - Al-durr

Alllero - A-le-row

Balllio – Bah-leee-oh

Bos - Boss

Bry-dar - Brigh-darr

Brynr - Brin-ner

Cales - Cale-es

Cento - Sen-tow

Citus - Sigh-tuss

Coldar - Coal-daar

Cria - Kree-ah

Eriz - Sigh-low

Danic - Dan-eek

Deeezo – Dee-zoh

Der - Durr

Diso - Dee-sow

Diyo - Die-oh

Eira - Eye-raa

Enyl - E-neel

Eriz - E-rizz

Garix - Ga-ricks

Gayn - Gain

Iddan - Ee-dann

Idon - Eye-donn

Illan - Ee-lann

Jarg – Jar-g

Jokta - Jock-tar

Kanzo - Can-zow

Keelu – Key-loo

Keryr – Kerr-eer

Ksal - Ka-sell

Lazu – Lah-zoo

Lurz - Lurr-z

Malo - Mail-oh

Matir - Mat-teer

Myan - My-ann

Myn-ras - Min-russ

Naio – Nay-oh

Nerx - Nurcks

Nuos - New-oss

Oyaz - Oh-yaz

Prex - Precks

Ronin - Row-nin

Saan - Sarn

Sena - See-na

Sy'mar - Sigh-marr

Syna - Sigh-na

Tamra – Tum-rah

Taro - Tah-row

Tenu - Ten-oo

Trav - Trahv

Tinh - Tin

Vytus - Vie-tuss

Vodin - Vo-din

Ulriq - Yule-rick

Vorn - Vawn

Vyar - Vie-arr

Xan - Zan

Xeus – Zeus

Zaro - Zah-row

Ziot - Zye-ott

Places

Argaxx – Are-jax

Crustiiu – Criss-tee-oo

Dyuqa - Dee-you-ka

Etteria – E-tare-rea

Galaza – Gah-Lar-Zah

Gikaet – Gee-ka-ett

Iphara = Ee-far-ra

Kulai – koo-ligh

Lysara – Liss-saa-ra

Mascroba – Mus-crow-ba

Resia Cay – Ress-Ee-ahh Kay

Sarvis – Sarr-viss

Sosu – Sow-soo

Tokauri – Too-cow-ree

Yithia – Yith-ee-a

Battleships

Chikara – Chee-kar-a - Force

Gladio – Glad-ee-oh - Sword

Kushin – Cush-shin - To Pierce

Surata – Soo-ra-tah – Beginning

Usaha – Oo-saa-hah - Endeavor

Shuttles

Celeeri – See-lee-ree - swift

    Denessi – Denn-ess-ee - sodge

    Eshima – Ee-shee-ma - respect

    Kevol – Kev-oll - agony

    Kuta – Koo-tah - modular shuttle.

    Liri-ny – Lee-ree-nye – freedom

    Misaia – Miss-aye-a - memory

    Sasay – Sass-ay - whispers

    Yakin – Yuck-kin - belief

Creatures

Asnu – Ass-Noo – buffalo/donkey

    Eiltur – Ale-turr

    Gracc – Grrr-ack

    Ilag – Ee-Lug– leggy slugs that feast on sol.

    Kreso – Kreh-soo

    Omeika – Oh-may-ka

    Pagsu – Pug-Soo - cocksuckers

    Reshy – Resh-Ee - huge, like the size of a kuta shuttle, with massive jaws and rows of sharp teeth.

    Sogair – Sow-gare

    Wilanegy – Will-anna-jee

ABOUT THE AUTHOR

SEVANNAH STORM IS A fiction writer who immerses herself in fantastical worlds both magical and science fiction. She has a flair for the creative having studied art and interior architecture and spends her time drawing, oil painting, and writing. An avid reader from an early age, Sevannah finds her inspiration from various sources: games, novels, music, and the land of make-believe. The unique versus the practical has brought on numerous debates.

In her spare time, she does Krav Maga, CrossFit, and rereads novels that snatch her breath away. Having embraced the social media world, you can find her on most platforms.

Her home is a land south of Wakanda, where animals roam free. Born in Zimbabwe, she grew up in South Africa. The crisp blue skies with cotton-candy sunsets expand her heart and soul, encapsulating a sense of freedom.

Words she lives by: "Know your pothole and dodge it. Don't work in a pencil factory if you're a vampire."

Sevannah loves to hear from her readers. You can find and connect with her at the links below.

Website/Newsletter:

https://www.sevannahstorm.com/

Facebook:

https://www.facebook.com/sevannah.storm

Instagram:

https://www.instagram.com/sevannah.storm/

Twitter:

https://twitter.com/sevannah_storm

Thank you for taking the time to read Soul Forged. If you enjoyed the story, please tell your friends and leave a review. Reviews support authors and ensure they continue to bring readers books to love and enjoy.

https://sevannahstorm.com

FATE FORGED

The Gifting Series #2

Jacqueline (Jack) Dunois struggles to find a man not intimidated by her career as a law enforcement instructor, especially in the small town she calls home. She would sacrifice a kidney to find someone who would make her ovaries clap and didn't live with his mother. Then she meets a supreme commander from another world who thinks the stars in the galaxies shine in her eyes... What's not to love about that?

Supreme Commander Ulriq doesn't believe in love, an archaic term for a volatile and untrustworthy emotion Etterians were no longer subjected to. Until he meets Jack who triggers the Ethera, the soulmate force that irrevocably changes a male when he finds his ideal female. At that moment, his world, his focus, his very loyalty shifts. But when she is taken from him, it is too much to bear. Under the influence of the Ethera, he launches a rescue. He'll start a war and kill anyone who dares stop him, just to have her back in his arms.

Read it here:

https://books2read.com/u/bMY09v

SUN FORGED

The Gifting Series #3

Meeting a drop-dead gorgeous man, who falls onto a knee the first time they meet, sounded too good to be true for Ava. Of course, with her luck, he had to be an alien. Thrust into an unknown alien world, meeting weird and scary creatures, and fearing for her life, Ava tries to survive as best as a hairstylist can.

Kanzo never expected to find a life mate, a Dar Eth. Since he was young, he was taught that pairings were rare with fewer females born. The statistics on finding his Dar Eth would be slim to none. Instead of dreaming and longing for companionship, he focused on being the best male possible, to end his life on a battlefield with honor. But when he experiences the Ethera—the life mate force, and is blessed with his female, he isn't prepared for the level of pain, pleasure, and need she invokes within him.

Unable to save her as she's teleported from him, the dark consuming pain in his chest drives him into a blinding rage. With no idea who stole her or where to begin the search, he will scour the known universe to find her, to hold the female he never wanted.

Read it here:

https://books2read.com/u/3n5vaB

WAR FORGED

The Gifting Series #4

Being kidnapped by aliens does not sit well with Quinlan. Not only would her seven guardians give her hell if she doesn't attempt some sort of escape, but she refuses to be at anybody's mercy. With her practiced military skills, the help of an underground lounge singer and a personal assistant, she takes over the alien slave ship. Not knowing how to fly the damn thing, she sends a distress signal. ...The rescue comes swiftly in the form of a bronzed man with exquisite ice-blue eyes. Leaving her to ask the true question: has she just given up her newfound freedom for a gorgeous man who seems determined to have her for eternity?

As Elite Supreme Commander of the Etterian Forces, Xan answers a distress call in Earth English. That is all he did. The female who captured the slave ship shows remarkable skill, making her a warrior in her own right. Said skills should be respected and honored. Except she is his Dar Eth, calling forth the Ethera—the soulmate bond. How can he protect his female when she can do so herself? What can she possibly need from him? What can he offer a female, not Etterian but human? Not that he can think clearly in her presence when she scents so good and makes him want to kiss all of her.

Maker help him.

Read it here:

https://books2read.com/u/bz1QGD

STAR FORGED

The Gifting Series #5

Macy is feeling a little left out, as usual. Who would have thought moving from one planet to another wouldn't change that loneliness? She is never alone these days since Etterians guard human women with an urgency she understands. But the lack of companionship is like a dark aching abyss inside her chest. On some days, it threatens to implode, and Macy Mitchell would cease to exist. Looming is her impending meeting with King Xeus of Etteria. How is she supposed to keep her shit together when presented to royalty? Not after she ran from the last king she met.

For Xeus, the void expands daily. Duty, honor, concern for his dying people, and endless loneliness fill his life. Having decided to search for pairings among other worlds, he is pleased his son found his soulmate among human women. It doesn't mean that Xeus's loneliness and longing haven't ended until he stumbles upon a crying female. Meaning only to soothe, he is spellbound when her presence brings him peace. Unable to resist, he forms an attachment to a female he can never have

Read it here:

https://books2read.com/u/3nXgp5

SHADOW FORGED

THE GIFTING SERIES #6

Forty-year-old Caroline is too old to start dating and too bored with her vibrator, but what other choices does she have. On the day she burns her shirt and breaks a fingernail, she meets Etterian warriors. As part of her job at E.S.A. (Earth Space Association,) she must 'entertain' the hot-as-apple-pie Chief Engineer she suspects isn't who he claims to be.

Operations Commander Malo, Head of Espionage, must act as an engineer and ambassador, hoping to invite human females to visit Etteria and save his dying race. From Princess Oriana, he has strict instructions to distrust humans. What he finds he cannot trust are his emotions and his body whenever in the presence of the human ambassador, Caroline. She does not believe in soulmates or in a forever with him. Convincing her to choose him is the greatest task ever set before him, one he cannot afford to fail.

Until she is stolen from him. He calls in favors, utilizes all his resources to find her. And *when* he does, he is never letting her off his battleship...or his bed.

Read it here:

https://books2read.com/u/bPNd8j

EARTH FORGED

THE GIFTING SERIES #7

Guilt hounds Izzy, who caused her sister's injury and subsequent blindness. But no matter how she cares for Simone or what she sacrifices, it doesn't ease the ache in her chest. With Simone and naive Caro, her best friend, Izzy's role as protector is fully realized. The cost? Hiding behind quirkiness, pseudo-joy, and giving up her hopes and dreams. What she needs is a knight in any armor. After all, beggars can't be fussy. She has no idea that armor, in her case, means black military and that a knight could come in any color, specifically bronze.

Oyaz wants to find his life force, his soulmate, and he'd like her to be human. Earth's females are soft, amusing, passionate, and their scents rival a garden of hahyt blossoms. His task is to guard their planet that promises so many salvations for his males. It's a duty he's pleased to perform, one he would die for. When Operations Commander Malo orders Oyaz to retrieve a human female, he's eager to oblige. That it would lead to his salvation is something he couldn't anticipate. What he hadn't planned for is an ambush that costs him more than his memory, the loss of his soulmate.

Now what? Nothing in their training prepared him for this.

And yet, despite not remembering kneeling for Izzy, he longs to claim her with every inch of his soul.

Read it here:

https://books2read.com/u/31V82D

LUST FORGED

The Gifting Series #8

Ex-socialite Leona wants nothing more than to enhance the mechanics within sex-cybs, not to mention improve their performances with their 'lovers.' It's a job where she's safe in an all-woman factory on Callisto, and far from her matchmaking mama. When the chief engineer is incapacitated, Leona's required to gift—her term would be pimp—sex-cyborgs to prospective clients. On an Etterian battleship, surrounded by gorgeous males, she tries not to think of sex when it's her work, especially with the Sub-Commander Aaro whose neon-blue eyes are the stuff of her erotic dreams.

As a diplomatic favor, Aaro must abandon his task to guard Earth, and perhaps find his Dar Eth or soulmate, all to protect cargo en route to many worlds, including the dangerous and unpredictable Yithia. Princess Oriana is most concerned for the two human female engineers determined to ensure the deliveries are successful. A simple enough mission until one human enters Aaro's cargo bay, dropping him to his knees.

But revealing to independent Leona that she's now trapped in a marriage isn't something Aaro can bring himself to do. He violates all he stands for, every ounce of honor by not telling her the truth. All in the hopes that she will choose to love him.

Read it here:

https://books2read.com/u/3LdA1w